PROLOGUE

Johnston Atoll, North Pacific Ocean
~ July 9, 1962 ~

I
T WAS 9 SECONDS PAST 9 a.m. precisely — Greenwich Mean Time — when the Thor Rocket, carrying a W49 Nuclear Warhead exploded at an altitude of 250 miles. Robert Cassidy clicked the stop button on his pocket watch to record the time. In the sky above, an explosion which would later be recorded as reaching 1.44 megatons, erupted — sending an artificial aurora borealis of splendid colors across the North Pacific Ocean.

Approximately 900 miles from the detonation point the city of Honolulu in Hawaii experienced the effects of the subsequent and powerful electromagnetic pulse. Approximately 300 streetlights went out in an instant and the island's only microwave tower was destroyed. The strange events were followed by the eerie sound of the air raid siren, sending terror into the hearts of those who had survived the attack on Pearl Harbor over two decades earlier.

On Johnston Atoll, Robert noticed beads of sweat form inside his protective goggles, which had allowed him to stare at the blast without incinerating his retina. He removed the eyepieces and let them hang below his neck. A few moments later his eyes adjusted to the new and magnificent horizon.

1

Filled with a myriad of reds, ochre, and yellow lines, the artificial aurora borealis dazzled onlookers from Hawaii through to New Zealand for the next three days.

Robert heard the loud ring of the launch station's phone. He answered it immediately. Listened to the report. Wrote down a few notes on a piece of paper, and then hung up. A wave of relief washed over him at the news. The military project, code-named *Starfish Prime,* had been a success.

But would they let him continue with his own special project?

His eyes turned to several observers twenty feet back. They were mostly military, but included some civilian engineers, politicians and science reporters. He could guess which of them worked for which organization. All except for one man.

He wore a big smile that expressed the wonder of science while at the same time saying, I told you we could do this. His brown hair was thick and tousled. Giving him the boyish good looks of a young movie star, despite his age possibly being closer to fifty. His brown eyes stared in awe of the event he'd just witnessed.

Above all, he had a deeply pensive quality about him — like he was trying to decide the fate of an extremely important decision. Robert watched the man speaking with some of the military brass involved in the experiment.

The phone rang for a second time.

There would be a number of reports coming in over the following hours. His pulse quickened. He calmed himself — it might not be the report he'd been waiting for. He listened intently. Wrote down a single line of notes. Then carefully crossed them out entirely.

He grinned with pride. *It worked! My equation is possible in practice.*

The man in the suit approached him. He looked like a bureaucrat not a politician, Robert decided. The man smiled at him. Robert thought it was a kind face. More like a model or

THE CASSIDY
PROJECT

CHRISTOPHER CARTWRIGHT

movie star. He couldn't care less which one he was. Someone had mentioned to him that the man was an independent civilian who was here to review the launch. Robert didn't care who he was, so long as the man gave him the green light to the funding needed to complete the project. The decision to fund the project was too important to leave in the hands of a pen-pusher or the military.

The man approached him. "Mr. Cassidy?"

"Yes, sir." Robert held out his hand.

The man took it. Gripped it with both hands and said, "My name is Ronald Reagan. That was quite a show you put on today."

"Thank you, sir."

"May I see the report?"

Robert handed it to the man. Reagan read the notes. Grinned. "The resulting electromagnetic pulse took out the lights as far away as Hawaii, did they?"

Robert wasn't sure if the man was pleased or upset by the discovery. No one could have predicted the EMP would travel that far. He looked at the man's eyes. They gave away nothing. "Yes sir."

Regan's almost permanent grin changed to a frown. "What about the second set of notes? The ones you crossed out?"

Robert remained silent.

The Commander of the Joint Task Force 8 approached. His ordinarily surly face, now beaming with pride at their success. "You can tell him, son. He's part of the secret committee reviewing your theory. His vote will ultimately decide if your project gets to continue or not."

Robert smiled. He'd made the right choice in picking out the man who held the power over all his hopes and dreams. He'd been polite, bordering on obsequious, to the right man. And then he told him about the unexpected finding.

Mr. Reagan stared at him. Sizing him up, as though he was

determining if he could be trusted. "I hope you understand this changes everything. None of this can be reported now."

"But sir, this only proves that my theory was correct! I must continue my research—now more so than ever. If we want to have any control over its outcome, we need to start now!"

Reagan's movie star smile returned. "Oh no, no. You don't understand me, son. I mean, your work definitely needs to continue. In fact I can guarantee the government will be willing to double your funding. Only that from now on, none of it can ever be made public. In fact, we'll need to move you, your team and your research to a secret location—another island. This one's a little more private. Somewhere you can commence preparations for your next attempt away from prying eyes. And you'll have to start immediately."

Robert laughed. "More private? What's more private than Johnston Atoll? We're in the middle of the North Pacific!"

Reagan ignored his question. "Someone will come shortly to pick you and the team up. Then you'll find out where our most top secret research and development in the history of the U.S. government will take place. I think you'll like the island." Reagan then embraced his hand again. "Well done, Mr. Cassidy. I wish you the best of luck with your research. The American people will never know how much you did for them, but just remember I will. And I thank you."

The man turned to walk away.

"Oh, Mr. Reagan. You know the project is going to take a long time to reach fruition, don't you?"

"Of course. Our entire plan may take decades to succeed, but it has to be done."

Three days later, Ronald Reagan, a lifelong Democratic Party member, became the most ardent supporter of conservatism, and a devoted Republican. He never spoke of the reason he left the Democratic Party.

There is no documented reason to suggest that he was involved in something much larger than an American political party. That he was involved in a league of men who wanted to change the world for the better.

Over the course of his political career, he would make many important decisions. But none of them would potentially have such far reaching effects as the one he'd just made. The decision to fund the Cassidy Project.

King Salmon Air Force Station, Alaska
~ January 4, 1983 ~

MAJOR JAMES MAVERICK STARED AT the B52H Stratofortress Bomber. She was the deadliest machine ever built and the head of the 705th Aircraft Control and Warning Squadron. Designed as a weapon capable of the extreme destruction required to provide a deterrent against nuclear attack, she protected the north-western corridor of the U.S. mainland. To Maverick, she was the single most beautiful machine in military aviation history.

She was certainly the largest and most formidable bomber in the history of the U.S. Air Force. Powered by eight Pratt & Whitney turbofans she created enough lift to allow for a theoretical maximum take-off weight in excess of four hundred and eighty-eight thousand pounds. Of course, some of the cowboys were confident that given the right length of runway, she could take-off with just about any amount of weight. She was equipped with an armament of both traditional and nuclear bombs, as well as a pneumatically driven M61 Vulcan, six-barrel, air-cooled, Gatling-style rotary cannon which fired 20 mm rounds at an extremely high rate typically exceeding 6,000 rounds per minute. A smile formed on his otherwise serious face — he was proud of her.

And she was his to command.

Outside the hangar the wind howled viciously. He thanked God his beautiful aircraft was protected tonight. Already registering gusts of up to eighty knots, the storm was by far the worst he'd witnessed during his total of twelve years maintaining aerial surveillance and security in the area. And it was getting worse. Predictions from the guys in meteorology suggested the strength was going to double through the night.

Maverick cautiously slid the large metal hangar door open a fraction to examine the force of the blizzard. It was a complete whiteout outside. The wind howled in through the gap with such vehemence it knocked him off his feet.

Three of his men rushed to get the door closed.

Maverick stood up and tidied his ruffled uniform. "Thank you gentlemen. I guess we can all go to bed early tonight. There will be no attacks in this weather — no one can fly in or out."

He finished dismissing his men and watched until the last had left. Maverick had the first watch for the night, ending at 23:00. Not that much could be seen with the weather the way it was. It was good for him. It would give him time to write home to his baby sister. The only family he still had. Married to the Air Force, he'd never felt it was quite right to start a new family of his own. He was close to his sister though. It was about time he wrote to her. The last letter he received was nearly six months ago.

He studied the picture of his niece in her new school uniform. *Cute kid. Striking green eyes. She's going to cause some man a lot of trouble someday, no doubt.*

He'd only met her once. It had been her second birthday. *Alexis Schultz* — her mother had kept the surname of the asshole who'd disappeared the same year she was born. Even back then, he knew the kid was going to be bright. She was a sweet kid, too. She called him Uncle Airplane because she struggled with the letter "J" in James.

He took the pleasure of re-reading the letter his little sister had written to accompany the latest picture. She'd written to say the teachers thought her daughter was *gifted*. Very gifted. Apparently, this meant that she shared the same sort of IQ as Einstein.

He watched the barometer drop further. The wind speed increased to 120 knots outside. He liked a good storm. It felt like it was his Maker providing him with protection and giving him some much needed rest.

His pen ran along the first line of paper–

Maverick stopped as the Staff Sergeant opened the door and approached him. There was a man with him. He wore a dark suit with a gray tie. Maybe mid-forties. Slightly balding in the middle, and his hair was noticeably combed over.

The Staff Sergeant saluted. "Sorry to interrupt, sir. This is Mr. Avery from the Pentagon. He says he needs to speak to you regarding something of national importance."

"Okay, thank you Brian. You may go." Maverick then looked at the stranger. "You got here rather quick."

The man stared at him with a vacant expression. "Quick?"

Maverick stood up and approached the man. He offered his right hand out. "I assume you're here about the photographs?"

Avery gripped his hand and shook. It was a weak handshake and further supported Maverick's impression the man was somehow slimy and had been sent to make trouble for his men. "I haven't heard of any photographs. I'm here about another matter entirely different."

"Sorry," Maverick said. He examined the stranger's face. It was impassive and hard to read. Perhaps he really didn't know about the photograph yet. *Well, he's about to find out. Then we'll see how collected he really is.* "We took the photographs of some men working on an iceberg in the middle of the Bering Strait a few hours ago. They're still being developed." Maverick smiled. "I figured with you being sent all the way here from the Pentagon the two incidences must have been connected."

"Men working on an iceberg in the middle of the Bering Strait?" Avery shook his head. "No one told me. Interesting."

Interesting what?

Interesting good. Or interesting we're about to see the missiles fly?

Maverick studied the man. He wore a dark suit. His smile was grimy, the type generals seemed to practice. It meant, we're on your side, just before they royally screw you by sending you on a mission where there's no chance of survival.

"All right. So tell me, what can we do for you?" Maverick asked.

Avery handed him a piece of paper. "I was told to give you this. And then stay with you to see that your task is completed."

Maverick didn't respond. He simply unsealed the envelope, and looked at it.

On official Whitehouse paper, in a hastily written scrawl, were the simple words,

Major James Maverick,

Your aircraft and men are hereby formally seconded for a mission of utmost importance. Please follow Mr. Avery's orders to their word. He will instruct you further on the details. May I please take this opportunity to thank you for your services? God willing, no one else will ever learn about them. Good luck. God bless you all. And God bless America.

At the bottom of the letter it was signed. *Ronald Reagan.* President of the United States of America.

Maverick grimaced. His day had just gotten worse. "All right Mr. Avery, what can we do for you?"

"That, I will explain in good time. But right now, we have to begin loading the Bomber."

"Can I ask what it is we're delivering?"

Avery took out a notepad and pen. It had the names of each of Maverick's aircrew. Avery placed a tick next to Maverick's name. "No. You most certainly may not."

Maverick took a deep breath through his nose and then breathed out through his mouth before he spoke again. "Can I at least ask where it's going?"

"Not until we're off the ground. Then I'll tell you everything you need to know."

"How do I know how much fuel we'll need? Flight plans, safety redundancies, etc. . . ." Maverick was angry at the man in front of him, but he was angrier at the machine he worked for. The U.S. Air Force knew best how to manage its missions. Only a bureaucrat would think a mission like this could be planned by a number of pen-pushers from the other side of the country.

"We have already planned that for you. You will have each of your fuel tanks filled to their caps. And your auxiliary tanks, too."

"We, who?" Maverick raised his eyebrow. "I thought you said you were from the Pentagon?"

"I'm afraid I only informed your Staff Sergeant that to maintain secrecy."

"So then, where are you from?"

"Langley."

"Langley? What the hell is the CIA doing borrowing a military plane?"

"As far as anyone's concerned, we never did."

"All right. So you're not going to help me with any of this are you?" Maverick sat down. Took notes. "When do we leave?"

"Tonight."

Maverick examined the man's impassive face. He was definitely serious. Even insane men believed with conviction things which simply aren't true. He laughed. "That's the best thing I've heard today. Have you even looked outside?"

Avery nodded his head. "I only recently drove through it with a Mack Truck carrying the cargo."

"There's a once in a decade blizzard raging. We wouldn't make it off the runway, let alone to our destination."

"All the same, we're going to need you to try."

Maverick stood up. Crossed to the other side of his desk and stopped just short of the stranger in front of him. The man was a good eight inches shorter than him. He had to duck just to look at the man's eyes. "No way. I'm in command here, and there's nothing you or any other idiot from the CIA can say to make me attempt to take off in this weather. It would be suicide. I'm not risking my life or the life of my men for no reason. And if you don't like that, I suggest you go back to Langley and talk to your boss. Good night."

The stranger smiled at him. It was coy and unctuous. "He said that you'd say that. Said that you'd need more convincing." The hangar phone rang. "That will be him now."

Maverick picked up the phone. Before he spoke he had a terrible feeling in his gut he was about to be royally screwed. "Hangar Three. Major James Maverick speaking." Maverick grinned as he listened to the man on the phone—someone who had learned the skill of persuasion from the best of them. To make matters worse, he felt honored to be so used. At the end of the phone call he said, "Yes, Mr. President. I will tell my men that, and we'll try our best not to get us all killed on takeoff."

Maverick taxied to the end of the runway. He pressed his left steering pedal to the floor and the B52H Stratofortress Bomber spun to face the center of the runway. The headwind was pummeling the windscreen. Sleet reflected off the bright runway red lights and ran across the glass like a series of tracer bullets. His vision was down—below fifty yards at best. He increased the pressure on the balls of his feet until he felt the brakes lock tight and the tires grip firm to the runway's blacktop.

With his right hand he moved all eight throttles to full. The eight Pratt & Whitney turbofans began to increase power until their high pitched whine drowned out the storm. He kept them there for a full minute. Checking all the gauges were in their correct ranges.

Davidson, his co-pilot looked at him with a worried look on his face. "We're losing nearly fifty revolutions off the starboard turbofans."

Maverick brought the throttles back to idle. "With this sort of crosswind? We should be thankful it's not closer to a hundred."

"Sure." Davidson replied. Gazing pensively out the starboard window, he said, "The question is—will she get off the ground?"

Maverick smiled. He'd flown these aircraft for nearly a decade now. More than twenty thousand hours. Fifteen of them in command. Instinctually he knew precisely how much she could take. "She'll get off the ground. It's keeping her off that's worrying me in this weather."

"Copy that, sir."

"Setting flaps down full," Maverick said adjusting the levers.

Davidson visually confirmed the correct setting had been achieved. "Flaps down, full."

"Adjusting the tail stabilizer upwards nine degrees," Maverick said sliding the lever upwards to the ninth upwards marker. The massive tail had nine degrees of movement upwards and a further four downwards, giving it thirteen possible settings.

"Nine up," Davidson confirmed.

"Rigby, please confirm the angle setting of the tail stabilizer."

"Nine up, sir," Rigby confirmed from the rear facing gunner's seat.

Maverick looked at Davidson. The man had just finished with the last of his Rosary and nodded his head.

They were good to go.

Maverick pressed the intercom. "All right gentlemen. We're ready to get this girl in the air. Mr. Avery, I hope you're strapped in tight, because I believe we're in for a bit of a rough ride."

The B52 Bomber, nicknamed *Maverick's Menace*, was loaded with a total of 312,000 pounds of aviation fuel, filled right to her filler cap. She was armed with nearly 70,000 pounds of nuclear and traditional bombs. And now a single 38,000 pound sealed crate — housing an unknown cargo had been taken onboard and secured midway along her fuselage, where their unwanted guest, Mr. Avery stared at it like it was the most precious thing in the entire world.

All in total she was 32,000 pounds overladen.

Maverick made a silent prayer, and then pushed all eight throttles forwards. The whine of the powerful Pratt & Whitney engines increased in pitch until they howled with the wind attempting to extract every single pound of thrust possible. He would need every one of their individual 17,000 pounds of thrust if they were to get off the runway.

The entire fuselage shuddered under the forces as *Maverick's Menace* edged forward despite the wheel brakes locked firmly in place.

Maverick released the brakes. "Here we go, Davidson."

The overladen aircraft crept forward. Slowly at first and then, building up momentum she began to revel in the challenge of the impossible task given to her.

He kept slight pressure on his left rudder. Trying to compensate for the additional torque of the strong crosswind on the starboard engines, which made *Maverick's Menace* want to yaw to the right.

Through the windscreen Maverick could only just make out the red running lights on the port side of the runway. His eyes darted between the instrument panel and the runway outside. Concentrating on maintaining a straight line along the guts of the runway.

"We just passed the third mile marker," Davidson stated.

"Halfway there," Maverick replied. His eyes glanced at the speedometer. *Maverick's Menace* had reached a sluggish pace of 90 knots.

For the first time he questioned himself if they would have enough runway. He pressed his left foot heavily on the rudder peddle trying to compensate for the crosswind, and keep them running straight.

"Five miles," Davidson said. "Speed: 130 knots."

"We're going to need a lot more than that if we want to stay off the ground."

They were approaching the minimum takeoff speed of the B52 Stratofortress Bomber under normal conditions. Overladen they would need to be traveling a lot faster. *Maverick's Menace* shuddered under the pressure, begging to be released from the confines of gravity. Maverick pushed the wheel all the way forward, trying to keep the nose from lifting. *Not until we're ready darling.* He needed all of the speed he could gather to get the overladen aircraft into the sky.

He looked down again. Their speed had just passed 140

knots — the minimum takeoff speed under normal circumstance, without any additional weight.

"We just passed the final mile marker," Davidson called out.

"Just a little longer," he replied.

Maverick knew this runway like he knew his aircraft. He'd used her nearly every day for five years. The runway finished with a flat field covered in snow and tundra. He was going to take *Maverick's Menace* right to the very end of the runway before trying to takeoff.

The final warning lights that marked the end of the runway glowed at him. He smiled. He had done all he could. Now fate would decide whether his aircraft could fly.

Davidson stared at him. Terror in his eyes. "End of the runway!"

Maverick grinned. He pulled the wheel ever so gently towards his chest. The nose lifted slightly off the ground and he felt the massive change in force as the aircraft altered its angle. He carefully maintained some forwards pressure to stop the nose from over extending and causing them to stall.

At the end of the tundra-covered field stood more than a thousand pine trees. By the time *Maverick's Menace* reached them its landing gear was just two feet off the highest tree.

"Gear up," he ordered.

"Gear up. I thought I'd never live to hear you say those words." Faulkner griped as he moved the lever. The motors whined at a pitch only just audible above the heavy pelting of snow on metal, and all ten wheels retracted into their wells. Four up front, four behind and a single wheel on each wingtip for stability. All safely stowed. "Gear up and locked."

With the drag of the landing gear removed, *Maverick's Menace* was finally able to pick up speed and gain altitude. He set a course for a steady climb until they reached a cruising height of forty-six thousand feet. Above the worst of the storm and the heavy buffeting the wings finally settled into an almost eerie calm.

Maverick handed over control of the aircraft to his copilot.

He pressed the intercom, "Mr. Avery. Get up here. It's time you tell me exactly what this mission is really about."

Major Maverick looked over his right shoulder. Avery stumbled into the cockpit. He was pale, sweaty, and looked like he was about to lose the contents of his last meal. Before takeoff he'd suggested that Avery ride in the instructor pilot's seat, but the man had refused stating that he'd feel more comfortable riding in the fuselage where he could keep an eye on his precious cargo. The outcome of such a decision meant Avery had to contend with an even more turbulent ride, and had just climbed through a series of ladders and maintenance vents to return to the main cockpit. Maverick thought the man was a fool, but had done nothing to dissuade him of his decision prior to takeoff.

Maverick looked at Avery and cursed. "You're not going to vomit in my cockpit, are you?"

Avery leaned forward like he was about to be sick. "I don't like to fly. And that was unlike any takeoff I've ever experienced, or ever want to in the future!"

"Nor any I've had either." Maverick tapped the metal lining of the hull with the back of his knuckles for good luck. "Like I said, it's a wonder we even got her off the ground, given her additional weight and the blizzard." Maverick felt no sympathy for the man. "So, are you going to tell me where we are headed?"

Avery handed him a scribbled piece of paper with some numbers relating to latitude and longitude. "We need to reach here by 0500."

Maverick took the piece of paper and looked at the coordinates. He knew the general location at a glance. "That's in the middle of the Siberian Straight."

"Yes."

"There's nothing there except water."

Avery shrugged his shoulders. "So?"

"So, whatever our cargo is — it's not currently set up to be deployed. Which means it's not a bomb. So, where are we landing?"

Avery pulled the zipper on his jacket up to his face trying to keep out the bitter cold. "I'll explain that when we get there."

Maverick finished circling the location with a pencil and then threw the map on the floor next to him. "You've gotta be kidding me! How do you expect me to plan anything like this?"

"I don't. I expect you to follow the President's orders." Avery then stumbled back towards the ladder and started climbing down without saying anything.

"Where are you going?"

"Back to the fuselage. Uncomfortable though it is I want to keep an eye on the cargo. It's more valuable than you could imagine." Avery then disappeared down the ladder without waiting for a reply.

Davidson looked at Maverick. "What an asshole!"

"Yeah, well President Reagan says that asshole might just save humanity." Maverick unclipped his seatbelt and climbed out of his chair. "I'm going down below to discuss these coordinates with Reynolds and Jacobs. I'll come back with a more detailed route shortly. Until then, set a course due west."

"Copy that. Setting a course — due west, towards Siberia."

Maverick climbed past the instructor pilot's seat, past the descending ladder, and poked his head into the rear facing gunner's compartment. He nodded his head at the two gentlemen sitting there. Wakefield, their Weapons Systems Operator, sat on the left seat and was carefully studying a series of electronic instruments checking on the stability of each armament. Rigby, their Gunner and youngest man onboard had settled himself into his seat and was trying to get some

16

early rest.

"Sir," Wakefield acknowledged him.

Rigby straightened himself out before saying, "Sir."

"At ease, gentlemen." Maverick crouched down beside the two men. "I just came back here to say that we made it through the worst of the storm. We should be all right from here on in."

"Do you know where we're headed, and what our mission is?" Wakefield asked.

"I'm afraid not. We're delivering our secret cargo to an island. According to Mr. Avery, it isn't on any map and without our cargo its mission can't be completed. He refused to say what its mission was, where the island is located, or what our cargo is. I'm in the dark as much as you both are. What I can say is President Reagan himself advised me that the outcome of this mission has by far the most far-reaching consequences of anything done since the start of the Cold War."

"So you haven't received any orders of a Nuclear Strike?" Wakefield asked.

"No." Maverick looked at his Weapons Systems Operator. "What do you know?"

"Mr. Avery spoke to me before we left King Salmon Air Force Base."

Maverick lowered his voice. "And—what did he say?"

"He wanted to confirm that we were fully equipped with our maximum armaments of nuclear warheads in case our mission fails."

Rigby cursed. "What is President Reagan planning?"

"I have no idea." Maverick shook his head. "All right gentlemen. I'll let you know more when I do. Get some rest while you can. It will be at least six hours until we reach the first waypoint."

Maverick returned to the middle compartment and climbed down the ladder. Jacobs, his Radar Bombardier stared vacantly at his radar screen. Reynolds was the first to spot him. "Evening, Sir."

"At ease, gentlemen."

"Do you have a location for me yet?" Reynolds, his Navigator, asked.

Maverick handed him the coordinates. "We're heading here. I've left Davidson heading due west for the time being."

Reynolds eyed the coordinates. "It's in the Siberian Strait."

"Yes," Maverick acknowledged.

"You know that's where they took the picture earlier today of the unidentified men working on an iceberg."

Maverick shook his head, and his eyes lit up at the new revelation. "Avery lied to me! He said he didn't know anything about the photographs. That son-of-a-bitch set me up. He knew damn well about the photograph."

"So. What are you gonna do about it?" Reynolds asked.

"I have no idea. But I have six hours to find out."

<hr />

At 0430 Maverick unclipped his seatbelt and made the cramped journey of ladders and maintenance gangways until he reached the cargo bay inside the fuselage. There his unwanted guest no longer displayed signs of motion sickness as he had earlier. Instead, he stared at the cargo as though it was the most valuable thing on the planet. Maverick had seen that sort of look in a person's eye before. It was the same sort of crazy luster one develops the first time they find gold.

"All right Avery, this is your show," Maverick said. "We're approaching the coordinates you gave me. What next?"

"Good. I'm going to need you to take us down to 1000 feet. Our guide will signal us from the surface."

"The surface of what?"

"I'm not sure. I'll fill you in when I know." Avery grinned with slimy satisfaction. "I'll follow you up to the cockpit. The next part of this mission might be a little delicate."

Maverick shook his head. "No way! We're a Bomber."

"So?"

"So I don't feel safe taking us that low. If there's an attack, we'll be struggling to win it from that altitude."

"There won't be an attack," Avery said, his voice slow and confident. "These are friendly waters — for the time being, anyway."

Maverick tapped his knuckles on the side of the steel hull. "For the record, I don't like any of this."

"I wouldn't expect you to. Even so, the precise location of what we are after can be a little elusive."

"And what are we after?"

"It's an island. A very secret island."

"A secret fucking island!" Maverick swore. "That's what this is all about?"

"It's not so much the island that we're interested in. It's what's stored deep inside the island — which the President is after."

"So where exactly is this secret island?"

"We lost it shortly after December 1962. At first we thought it had been destroyed. Then we started to see evidence it might have survived. Then we prayed it had been sunk in the North Atlantic."

"North Pacific?" Maverick complained about Avery's inconsistency. "But we're in the North Pacific — and last time I checked, islands don't move?"

Avery ignored the question. "We'd better get back to the cockpit. I don't want to miss the signal. Your concerns are duly noted, and you're welcome to take them up with President Reagan, but for the time being, we need to complete the mission. This might be our last chance."

Maverick swallowed his concerns without saying another

word. He returned to the cockpit, strapped himself in with his harness and took over command of the aircraft's controls again.

Commencing their descent in a steep decline, Maverick gently pushed the wheel away from his chest until he felt the nose drop off the horizon. He depressed the intercom. "Gentlemen. We are dropping to 1000 feet to receive a coded message from the surface. Maintain extreme vigilance. I have been kept in the dark as much as you have about the real purpose of our mission."

Maverick watched the altimeter click below 30,000.

He swallowed trying to allow his middle ear to equalize with the sudden change in air-pressure.

Despite his outwardly calm appearance, Major Maverick was nervous as all hell. The B52 Stratofortress Bomber had a combat height of 48000 feet. Every 1000 feet below that its maneuverability decreased and it had less use for its bombs.

He swallowed harder when the aircraft descended below 5,000.

"All right gentlemen. Look sharp. We're descending past 5,000 feet. Keep your eyes out for trouble."

It made him nervous to fly so low.

"We have an incoming bird!" Jacobs said. "Bearing: 270 degrees. Height: 2,000 feet and climbing! Current speed: 95 knots."

Maverick glanced at the altimeter. They had just descended below 3,000 feet. He looked out the left window "Anyone got eyes on it?"

"I've got it," Davidson yelled. "Golden speck on the horizon—at your six o'clock."

Maverick rested his right hand on the main throttle, preparing to increase power to the engines. "Is that what I think it is?"

Avery unclipped his seatbelt and leaned forwards to get a better sight of the incoming plane. "What is it? What do you see?"

"Looks like an old warbird from World War II," Maverick said. "Something like a Spitfire or a Messerschmitt."

"Don't be ridiculous," Davidson said. A large grin forming as he shook his head in disbelief. "That's a de Haviland Tiger Moth. My old man used to own one when I was a kid. First thing I ever learned to fly. Although, what the hell its doing a thousand miles from land beats me."

The tension in Maverick's neck and arm reduced immediately. He took his right hand back from where it was resting on the throttles. He could see the plane clearly now. It was a bright yellow bi-plane. No way could it carry anything capable of piercing their armor let alone causing them any real threat.

"A yellow Tiger Moth." Maverick looked at Avery. "Is that the guide you were expecting?"

Avery stared absently at the tiny aircraft. Sweaty beads of fear formed on his pale forehead. His jaw was rigid and his eyes appeared lost in an unknown horror of his past. "No. We were to pick up a signal from a submarine . . ."

"So where did this Tiger Moth come from?" he asked.

Avery ignored the question. He withdrew from the sight of the approaching aircraft. "No. It can't be! They were certain they destroyed you — all those years ago!"

Maverick grabbed Avery's jacket with his free hand and twisted until the man looked at him with the confusion of a person woken from a bad dream. "What happened with the yellow Tiger Moth?"

"That aircraft is not what it appears," Avery said. "Major Maverick, tell me you have something capable of shooting it down before it reaches us?"

Maverick started to laugh, but stopped himself as he looked at Avery's face, rigid with fear. "That's an old plane. It probably isn't even equipped with any weapons. And if it was, they wouldn't be large enough to inflict any real damage on one of the most powerful bombers ever built!"

"Good." Avery raised his voice in a confidence previously not displayed. "Then I suggest you shoot it down before you discover just how wrong you are."

Maverick grinned. It pleased him to watch the discomfort in his unwanted guest. He almost wanted to wait it out and see what the strange aircraft wanted. "All right gentlemen. Let's see what this old relic wants. Rigby, if it comes within range — take it out." He depressed the radio transmit button on the side of the wheel. "Unidentified aircraft. You are approaching a U.S. Air Force B52 Stratofortress Bomber. Please turn 90 degrees to your right immediately."

No response.

He depressed the radio transmitter again. "Unidentified Tiger Moth. You are on a collision approach with a U.S. Air Force B52 — I say again, please deviate direction to your right."

The radio remained silent.

At the same time the Tiger Moth continued to narrow the distance between the two aircraft.

"Holy shit!" Avery swore. "What are you waiting for? Destroy it!"

Maverick ignored him and depressed the radio transmitter once again. "Tiger Moth divert or we will fire upon you."

More silence.

Followed by the sound of corn popping in the distance. It came from the barrel of an old World War II hand held machine gun raking the side of the fuselage. The other pilot could do so all day and it wouldn't penetrate the B52's armored exterior.

Who fires a hand machine gun at a bomber?

Maverick increased power for the engines to full. Then pulled the wheel back towards his chest, lifting the nose as far above the horizon as he dared, and sending the Stratofortress bomber into a steep climb. "Rigby, don't let them take another shot at us!"

"Understood!" Rigby grinned as he gripped the targeting arm of the aft mounted, remotely controlled six-barrel Gatling-style machine gun, and searched for his target.

Maverick held the bomber in a climb rate as close to its stall angle as he dared. He glanced out the left side windshield. The yellow Tiger Moth was so close he could make out the pilot's face. The man, if it was a man, wore an old fashioned, leathery pilot's cap and goggles. Maverick thought he could just make out a deep smile on the person's face.

The pilot's smile made him feel particularly uneasy. There was something wrong about the situation. Everything about it didn't seem right. In an instant he wished he'd taken Avery's advice and shot it down without attempting to communicate. Maverick strained his eyes to make more sense of the pilot's expression.

And then the horizon disappeared and the entire windshield turned white. The flash was so bright it blinded everyone in the cockpit. Maverick didn't have time to consider if they'd been destroyed by a bomb, before it was followed by a sonic boom a split second later.

Maverick felt the slight jolt on the wheel. Nothing large enough to affect his ability to fly, but evidence the Tiger Moth had definitely hit them with something significantly more substantial than a hand machine gun. *But with what?* It was too small to be carrying anything capable of considerable damage.

The lighting behind the instrument panel went completely dark. Possibly the result of a power surge after a direct hit on one of the main batteries. Maverick made small adjustments to the aircraft's controls. His confidence returning as he discovered he still had full control of the B52 — *For now.* Rigby wouldn't let the Tiger Moth survive long enough to take a second shot at them. Even so, there was something terrible about the fear in Avery's eyes which told him to be frightened.

In the aft facing weapon's room behind them, Rigby looked at the small aircraft approaching. He lined the golden speck of the Tiger Moth, superimposed upon the horizon, with the cross hairs of his remotely controlled six-barrel Gatling-style machinegun.

Without hesitation, he depressed the firing nipple.

Immediately the defensive fire control system directed all four .50 caliber machine guns to fire. The entire cockpit vibrated to the sound of more than a thousand rounds of bullets being expelled in a matter of seconds.

The Tiger Moth disintegrated in a blaze.

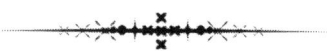

A moment later the massive B52 banked heavily towards the left. Maverick dipped the nose below the horizon to pick up airspeed. He fought violently with the wheel, which buffeted under the new strain. His right foot pressed hard on the rudder pedal in an attempt to stave off the imminent stall spiral known as a death spiral.

"What the hell's wrong?" Avery yelled. His face red with anger.

"Your damn load's shifted. That's what's wrong! Whatever it is you've got back there has now moved to the port side."

Avery didn't wait to respond. He unclipped his seatbelt and moved fast. Racing towards his precious cargo.

Maverick depressed the intercom. "Rigby, Wakefield! Get back there with Mr. Avery and see what you can do to stabilize the load before it sends us into a deadly spiral!"

Davidson looked over. Concern painted heavily on his face. "What do you need me to do?"

"Slowly decrease power to the starboard engines. See if we can compensate for the shift of our load with a change in engine torque."

"Copy that," Davidson said. "Decreasing power to sixty

percent for all four starboard engines."

Maverick felt an immediate change in the aircraft's maneuverability. Less pressure was required to adjust the movement to the wheel. The rudder pedals became easier to manage. It was working. He glanced at his instrument panel. The lighting behind was still out.

Nearly twenty thousand flying hours reassured him by the weight in his seat that he was currently flying straight and level. "Davidson, see if you can replace the blown circuit breakers. It would be great to be able to see the instruments again."

Davidson moved quickly. "I'm on it."

A few moments later the light behind the instrument panel returned to its usual red glow. Maverick grinned. Everything was going to be all right. "Good work, Davidson."

The reassuring sensation was fleeting. Maverick took one glance at the instruments and knew his day was about to get worse. Every single one of them was broken—or worse, functioning correctly. He ran his eyes along them.

The altimeter ticked slowly in a counter clockwise direction. He adjusted the pitch of the nose and it made no difference to their rate of descent as far as the aircraft's electronics were concerned. Even when he dipped the nose downwards, the rate of descent should have sped up, but instead it remained steadily rotating counter clockwise.

Maverick straightened the aircraft into what felt like straight and level flight. Then tapped on the altimeter. "What the hell's wrong with it?"

Davidson shook his head. "Beats me."

"All right, let's set a course east and head for home. I'm done with this stupid mission!" Maverick glanced at the compass. Double checked it and then swore. It was the first time he'd ever cursed in front of his men.

The gimballed compass arrow rotated counter clockwise in

the exact same slow and steady manner as the altimeter. He looked at Davidson. "What's your compass doing?"

Davidson checked the second compass. The one on his side of the cockpit. "Something's wrong. It's just ticking counter clockwise."

"Yeah, mine too."

Maverick scanned the rest of the instruments. Every gauge, ranging from airspeed to oil pressure and right down to fuel readings was broken—they all simply rotated in a counter clockwise direction.

At least a thousand miles out from King Salmon Air Force Base, above only water, and with no means of calculating their direction, Maverick knew only too well that they were out of luck. He was about to start working the problem when the aircraft's controls became cumbersome.

"We've got the load secured, sir." Rigby's voice was rushed and panicked over the intercom. "I'm afraid Mr. Avery was crushed in the process."

Maverick cursed. Then, correcting his settings to maintain straight and level flight, he said, "I'm sorry to hear about Mr. Avery. Good work securing the load. Get back up here—we might be in for some rough flying."

Rigby's voice was softer this time when he spoke. "There's something else, too, sir."

"What now?"

"The cover for the cargo came off during the move."

"And?" Maverick's heart pounded heavily in his chest.

"You're going to be mad as hell when you see what we've been carrying."

"A nuclear bomb?" Maverick stared vacantly out the windshield. "You've gotta be kidding me! That's the most ridiculous thing I've ever heard. We're a nuclear bomber for goodness sake! If President Reagan wanted us to destroy an island, why all the cloak and dagger spiel? I mean, he could have just told us he needed a secret island nuked and we'd have done it?"

"What if it was one of our allies he wanted removed?" Davidson asked.

Maverick adjusted the aircraft's nose so it balanced on the horizon—the only accurate means of maintaining straight and level flight without instruments. "Doesn't make any sense. He could have sacrificed us, but why would Avery have gone along with the plan knowing it was a suicide mission?"

No one had the answer.

"There's another thing, too," Rigby said.

"What?" Maverick and Davidson said in unison.

"There's a timer. Wakefield is looking at it now, trying to see if there's a way to disarm it. He says it's doubtful. Whoever built it wanted to make it impossible for anyone to make changes while the plane was in the air–"

"How much time?" Maverick interrupted.

"Fourteen hours," Rigby replied. "But Reynolds says not to worry because our fuel will run out after ten hours, which means we'll be on land with plenty of time to get this thing off, right?"

Maverick looked at the young gunner. Nineteen years old, this was the boy's first rotation of active service. He pointed at the instrument panel. "Every single reading is wrong. We're flying blind. We should have enormous fuel supplies, but that won't help much if we can't point ourselves in a straight direction towards land—our land. If we go anywhere near the soviet bloc we're going to get ourselves shot down. Without a working compass we're just as likely to fly in circles."

"Are you saying, you can't land without instruments?" New beads of sweat formed above Rigby's brow.

Maverick grinned. "I can land this bird without anything

else so long as I can see out the windshield. The problem is, I have to find somewhere to land first."

"Whoa!" Rigby looked like he was just coming to realize the severity of the situation.

Maverick ignored him, trying to concentrate on the bigger problem. He looked at Davidson, the next person below him in the chain of command. "Broken Arrow!"

"What?" Davidson said.

"We're carrying twenty AGM-69 SRAM nuclear missiles. If we don't find land before we run out of fuel they're going to the bottom of the ocean." Maverick thought about the next step. "When the Strategic Air Force Command finds out they've had a loss of 20 nuclear weapons over Siberia, they're going to think the worst!"

"They're going to think we've defected?" Rigby pointed out.

"If we're lucky," Maverick said. "If not, they're going to think Russia was responsible. This could trigger Armageddon."

A red telephone handle and wire was attached to the ceiling of the cockpit directly above his head. It represented the most secure communication line directly to the Strategic Air Force Command — used only as a means of confirming nuclear attack orders.

Maverick picked up the phone and pressed the connect button. He shook his head, unable to comprehend a disruption in the secure link, as he heard only static. He spoke clear and firmly. "Strategic Air Force Command. This is *Maverick's Menace*. Requesting break in radio silence for immediate assistance."

More static.

He repeated his request. Waited for a response. And then hung up the phone.

"What did they say?" Davidson asked.

"Nothing. All I got was static." Maverick didn't wait for

Davidson's response to the news. With his right hand he flicked the radio over to 122.750 MHz—the standard channel for air to air communications. "Mayday, Mayday. This is U.S. Air Force Aircraft Maverick's Menace. Seeking radio transmission from any aircraft or radio station in our vicinity. We have lost control of our navigational instruments and are seeking a radio signal to set our bearings. Over."

The radio returned heavy static. Davidson increased the volume. The static seemed to worsen. "There's nothing but white noise."

Maverick reached forwards to rotate to another channel. Rigby put a hand on his shoulder and said, "Just wait a second. I think I hear something."

"What do you hear?" Maverick asked, studying the face of the youngest man in the room. He could be the only person onboard whose ears hadn't yet been damaged by the ever-present sound of the eight turbofans. Or his mind was already shot by the recent series of events and he was now delusional. Maverick couldn't determine which category Rigby fit into, so he let him keep going. "What do you hear?"

"Music," Rigby said, with certainty.

"You hear music behind the static?" Davidson looked doubtful.

"Yes. It's very light, but I can hear piano music!" Rigby searched their faces for recognition. Finding none, he continued. "I played piano my entire life. I was quite good, too. My mother wanted me to go to Juilliard. She drove me hard and I ended up joining the Air Force out of retaliation."

Maverick took a chance the kid might be telling the truth. "What's the song?"

"I don't know. It's old, but not as old as the classical greats such as Beethoven or Chopin. Sounds sullen, almost depressing."

"Well, that's going to do us a lot of good!" Davidson flicked to the next channel. It was broken with the same heavy static. He switched between more than a dozen before leaving it on the original channel. "It's useless. There's nothing on any of them."

"Except that damned music!" Rigby replied.

"The music's on all of them?" Maverick asked. "Are you sure?"

"Yes, I'm sure. The same song. Every time. Same melody."

After nearly twenty two hours of continuous flight the four turbofans on the right wing, unable to draw any more aviation fuel, misfired and failed. The engines on the left wing continued for a total of six more minutes, sputtered and then stopped completely.

Maverick naturally dipped the nose of the aircraft to avoid an immediate stall. He then brought *Maverick's Menace* into a controlled glide. But without any land in sight, they were destined to end in the water.

"All right gentlemen," Maverick said. His voice calm and confident. "We knew the fuel would run out eventually. Rigby, I want you to prepare the life raft, but don't deploy it until right before we're ready to eject or you'll never see it again."

Rigby nodded his head in silence.

"I want you all to know it has been a privilege and an honor working with you. We have a week's supply of water and rations inside the life raft. Depending on the temperature, we might just live long enough to be picked up by a search crew." Maverick grimaced. "Let's just hope it's one of ours."

"Is that an island?" Davidson stared vacantly out the left windshield.

Maverick looked as the tiny island came into clear view through the port windshield. At a guess, it was somewhere in the vicinity of ten miles in width and perhaps eight in length.

A small mountain, no more than a couple hundred feet tall could be observed at the far end of the island. The island was covered in snow and ice at least several feet thick. With the exception of the small mountain it was entirely flat. The only man-made structure he could see was a single runway which ran the entire length of the island. Although the island looked deserted the strip of blacktop appeared to have been cleared of snow only hours beforehand.

"My God! Thank you!" Maverick said. "If that isn't some sort of Divine Intervention, I don't know what is!"

The entire crew cheered.

Maverick made a shallow bank to the left, losing more altitude and lining up for an easy approach. He knew he only had one chance. In the process it gave him a clear view of the island. A small lake lay, unfrozen, near the middle of the island. Thick snow and ice reached the lake's edge and then stopped short of the water, as though someone had taken a carving knife to it. It appeared in striking green and purple colors — most likely a sign it was made by a geothermal spring, releasing mineral rich warm water.

Through the port side window, Maverick was startled to see how deep it went. At a guess, it could be as much as 100 feet.

"Looks like a nice island," Davidson said.

Maverick adjusted the flaps another ten degrees. "Yeah. Shame we're unlikely to live long enough to enjoy it. We've got less than four hours to work out how to get rid of that bomb, remember?"

Davidson kissed his Rosary Beads for good luck. "Just get us on the ground and I'll get rid of it myself even if I have to carry it by hand."

Maverick banked left until he lined the B52 up perfectly to the runway for the final approach. He leveled both wingtips. Confident that he had been saved for a higher purpose, he said, "I'll put us on the ground. Don't you worry about that!"

The nose passed the edge of the island and he saw the start of the runway. Even without the instruments to tell him, after more than 20,000 hours in the cockpit Maverick instinctually knew his beloved aircraft was close to the ideal 136 knots recommended for landing.

He moved the wheel just slightly towards his chest, raising the nose of the aircraft, slowing his descent rate, and settling perfectly level to touchdown.

After nearly twenty-two and a half hours in the air, and 312,000 pounds of aviation fuel lighter, the ten landing wheels of *Maverick's Menace* made contact on the runway of the unidentified island. The brakes locked and the tires gripped the blacktop sending a dark cloud of burnt tires into the surrounding air as the monstrous aircraft slowed to a final stop no more than a hundred yards from the end of the small runway.

Maverick applied the park brake and unclipped his seatbelt. "All right, Davidson. We're on the ground. Let's work out what we're going to do about that bomb."

Maverick gritted his teeth and used his shoulder to help his men slide the crate free of the fuselage. It slid down the grated steel ramp along a series of wheels and the momentum carried the heavy bomb nearly twenty feet along the runway. He stepped down the ramp and on to the runway's blacktop — only it wasn't blacktop. He grinned at the surprise finding and pressed his hand against the runway. It was smooth. Almost glassy like obsidian or polished ebony and despite the icy cold ambient temperature the stone was warm, bordering on hot to touch.

"What the heck is it?" Davidson asked.

"I have no idea," Maverick replied.

His men worked quickly with electric screwdrivers to remove the bomb's safety panels. Wakefield, his weapons systems operator, was the only one on board who might have a clue what he was looking at on the inside of the nuclear bomb. It was a far stretch to imagine he would be capable of disarming it, but so was finding a safe landing spot at the precise time the fuel ran out.

It was the first step, and a long way off saving their lives. Unless they could disarm the bomb in the next three hours they were all going to die. There was nowhere on the island that would keep them safe from its blast.

Maverick smiled. Today was a day of miracles. He sat down on the warm runway and simply looked at the island. The warmth made him feel safe for the first time in the past 24 hours since he was introduced to Mr. Avery and this bizarre mission.

The sensation was short lived.

Maverick stood up and swore loudly. It was the first time he showed his men he'd lost control. He didn't care. It was over and he and his men had lost. He walked over towards the bomb. "You can stop working on the bomb, Wakefield."

"What on earth you mean?" Wakefield laughed uncomfortably. "I have less than three hours to disarm this thing and I don't have a clue where to start."

"It doesn't matter. I think I just worked out exactly where we are, and whether you disarm that bomb or not won't change a thing."

"Why?" Rigby asked. "Where are we?"

"Wait here and I'll show you." Maverick climbed back into the cockpit, and returned less than a minute later with a cup and bottle. He carefully poured the contents of the bottle into the mug. It was a dark, rich, coffee. He filled it until the contents formed a narrow film on the surface. "Look at that."

It was perfectly still.

"What is it? I don't see anything, sir?" Wakefield asked.

"Just watch."

A slight tremor caused the liquid to move.

He waited slightly longer.

A second ripple formed. This one was slightly larger.

Davidson was the first to realize the significance. "I don't believe it! Of all the shitty luck—we had to pick this island to land!"

"What is it?" Rigby asked. "Where are we, sir?"

Reynolds was the next to fathom the depth of their desperate situation. He was the first to accept his fate with equanimity. He had survived ten years as a pilot during the war. Even if it was a cold war so far, he knew that he'd been living on borrowed time. He'd flown more than four hundred missions without significant incident. It was simply his time to lose. "We're never going to be allowed to go home, are we?"

"No, son. I'm afraid this is it. On behalf of the President himself, who spoke to me before we left—I thank you all for your service."

Rigby was the last to understand. At nineteen years of age he was by far the youngest man on board. His face shriveled in abject horror as understanding finally reached his simple mind.

"We're on *The Island*, aren't we?"

Maverick felt at peace. At least he finally knew what this was all about. Why it had been kept secret to them all. He didn't even condemn the President for doing so. He just wished he'd had a chance to speak to his kid sister once more and see his niece Alexis, who he'd been told was going to do great things for the world one day.

He then spoke with the calm, reassuring authority of a man who'd spent the greater portion of his time on earth in command. "Yes, son, I'm afraid we're on *The Island*."

CHAPTER 1

Antarctic Coast
~ Present Day ~

H ER WHOLE BODY ACHED AS she rolled over and looked at the bedside clock. It was 10:35 a.m. and still there was no sign of them. They normally came in at 8 a.m. on the dot every morning to check in on her and insist she try to eat and drink something. She was feeling better and thought maybe today she would try getting up and leaving her room — if they let her.

Quarantine was a big issue on a cruise ship. And any incidence of gastro meant passengers forfeited their right to leave their stateroom. She picked up the phone and pressed nine. No answer. The Indonesian service staff on board the *Antarctic Solace* had the highest ratio of staff to passengers of any cruise ship on the ocean. They were always attentive to her every need. She checked the number. Tried again. Still nothing.

Perhaps I'm ringing an old number?

She tried the Beauty Therapy, followed by the team from Fine Dinning reservations. Their prices were so extravagant they could afford to offer twenty-four-hour service. Still no response. *Maybe there's a fault with the internal phone system.* She waited some more and then tried again, before deciding it was time to get out of bed anyway. She was feeling better. Not well, but better.

She'd already missed the first three days of her voyage by being confined to her stateroom. It was nice, but even the best prison can become torture. In this case, one she'd paid big dollars to enjoy. She rolled onto her side. One long, and slow movement. She'd spent nearly three straight days in bed, and now everything was sore. Then, in another single movement she slipped her legs out from under the blankets. Her whole body felt cold. She took four steps to the door of the ensuite bathroom, stepped inside and turned the shower faucet to hot.

Steam began rising from the shower. Confident it was warm enough, she undressed and stepped inside. As the water warmed her body, she felt like she might pass out. She sat down in the shower and the feeling slowly went away. For three days she'd had nothing to eat and barely anything to drink. Once the seasickness had dissipated she just wasn't interested in trying any food again.

After about ten minutes, she reluctantly turned the shower faucet to off. Closing her eyes for a moment, she waited while the last of the hot water ran down her back, and then stepped out. Her ordinarily white skin, pale from years of work with limited natural light, appeared red and angry; having run the shower as hot as she could withstand.

Alexis Schultz stared at herself in the mirror. Her intelligent emerald green eyes stared right back at her with scientific accusation.

How in the world did I end up in this fucking mess?

Her otherwise perfect life had taken a stunning series of downward turns over the past five days, culminating in her present situation—three days of being sea sick and quarantined to her honeymoon suite aboard the overpriced cruise ship, the *Antarctic Solace*.

It was the large swell as the ship entered the latitudes south of forty degrees that had stirred the tremendous seasickness she never knew existed. The cruise ship doctor, worried about a spread of gastroenteritis, had quarantined her in the honeymoon cabin. For eight hours they had come to check up on her constantly, being more of an annoyance than of any real benefit. Then, she'd been given a series of painful antiemetic injections, which had finally allowed her stomach to settle, and then she slept almost continuously for the past forty eight hours.

Since then, no one had come to check up on her. Despite her multiple calls to every service department she could think of, her calls went unanswered. She dried her curly brown hair. Then pulled on a pair of black denim jeans, a white tank top, and dark green skivvy. Her myriad of freckles reached to her small dimples, giving her face a cute, albeit erroneous, appearance of innocence. She didn't put makeup on. Never wore any. Didn't need to—and if she did, still wouldn't have. As a scientist she didn't care for vanities. She forced herself to smile—even to her, it looked contrived; the sorrow of a lost puppy unmistakable in her otherwise striking green eyes. She tied the laces to her boots, opened the door and stepped out into the empty hallway.

She was on her honeymoon—and all alone.

CHAPTER 2

THE *ANTARCTIC SOLACE* WAS AN eight hundred and twelve-foot adventure cruise ship. Designed specifically for navigating waters in some of the world's most remote and inhospitable destinations, including both of earth's Polar Regions. The 85,072 ton vessel boasted a strengthened hull with a Lloyd's Register ice-class notation 1A for passenger ships, authorizing her to take commercial passengers to areas otherwise reserved for icebreakers.

She spent the summer months in each polar region providing luxury travel in the lucrative trade of Arctic and Antarctic adventure. This was the last of her trips in the southern hemisphere for the season, and probably a little too late. She carried a hundred and fifty paying guests and nearly twice that many crew and entertainers to ensure her passengers experienced the world's best in luxury cruising.

Alexis took a few steps down the empty passageway without falling. She smiled. *Perhaps I'm finally getting my sea legs?* At the end of the passageway she paused and looked back. No one had stopped her yet. She felt slightly nervous. Like a school girl sneaking out in the middle of the night on camp to meet a boy, she half expected one of the staff to catch her at any moment and send her straight back to her stateroom.

But no one came.

She tentatively looked over her shoulder where she had just

come from and then started to climb the stairs towards the sixth level. Her stateroom was situated near the very front of the ship, on the portside of the bow. She headed towards the aft of the ship. The main restaurant stood empty. It was often filled to bursting with exceptional food, delivered in both buffet style and a la carte—three times a day. Each sitting provided a two-hour window to enjoy the food. There was unique and even finer dining on top deck above, but this was where the main meals were served.

Alexis looked at the empty restaurant. She didn't wear a wrist watch, but could tell instantly that the time was outside one of those three meal windows. She'd never seen the place so vacant. Normally there's a straggler who's simply remained to have a coffee, or finish reading the newspaper. But today the place was completely empty.

She walked inside. Past the rows upon rows of stainless steel buffet serving tables and dispensers, all empty and polished clean so that the metal shined in preparation of the next meal sitting. At the end of the room she stopped before the kitchen door.

Her eyes glanced at the small opening where special orders were delivered to picky passengers. People who didn't like the normal, delicious food. Vegans, people who were gluten-free or had allergies to everything, and just plain whiners. During meal times the place was filled with chefs working vigorously to meet the demands of the passengers whose vociferous appetites for perfection drove them to work ever harder. Between meal times, you could ordinarily catch the occasional chef coming and going, or some of the junior kitchen staff performing the menial tasks of food preparation for the next sitting. Today, she saw no one.

She tentatively ducked her head into the kitchen window, hoping to catch someone who could make her something more interesting than the diet of plain toast and water, which she'd subsisted on for the past three days. "Hello. Excuse me . . ." she said.

No response.

"Is anyone there?"

Silence.

Well that's odd. Where is everyone?

Alexis continued walking aft. She was tempted to take the stairs up to the seventh level—where the finest foods in the world were served at a premium price, twenty-four hours a day. She would have too, if it wasn't for her fear that the deliciously rich gourmet meals would irritate her empty stomach and send her back to her stateroom in a quarantined status.

Behind the restaurant the ebony grand piano stood alone in an empty bar. The racks of alcohols used to blend expensive cocktails hung in preparation for the drunken revelers who would soon follow. Alexis guessed it must be before 1130, because that's when the pianist started. The bar usually didn't gather many patrons until then.

On her first day, before the sea sickness caught her, she had met James there. He was a Jazz pianist from New Orleans, playing music on the grand piano. He was a passenger but the staff let him play, and a crowd quickly formed to listen. Like everyone else, he appeared to have slept in today.

Alexis kept walking aft of the great ship, past the empty library. She stopped at the concierge and on shore adventure desk. A little yellow sign with a handwritten note stared blankly at her in the middle. She picked it up and read the note—*back in fifteen minutes.*

It reassured her nothing terrible had happened. No one bothers to leave a note if they're abandoning a ship.

She took a seat at the desk and waited. After a few minutes she stood up and laughed at herself. *What was I thinking?* A ship like the *Antarctic Solace,* with modern technologies and a reinforced steel icebreaking hull, doesn't just break apart at sea, or lose all its passengers to some freak accident while leaving everything perfectly intact. She was being overly paranoid. There was a perfectly logical explanation for where everyone had disappeared to. And she would discover it at any moment.

Alexis considered the only places aboard that could draw so many people away from the main areas of the ship. There was only one that she could think of — the theatre.

Maybe there's a big performance in the theatre? The entertainment department boasted some of the best shows of any cruise ship, ranging from current best-selling musicians to performances by Cirque du Soleil. The name struck a chord in her memory. She looked at the entertainment's board. Cirque du Soleil was on the list. They must be performing today, and drawing big crowds.

Of course, Cirque De Soleil was performing. This must be the day for the main show. She didn't even consider why the main performance would be showing during the morning, when traditionally they were always performed in the evenings. Even so, she couldn't get past the impending sense that some great calamity had affected everyone aboard the ship with herself the only exception.

Alexis continued to walk towards the back of the ship. Next to the empty library a door labeled Fitness Center was closed. Ordinarily she wouldn't have taken notice, but the series of strange events had led to a heightening of her senses.

She stopped and tried to open the door or turn the handle. It clicked as she went to turn it. Someone had locked it. Below was a sign which read, *Open 24 Hours*. She felt that uneasy sensation one feels when they are about to discover something very bad has just happened. She felt tight in her chest and her heart fluttered.

The *Antarctic Solace* provided luxury cruising to adventurers. Anyone interested in hiking across the Arctic Circle or climbing glaciers usually likes to exercise when they're confined to a floating hotel. Like everywhere else onboard, the cruise ship provided state of the art training equipment and industry leading fitness instructors and exercise physiologists.

She knocked on the glass door loudly. "Hello. Anyone in there?"

Silence.

Alexis sighed. Maybe her life wasn't quite ready to return to normal. She then continued to walk towards the theater. Her previously relaxed and casual pace now brisk. This time she didn't detour at any of the usual places where people could be found along the way. She passed the beauty salon, health retreat and spa.

Alexis ignored the boutique shops. All of which displayed the customary yellow 'closed' sign she had become used to seeing. That in itself didn't worry her. The shops often only opened during the evenings. She didn't once stop to question if she'd ever recalled seeing a yellow 'closed' sign on anything previously—which she hadn't. Subliminally, they simply contributed to her sensation that she was on some sort of deserted ghost ship.

She finally reached the entrance to the grand theater.

The golden doors were closed. It was a good sign. The amphitheater doors were left open when not in use so that guests could come and go. The fact they were firmly shut implied a show was currently being performed. Her ears perked trying to listen for sounds, but found only silence. She hoped that was related to the heavy soundproofing of the theater.

She tried the door handle. It was locked.

Then she noticed the yellow sign on the floor. The string which appeared to have previously held it over the door looked like it had been broken. Her heart pounded as she knew before she turned the yellow placard over, what it would say—
Closed. Back in 15 minutes.

She banged loudly on the doors.

Then saw the axe on the side of the wall. It was there in the case of fires. *I'm done waiting. It's time to see what's behind closed doors.* Alexis grabbed the small hammer on the side of the unit and then broke the glass cover of the fire axe. She reached inside and took the axe from its alcove.

No longer afraid of the repercussions of being caught, she lifted the axe high above her shoulders and swung it so the head struck in between the large doors. It cut a small slice out of the door, but nowhere near enough to open it. She repeated the process again. And again. By the fifth attempt, something gave way in the locking mechanism and she was able to open the doors.

She stepped inside the two hundred seat theater. Completely empty, the place echoed with her footsteps.

CHAPTER 3

HER HEART QUICKENED. *HAS THERE been some sort of disaster and I failed to receive the order to abandon ship with the others?*

She held onto the axe for reassurance. Then ran to the edge of the room and opened the thick glass doors to the exposed deck, which wrapped around the sixth level. Alexis stepped out into the freezing cold air. It was a technically a few degrees above, but that didn't make it feel any warmer—and she wasn't dressed for it whatsoever. Even so, she didn't feel the cold in her rush to learn the truth.

She ran to the portside where her designated life raft was supposed to be. She had performed a practice drill to reach it on her first day at sea. It rested at the edge of the 80 foot marker. Before she even reached it she'd imagined all the life rafts missing. Alexis anxiously passed the heavy bulkhead and found her life raft still secured inside its cradle.

The sight gave her a small amount of reassurance.

Her eyes scanned the vacant sea for other life rafts or signs of a tremendous calamity. None were seen. Instead all she could see was dark blue water, mostly still and reaching the horizon in every direction. She walked along the deck in a counter-clockwise direction. There were multiple life rafts situated in their cradles and suspended above the edge of the deck. By the time she'd reached the starboard side life rafts she accepted nothing terrible had happened to cause everyone to abandon ship.

There must be another explanation. One that didn't include anyone getting injured or hurt. She just couldn't think of any.

She stared at the water. There was something different about it. The dark blue water still filled her vision to the horizon in each direction, but there was something else. Then she realized what it was. The sea water was dead calm.

It was the first time she'd given the concept any thought. She looked at the horizon. It appeared almost perfectly horizontal, which meant the ship was still. There was barely even a gentle rocking motion. Even a ship at anchor swung around a little.

Have we run aground?

It was an impossible explanation. If they'd run aground surely there would have been signs of the impending disaster. Life rafts missing. Life jackets dropped as passengers tried to hastily don their survival devices, which would serve little use in an area with water temperatures approaching freezing.

So, if the Antarctic Solace hasn't run aground, where did everyone go?

Alexis opened the glass doors on the starboard side and entered the main entertainment level on the sixth floor again. Her eyes scanned the empty ship for any signs of recent activity. The lights were on. The fridges in the bar were running. The jukebox rattled as it waited for someone to choose the next song.

She yelled, "Hello. Is anyone still here?"

The sound echoed.

I'm thousands of miles away from civilization — and I'm totally alone.

Like a frightened child left alone in a strange place, she shrunk.

What if it wasn't the sea that got them?

What if the Antarctic Solace has been attacked and the passengers are all hostages?

The thoughts made her quickly realize that she needed to be

quiet, careful and sly in her movements. But even those thoughts only provided her with more questions.

Why would anyone attack them?

And if they did, why leave the ship completely empty?

She walked down to the fifth level and carefully slunk towards the bow of the ship again. Each of her senses heightened by fear, searching for anything that sounded different. Smelled different. Or looked unusual. Her confidence grew with each movement.

Over the course of the next two hours she searched the ship and found nothing. The ship was stopped at sea, with all passengers bar herself missing. With the exception of the crew's quarters on the lower decks, she'd searched everywhere. She would have searched the crew's compartments but they were only accessible by the elevators and required security access cards.

She returned to the bow of the ship, along the deck on the sixth level. There, she took the outside stairs that led to the seventh level. At the top she found a solid glass door. A prominent white sign with the words, "Cruise Ship Staff Only" barred the door. She ignored the sign. It was time to find answers. She hacked at it with the axe until it smashed to pieces.

Alexis opened the door and entered the bridge. It was entirely empty. Perched at the bow of the ship with glass windows surrounding the walls it allowed a three hundred and sixty degree view of the horizon. All she saw was an empty ocean.

Alexis walked over to some computer screens. A gimballed compass rested next to a small joystick. It was probably the only remains of sailing from another generation and looked ornamental more than for navigational purposes.

She glanced at the compass for a moment. She felt a sudden uneasiness at the sight. The compass arrow spun in a slow and continuous anticlockwise direction. Surreal in its constant movement, the compass appeared like it had been rigged as a gimmick.

Next, she examined the two computer screens beside the joystick. Navigational charts covered the screen. A tentative glance from the least astute bystander showed these two computers and their state of the art global positioning systems were what the pilot really used to navigate the ship.

The sight brought the tiniest bit of relief to her. Although she'd never been on a cruise before, there was no doubt in her mind she could at least work out from the GPS where she was. She scrolled across the touch screen.

It looked dark blue, the sign of deep water, wherever she went. As though the program had become caught up in a loop where each new screen simply mimicked the previous. Frustrated she clicked the image of a single ship—below it, were the word, "Locate Ship."

Where am I?

A moment later the computer began automatically scrolling through reams of information. When it stopped, the image that remained sent a tingling sensation down the back of her neck, as though her lost relatives of generations past were now warning her.

UNABLE TO LOCATE SATELLITES.

CHAPTER 4

Ronne Ice Shelf, Antarctica

W ITH HIS DEEP BLUE EYES hidden by the glossy reflection of snow goggles, he stared into the distance. The dry snow reached for miles. Over the ice covered crest and towards the horizon, the Pegasus science station stood hidden; concealed by snow. It was there, he knew it was. He just didn't know how to reach it.

His first attempts had failed because the strange floating iceberg ended in a thirty-foot chasm which separated it from the mainland continent of Antarctica. After leaving the *Maria Helena* on a snow mobile, he'd ridden to the very end of the island, and then followed the chasm in a westerly direction. The deep ice calving cut jaggedly inward with tiny faults in the floating landmass's structure.

Sam Reilly swung the snow mobile inward again. Swore, and then continued in search of another place to cross. It was clear he was going to need more equipment to pass the chasm and reach the trapped scientists in the Pegasus station.

All that would take time. No one had heard from the scientists, whose vessel had become trapped in the ice between the coast and the newly arrived iceberg, for more than ten days. They had previously advised their rescuers they were running low on supplies and were not equipped to survive the harsh winter.

He came around the second jagged fault line and then south again; this time towards the hill. It couldn't quite be called a mountain, but it was by far the highest point for miles. And it was on the edge of the giant iceberg.

Sam drove the snow mobile towards it, and rode up the base of the slope as far as he dared before the incline became too steep. He stopped about halfway up. Approximately a hundred feet he guessed.

He looked back. The shape of the ice island stretched for miles, and for the first time, he could gain a rough idea of its size and outline. It stretched at least five miles in width and possibly double that in length. Sam watched as the jagged edge of the chasm followed the entire length. He then looked towards where he had come from. About five miles back, the *Maria Helena* stood still, anchored alone in the bay.

Sam kicked himself for not preparing the Sikorsky Nighthawk better for transport. During the travel into the deep Southern Ocean, the *Maria Helena's* helipad became covered in snow, freezing many of the vital parts of the helicopter. The consequence of which was that only a land based rescue party was capable of reaching the ice station. He swore again, as he realized he'd already be back onboard if he'd been able to take the helicopter.

As it was, there was only one snow mobile on board. It could take two or three people at a stretch. He and Tom had played Rock, Scissors, Paper to see who would go and retrieve the scientists. Sam had lost, and Tom had agreed to help Veyron try and get the Sea King back in the air. Sam had left a few hours earlier, loaded with food supplies and medicine. Based on the GPS coordinates given and his current satellite imaging of the area, the Pegasus science station was approximately fifteen miles to the south.

No one had heard from the scientists for a total of ten days now. Matthew, on board the *Maria Helena,* had tried the VHF radio hoping they might pick up local communications. But all anyone could hear was static.

Sam still held high hopes he would be back within a few hours. Instead, he still couldn't work out how to reach the research station. He continued to climb the hill in the hope he would spot a safe place to cross the ice rift. Trudging through the deep snow, he continued his ascent to the tallest peak of the floating landmass of ice. As the incline increased the wind scattered snow from the crest which constantly appeared harder to reach.

Each step, he needed to consciously dig his ice boots in, and place the ice pick before making another move. He knew he should have gone back for more help, but his need to know what had happened to the scientists consumed him. With each step, he was certain he was going to make the 200-foot precipice. There he would be able to see the station at least. Then, with a direct line of sight he should definitely be able to communicate with the scientists via his hand held VHF radio.

Sam pulled himself over the last section of solid ice and reached the peak. The coast of Antarctica came into view. He struck his icepick in hard and tethered himself to it for safety. Not far in the distance, perhaps another few miles on the other side of the small ice mountain, he spotted the Pegasus Station.

It was little more than a dome shaped mound of snow, too symmetrical to be anything other than manmade. He adjusted the binoculars to see if he could make contact with any of the scientists. The place looked deserted. A single French flag was the only evidence of human involvement at the camp. He wasn't sure what he expected, but he was certain there should have been more than this.

Above the science station and spread out along the horizon, a timid display of colorful lights took his breath away. An Aurora Australis, the southern version of the Northern Lights filled the dark sky with vivid reefs of green, blue, red and purple.

Sam opened up the antenna for his portable VHF radio and depressed the transmitter button. "Pegasus science station. Does anyone read me?"

The radio made the sound of constant static. The same as when someone accidentally leaves the button for the microphone open, and it picks up every sound. Instead of being able to hear anything comprehensible, it produced a garbled mess of white noise.

He tried again. "Pegasus science station. This is Sam Reilly, from the *Maria Helena*. Can anyone hear me?"

More static.

He turned to face the *Maria Helena*. "*Maria Helena*. This is Sam Reilly. Come in for a radio check, please."

He received the same, constant garbled response he'd heard before.

Sam tried once more, and then gave up.

The heavy ionization of the spectacular display of lights were probably wreaking havoc on the transmission of radio waves. He lifted the binoculars back to his eyes, and traced a route back from the Pegasus station. When he reached the impassable chasm that split the Antarctic continent and the iceberg, Sam stopped. He studied the chasm. The iceberg ran east to west. From the east, where he'd recently searched, the gap was too large to cross and continued all the way to the ocean. From the west the chasm narrowed until it was no more than a foot or so wide at places.

Using the binoculars, Sam followed it backwards from the western end to the base of the hill he was standing upon. He stopped when he found a single portion of the iceberg where the distance within the gap had narrowed to the point where the top had covered over with ice. *There, I can get across there.* It would be dangerous, but he should be able to ride the snow mobile over it.

Sam turned around, preparing for the slow journey to the

bottom of the hill. Something reflective caught his attention in the distance. He pulled up the binoculars to his eyes and searched the horizon. The *Maria Helena* rested at anchor, alone in the bay — then behind her, maybe another few miles out, he saw a second vessel. It was covered in yellow paint; probably a cruise ship.

He put the binoculars away. *I wonder if they too have responded to the call for help.* Sam dismissed the casual thought from his mind as a sudden burst of wind gusted. It was so powerful it nearly knocked him off the hill.

Sam looked at the snow mobile at the base of the hill. It was more than two hundred feet away. Behind it, a localized storm rapidly whipped up the previously clear sky into something dark and evil.

Sam stared at the approaching monstrous wall of ice and snow. *Where the hell did you come from!*

He started to run.

CHAPTER 5

S AM CHIDED HIMSELF FOR NOT taking more caution. A snow storm in the Antarctic winter would kill quickly. The storm approached like a violent wave of destruction. He moved rapidly down the steep slope.

At first he tentatively chose each large step down. Then as the storm closed in on him, he started to climb down at speed. Careful at first, Sam quickly took greater risks with each stride, until he was running down the steep hill.

About two thirds of the way to the bottom, he lost his footing. It was a momentary mistake, which might end up taking his life. Sam's left leg slid on the ice and to compensate he threw the bulk of his weight on his right. It was too much. He toppled over and started to roll down the steep slope.

He gripped his snow pick in his right hand and tried to jam it into the snow — hard. The pick caught, but the momentum was too much and the handle ripped out from his hand. He started to slide like an uncontrolled toboggan, gaining momentum fast.

At the bottom of the hill he slid to a stop in deep snow.

Sam wiped the snow off his goggles. He waited for his eyes to adjust for a moment and then realized the storm was obscuring what little light had remained for winter. He stood up. Panicked, he looked for his snow mobile.

His vision was reduced to five feet. Sam couldn't see the

snow mobile anywhere. He wore snow clothes designed for the sub-arctic weather. They were rated to conditions as low as minus forty degrees Fahrenheit. He zipped the jacket up to his eyes. He wore a ski mask underneath, but with the increased force of the wind, it did little to protect his face from the stinging shards of ice.

He needed protection if he was going to survive the next few minutes, let alone the hour it would take for the storm to pass. Sam crouched down in the thick snow. Using only his gloved hands, he tried to dig a hole into the snow. His cave struck solid ice about two feet down. It wasn't perfect, but it might still save his life.

He huddled down with his face at the lowest point in the tiny snow cave until he reached something that resembled comfort. If the storm passed quickly, he would live. If not, he would freeze to death. It was that simple. Protecting himself as best he could Sam hoped like hell the storm would pass as quick as it began.

The previous gray of the winter's day turned to a constant darkness. Sam's mind drifted in and out of consciousness. Remembering some of the good times and the bad, and wondering how it all ended here—no more than five miles from the warmth and safety of the *Maria Helena*.

The storm raged for an unknown time. It could have been hours or days. Huddled up as low to the ground as he could manage, Sam had no way of telling the time.

He wiped off the snow built up along his goggles. The storm wailed ferociously. Somewhere in the darkness, his eyes caught sight of something. Sam couldn't quite tell what it was. He lost it a split second later. Then he saw the flicker of a strange glowing orange light. It was most likely a fanciful figment of his imagination.

And it was getting closer to him.

Sam's heart pounded. He knew he was beginning to feel the

symptoms of profound hypothermia. Despite his protective clothing the wind-chill ripped through and tore at his bones.

"No, go away!" Sam wasn't ready to welcome the bright light.

He reached for his ice pick. Forgetting he'd lost it when he fell, Sam swung his arms up at the glowing light.

"I'm not done yet!" he said, stupidly.

The orange light then reached down with a giant hand and grabbed him. It lifted him up as though he weighed nothing at all. "I'll be damned Sam. I don't know how many times I have to tell you — if you go off doing something stupid on your own, you're gonna get yourself killed."

"Tom?"

"Who else would be stupid enough to come searching for you in an Antarctic blizzard?"

CHAPTER 6

S AM OPENED HIS EYES. HE was in some sort of vehicle. His mind couldn't instantly determine what or where it was. The headlights were on, but they barely penetrated the darkness. Windshield wipers swung back and forth. The blizzard was going to bury them if they didn't find shelter soon.

"Can we make it back to the *Maria Helena*?" he asked.

Tom shook his head. "No way, the wind is gusting towards us at 120 knots. There's no way we're going to be able to drive into it. We're going to need to find somewhere to ride out the storm."

Sam thought about the landscape he saw from the top of the mountain. "I think I know a place."

"Where?" Tom asked.

"The Pegasus science station. It's just on the other side of this hill. If you keep it on your right until we round it, and then head due south, we'll hit the research station."

Tom pressed the main starter switch and an engine began to whir below them. The entire vehicle lifted off the ground as though they were riding a fluffy cloud. "Sounds like a plan."

Sam grinned. Everything was going to be all right. "You got the hovercraft engine to work in this weather?"

"Veyron did."

Tom threw the gear forwards and the hovercraft lurched

ahead. It picked up speed; going with the wind instead of being thrashed by it like before. The base of the small ice mountain came into view, while the rest of it remained hidden by the storm.

"Keep it on your right until we reach the other side," Sam reminded him.

"Gotcha, Sam."

A few minutes later they rounded the mountain. Tom turned the hovercraft due south and then increased power to full. They picked up speed. Designed to be used on water and sand, the hovercraft raced along the icy surface.

Sam looked behind him, where a large electrical heating element had been added. Feeling the warmth on his back, he removed his gloves to absorb some of it. His hands burned as sensation returned. "I like what you've done to the hovercraft."

Tom turned his head to the right and looked at the glowing heating element. "Veyron's idea. It wasn't for our comfort though. He's not that considerate. Says it has to stay on so long as we keep the hovercraft out here. Otherwise, the engine will freeze and we won't be going anywhere."

"All the same, I appreciate it."

Sam felt himself relax. The warmth bringing a certain level of reassurance that everything was going to be okay.

He closed his eyes.

The loud bang was instantaneous.

Sam felt the jarring all the way through his spine. "What the hell was that?"

The hovercraft slowed, settled and then kept going. "I've got no idea! We lost contact with the ground for a while. Launched by one of the small mounds of ice I suppose. Landed pretty hard, but I think we'll be okay."

Sam grinned. "Sorry. That was the chasm. I forgot to mention there's a slight gap between the island of ice and the Antarctic coast."

"Right," Tom shook his head. "Should I expect any more gaps?"

"No. We should be good. We'll reach the Pegasus station any minute now."

Tom touched the brakes and the hovercraft settled to a crawl. Directly in front of them, buried to its roofline with snow, was what they had crossed the southern ocean to reach — the Pegasus science station.

Ordinarily, Sam guessed, the scientist would have taken it in turns to clear the front area of snow. It was an immediate bad sign that the snow had been left to build up.

"This is it?" Tom asked.

"I'm afraid so."

Tom flicked the power to off and the hovercraft sunk into the ground. "Any idea how to get in?"

Sam put his gloves on. "Now we dig — for our lives."

Over the course of the hour the two men dug deep into the snow. By the end of it, Sam had cleared enough snow to reach the door. He pulled at it, and entered the French science station — Pegasus.

CHAPTER 7

SAM PUSHED HARD ON THE door. It was enough to slide through the gap and enter the science station. The building had a dome shaped ceiling and stretched about eighty feet long. There were four archways that led to other rooms. The lights were all switched to off.

Sam found the light switch and flicked it to on. "Hello."

No response.

He heard Tom huff as he squeezed his large, muscular frame through the narrow opening. Tom looked at him. "All this effort and nobody's home?"

Sam shrugged his shouldered. "I don't know."

"Hello. Anyone still here?" Tom said loudly.

Silence.

Sam walked forward. "Come on. Let's go see what we can find. Maybe they left a note or something?"

"Okay."

Stepping further along the room it all appeared normal. A moment later he heard the automatic electric generator start up. "They must have it set to automatic when the amp-hours reached a certain level. Turning on the light switch must have activated it."

The first room was small with a second doorway about ten feet in. The room most probably served as a pressurized room to stop the cold air flooding the inside living quarters. Five full sets of snow clothes, including overalls, jackets, and boots all stood on their racks. Above each one was the owner's name.

"If their outside gear is in here, they must be home?" Sam said.

Tom looked at the boots. They were clean and polished. He picked one of them up. The boot looked like it had barely been worn. The smell of black boot polish instantly brought back memories of basic training in the Corps. "I guess they've had a lot of time on their hands down here. The question is, if they're here — why aren't they answering?"

"No idea. Let's go find out."

Sam opened the next door and entered the main living room.

Stepping further along the room it all appeared normal. It wasn't huge, but it was big enough to be comfortable for the five scientists who were supposed to be working there. A small kitchenette with a kettle stood at the end of the room. Fold out camp chairs sat in a semicircle. A small bathroom was at the end of it. A bed hung from the ceiling like a hammock. Inside, a single book rested open. A single dog's ear noting where the last reader paused. Sam picked it up. *The Old Man and the Sea*, by Earnest Hemmingway. He smiled. He'd read it as a kid, and felt a natural attraction towards it.

Tom came back into the room. "There's no one here. The food stores are packed with enough rations to keep a group of five men fed for months. The bathroom's empty. There's no sign of the scientists or where they went."

"Strange. Why would the scientists just leave?"

"No idea. And while we're at it. What did they leave with if they didn't wear their snow protection gear?"

"Any idea what they were studying here?"

"No. The rooms are all virtually empty. They must have had laptops with them. They're nowhere to be seen. Maybe they had to leave suddenly, and that was all they took with them."

"All right. What about their radio?"

"What radio? I didn't see any."

Sam walked back into the main living room and started opening up cupboards. "It must be somewhere here. They were able to radio for help when we were still in the Falkland Islands."

"Good point. I'll have another look."

"It would be good to contact the *Maria Helena* and get word to them that we're okay. We might be here a while before the weather clears up."

"I agree, but don't sweat on it too much. I spoke with Veyron before I left and made him promise not to come looking for us if we don't come back before the storm finishes. I told him we'd find somewhere to bunker down and ride out the worst of it."

Sam opened the fourth cupboard. A series of VHF and HF radios were bolted to the internal wall. "All the same, it will be good to let them know we're safe in the Pegasus station."

"All right," Tom said, "You let them know we're okay. I'm going to go cover the hovercraft with some tarpaulins, then I'm going to raid their stores for something to eat."

Sam smiled. "Sounds good. See if you can find me some chocolate, too."

He watched as Tom opened the door and disappeared into the store room. Sam picked up the VHF radio microphone. Switched to channel sixteen. "*Maria Helena,* this is the science station Pegasus. Are you receiving me?"

No response.

Sam increased the volume and adjusted the squelch. The static became louder. "*Maria Helena.* This is the Antarctic science station, Pegasus. Can you hear me?"

He waited for a reply.

The same constant, garbled, static whirred indecipherably from the radio. He was about to turn it off. *I guess none of the radios are working out here.* Sam thought about the first time he ever saw an Aurora Borealis. It was in Fairbanks, Alaska and his brother and he had gone on a team-building orienteering exercise in the wilderness. When the amazing night's sky was filled with the strange and colorful phenomenon, he'd tried to radio his brother to find out if he could see it too. All he received was radio static. He recalled it had something to do with the high altitude ionization affecting the transmission of radio waves.

Does the South Pole have an equivalent problem with its lights?

He'd seen the Aurora Australis from the mountain earlier. He reached forward to turn off the radio, and then stopped. It wasn't transmitting pure static. Although it appeared garbled, the sound had a distinct and repetitive nature to it.

Has someone overlapped the radio channel with a constant message?

Sam flicked to the next channel.

It displayed the same repetitive crackling sound, and so did the next channel. He tried another three before he gave up.

Could there be a subliminal message behind the static?

If so, what is the message?

CHAPTER 8

T OM WALKED INTO THE ROOM. He took one look at Sam's face and knew something was wrong. It was pensive, and his usual curiosity appeared to have been replaced by a new worry. Sam had his head turned slightly to the left, with his ear right up against the radio speakers. His eyes were closed as though he was straining to hear the sound or recall a song.

"What do you hear, Sam?"

Sam ignored him. His right hand tapping a slight beat onto the side of the wooden table. It was slow at first, then increasing in its tempo. The sound reminded him of classical piano as it changed from fast to slow, and then soft to loud. It sounded mysterious, more like something by Debussy rather than Bach or Chopin.

Tom waited.

Sam turned the radio to off and tapped the same tune with his fingers. The tone was distinct, rhythmical, and compelling.

"What is that?" Tom asked.

Sam stopped what he was doing; his eyes wide with interest. "I have no idea."

Tom sat down on a chair next to the radio. "I guess you couldn't get through to the *Maria Helena*."

"No," Sam replied. "All this static is blocking everything."

Tom looked at the table where Sam had started to drum the same, compelling beat with his fingers again. "Not everything."

Sam grinned. "I didn't even realize I was doing that. No, not everything was blocked. Behind all the static this tune seems to be on a continuous transmission."

The microwave at the other end of the room beeped. Tom stood up again. "That's our lunch. Dehydrated macaroni and cheese. I would have expected more from the French scientists. Don't worry about the radio, this storm will be over soon and then it won't take long for us to return to the *Maria Helena*."

"I'm not worried," Sam replied. "Just curious what that sound was, that's all. It seems familiar to me. I can't place it, but I'm sure I've heard it before. Somehow, it doesn't fill me with warm feelings. Instead it reminds me of something terrible that's happened. A part of my life my mind's tried to cover up. I just can't for the life of me think what that is."

Tom shrugged his shoulders. "It might just be music being broadcast by one of the other science stations. That's all."

"You're probably right."

Tom and Sam spent the next two days waiting for the storm to subside. The food was boring, but plentiful. Tom spent the time reading a good book. Something about a futuristic world called Prism, by Alan Dean Foster. He enjoyed it. Sam on the other hand, squandered his free time trying to write down the musical score to the sound he'd heard.

It was seven a.m. when the storm passed and they were able to remove the covers off the hovercraft. The Southern Lights display had finished. The sky was dark and crystal clear, providing a horizon filled to the brim with stars.

Tom switched on the electric heating element inside the hovercraft. Within a few minutes it glowed like fire. Twenty minutes later, the important components were warm enough to start the engine. Tom sat in the driver's seat and flicked on the master switch.

The engine started slowly.

He let it warm up until he was confident that it would make it back to the *Maria Helena*. Sam left a note for the absent science crew to contact the *Maria Helena* if they returned, using VHF channel 16. He then closed the front door.

Tom switched the headlights on and the white, fluffy snow reached the horizon. He placed the hovercraft into gear, and the entire thing lifted off the ground as its skirt inflated.

It would be an easy run back to the *Maria Helena*. The crisp snow covered the undulating landscape for miles. Tom increased the speed of the main propeller, mounted at the rear of the hovercraft, until it reached maximum RPM.

They would reach the *Maria Helena* soon.

Tom came over the next hill and landed into the icy waters of Weddell Sea. The spray of water shot out in all directions. Next to him, Sam braced his hand on the dashboard as the change in momentum threw him forward.

Tom brought the hovercraft to an idle. In the distance, miles out to sea, he saw the faint outline of a ship—most likely the *Maria Helena*. "Where the hell did the giant iceberg go?"

CHAPTER 9

S AM BROUGHT OUT HIS COMPUTER tablet. He swiped to the side until he found the icon he was looking for and pressed to open it. A moment later the GPS App opened. It positioned them on the very edge of Weddell Sea. He was initially worried they'd approached from a different angle or something and was off course.

He looked at the ship in the distance and correlated it with their current position. "That must be the *Maria Helena* out there, Tom."

Tom shook his head. "I gathered that. What I want to know is where the damned island of ice disappeared to? I mean the place was massive. It had a small mountain and everything!"

"Maybe the storm blew it out to sea again?"

"Elise never did work out where the ice had come from, did she?" Tom asked.

"No. Despite reviewing a series of current and recent satellite images of the surrounding coastline and the ice shelf, her computer programs couldn't determine where the ice mass had come from. It was like the entire landmass of ice just appeared out of nowhere." Sam shrugged his shoulders. "Maybe it returned there."

"It came from somewhere. Most likely the bulk of its mass was underwater. That's the reason Elise's program can't find a match on the ice shelf where it broke away from."

"So then, where did it go now?"

"The storm probably blew it out to sea. I wouldn't worry. Let's get back to the *Maria Helena* and work out what we're going to do about those missing scientists."

Sam felt his shoulders sink back in his seat as Tom accelerated again. The hovercraft skimmed across the still water of the bay. Within minutes they were slowing down again, coming to a complete stop on the portside of the *Maria Helena*. "At least she's still where we left her."

"Yeah, she's one trustworthy girl."

Sam opened the side hatch and climbed out onto the hovercraft's rubber skirt.

Veyron peered at them from the side of the *Maria Helena*. "You two gentlemen picked one hell of a weekend to go camping. Did you find the scientists?"

"No," Sam said. "We'll tell you all about it shortly."

Veyron lowered the winch cable and Sam connected it to the hovercraft's chain link. Ten minutes later the hovercraft was being secured on the aft deck. Sam and Tom walked into the bridge with Veyron. Matthew and Elise greeted them once they were inside. And a moment later Genevieve brought them both warm minestrone soup.

Matthew smiled at them. "Good to see you made it back. Are all your fingers and toes still intact?"

Sam held up his hands. "No frostbite. Warm hands warm heart."

Tom grinned. "You don't have enough good sense to freeze."

Sam ignored Tom's comment. He looked at Matthew. "Where the hell did that storm come from, anyway? I thought you said there was nothing significant on the synoptic charts for the next few days?"

"Sorry Sam. There weren't any signs of the storm on the synoptic charts, radar or satellite weather prediction software.

It must have been a localized weather pattern."

Sam raised his voice, slightly. "It sure didn't feel like any localized weather system."

"No. It started fast and it became big," Matthew agreed. "I'm sorry."

"Don't worry about it. At least Veyron got the hovercraft to work in time." Sam stared at the radar screen. "Any sign of the ice mass which looks like it disappeared just as quickly as it appeared from nowhere?"

Matthew increased the distance on the radar to five miles, and then to ten. "No. We anchored back from it at the start of the blizzard. Throughout the storm we couldn't see anything more than two feet in front of us. When it all died down and I stepped out on the front deck, the entire iceberg had disappeared. My guess, the storm blew it away."

"I agree," Sam said. "You'd better notify the National Oceanic and Atmospheric Agency and any local ships that the massive iceberg is now drifting along the coast somewhere. It may very well cause a similar problem to some of the other science stations further along."

"I already have," Matthew confirmed.

"Thanks." Sam clicked on the second man-made structure he could see on the radar. A large ship—most likely a cruise ship. It was much too large to be an icebreaker or a research vessel. It was probably the same one he'd seen from the top of the small ice mountain he'd climbed two days earlier. "What's their story, they haven't moved for days now?"

"No idea Sam," Matthew replied. "It's the *Antarctic Solace,* a cruise ship that caters to the adventurous sightseers."

"Have you tried radioing and seeing if they need any help?" Sam knew that even for a well set up cruise ship, Antarctica could prove fatal to the slightest of mistakes. And being caught in the recent blizzard was a mistake for any captain.

"Yes. Three times. No response whatsoever."

"That's unusual. Do you think they're in some sort of trouble?"

"The funny thing is . . . you said you saw the cruise ship out there two days ago when you were on the ice mountain?"

"Yes. What difference does it make?"

"Well, our Automatic Identification System didn't pick them up at all until a couple of hours ago. Even then, when I looked at her automatic logging information, her last known location based on her satellite tracking was more than six hundred miles to the north of us."

Sam consciously thought about how such an advanced system could be so confused. "Not a problem. This is what happens when people let computers take over sailing. What about our radar log. When did it pick them up in the distance?"

Matthew squirmed and then replied. "I'm afraid it too seems to have the same confusion about the facts. It only picked them up two hours ago. It's like it just materialized from thin air."

"Strange. Have you tried contacting her shore side operators?"

"Yes," Matthew replied. "According to their company, they were supposed to anchor in McMurdo Sound three days ago, but never showed."

"Are they at anchor?"

"No, from what we can see using current satellite imaging they're drifting."

"All right. We'd better get over there and have a look. Tom and I will take a runabout in case the cruise ship is trapped in ice. Where's Elise? Her medical skills might be required. Also, I want Veyron—if it's an engineering problem I want him with us."

"When are you leaving?" Matthew asked.

"Now, of course."

CHAPTER 10

A LEXIS SETTLED INTO A ROUTINE on board the *Antarctic Solace*. She'd given up fearing what she couldn't see and simply accepted the fact the ship had become stranded. The anchor chain was fully coiled and the steel anchor was in its cradle. As far as she could tell the bow of the ship swung round with the change in wind and currents, but she was certain the ship hadn't moved. The *Antarctic Solace* wasn't aground, but something else, almost intangible was holding her at bay. She was still buoyant, but an invisible restraint stopped her from floating away.

She didn't believe much in the religious views of life and death, so she doubted very much she'd found herself in some sort of unfortunate limbo of the afterlife. No, she was still alive and someone would come for her. There was infinite food aboard for one person, and even if the power ceased, she would have provisions for keeping the food stores cold on the deck. She settled into a routine of morning exercise, cooking, reading, and generally making use of the freest time she could ever recall having. She even used the swimming pool while it remained warm. She felt a strange comfort in her situation—until the storm began.

The outside world darkened to the blackest of nights in an instant. The noise followed next. It was the sound of gale force gusts of wind and ice pummeling the windows with such ferocity she could have been mistaken for it being produced by machine gun fire raking the *Antarctic Solace*. Worried the windows would shatter and destroy what little refuge she had left, Alexis climbed the external stairs on the protected side of the ship, and into the secure bridge. With large reinforced glass windows it gave her a clear view of the impending tempest.

She watched the storm unfold. Quickly the swell amplified into large crests of ice and water which raged towards the bow of the ship. Tentatively she watched them crash along the bow, unable to quite see the extent of their destruction from the dark confines of the bridge. Alexis carefully held the side of the navigation table, bracing for the sudden movements that must surely follow each strike.

Blinded by the darkness of the storm her sense of hearing compounded the sounds of the ghastly tempest. She searched the instrument panel and found a section labeled external lighting. Alexis flicked on all deck lights.

The bow of the *Antarctic Solace* lit up with the warm glow. In the ocean ahead a shadow approached. Only it wasn't a shadow at all. Instead it was the largest wave she'd ever seen and on its crest were several icebergs, as large as houses.

This is it! Nothing can survive that!

Alexis cowered under the navigation table, certain the entire bridge was about to be destroyed. Her knuckles turned white as she gripped the edge of the table and held her breath in anticipation. She then waited for a certain death—that never came.

After a few minutes she let go and then looked at the decking of the bridge. Unable to see the horizon or the outside world, it appeared almost perfectly still. Maybe not quite still, more like the deck of a boat tied up in protected harbor.

When she was certain the wave wasn't going to crash through the windshield she slowly stood up. Outside the large swell could still be seen. Alexis didn't believe for a minute the *Antarctic Solace* was built with such strength to render the massive waves harmless. A ship ten times her size would be thrown around like a toy boat in a storm and yet it was obvious the storm wasn't affecting the ship.

She closed her eyes and tested the theory. At first she held onto the navigation desk. When it didn't feel like it was moving, she let go. With her hands held in front of her for protection, she took a wide stance and balanced.

The ground below didn't move. She opened her eyes. Another large wave approached the bow. She stared at the ground instead of looking out and nothing happened. It confirmed the truth—the ship was stationary, despite the waves crashing into her bow.

Was it all an optical illusion?

She wondered if she was in the midst of a particularly bad dream, or perpetual recollection of the ending of her life.

Almost in response to her question, the violent tempest ceased as quickly as it had manifested. The deadly sea before her being replaced by the calm of an icy millpond, which appeared placid and inviting. The darkness disappeared and once more she was in the perpetual twilight of the approaching Antarctic winter. The water below suddenly so clear she could see the bottom.

So I must be close to shore – but which one?

It might be a hundred feet, maybe two hundred. Its clarity so intense she couldn't tell for sure. She studied the icy sea, waiting for some sort of sign the storm had returned. Part of her thought for certain she was now only in the eye of the storm, awaiting for the real damage to occur.

But it never came.

Instead, she heard banging.

The continuous banging came from the level below. The *Antarctic Solace* had a number of automated mechanical systems that made a multitude of clanks and bangs throughout the day and night. Her ears, now highly attuned to the strange sounds of a working ship, recognized the introduction of a new one immediately.

What is that?

It was coming from somewhere below; that much she was sure of. Alexis walked down the stairs and into the level below. Confusion was replaced with fear as recognition dawned. The bangs were coming from the locked door next to the Grand Staircase. *The new door* — it was yellow, and had been purposely sealed from the inside.

Alexis looked at the door.

Her mind instantly recalled the first time she'd noticed it. She'd been searching the *Antarctic Solace* for any other survivors and found it. She'd tried the handle but found it was locked from the inside. She had taken interest in it only because she thought she'd previously noted it as an emergency doorway to the lower decks in the same place.

In fact she was certain she had identified the door as an emergency exit that led to a small decked area just above the waterline that could be used in an emergency and as a means of traversing onto another small vessel.

She'd wondered at the time if someone had indeed gone to the trouble of locking it. Was it because they wanted to keep her from getting inside? Or, was it because they had wanted to keep something from getting out?

The door banged again and Alexis returned to the present.

She tentatively placed her hand on the door. It vibrated with the sound of a steel striking steel. She removed her hand instantly. Someone was trying to get in. The banging was clearly the sound of a person intentionally driving something to the end of it.

She heard each clank with the combined sense of excitement and fear that she was going to find someone.

But would she want to be left alone with this person?

The door's large hinges broke free, leaving a slight gap

between the door and the steel frame it was bolted to. She saw fingers slip through the gap, feeling their way to the bottom and then back up again, where they stopped at the second hinge. And then disappeared again. Only to be replaced by the edge of a crowbar.

"Hello?"

No response.

She gripped the hilt of the small fire axe she'd been carrying with her wherever she went for protection. It gave her little confidence as she knew, one way or another, she was about to discover what this was all about.

The edge of a crowbar slipped into the gap and was followed by the commencement of the previously mysterious clanking sound—someone was driving the steel bar into the hinge. On the fourth strike, the hinge gave way.

A moment later the yellow door opened and two men walked through. One of them average height with a solid build. The other, the height and size of a giant. Both wore thick snow jackets and goggles.

The first man stepped forward and removed his snow goggles, revealing startling deep blue eyes. "Good morning, my name's Sam Reilly." He smiled kindly, revealing perfect white teeth. Natural creases formed on his cheeks where he appeared to have a big, perpetual smile. "Some crazy weather we've been having, hey?"

CHAPTER 11

S AM LOOKED AT THE BEAUTIFUL woman in front of him. The first survivor he'd found since boarding the cruise ship. She had dark brown, curly hair and pale skin which looked at odds to her otherwise Mediterranean ancestry. Freckles covered her cheeks where dimples formed at the edge of a nervous smile, which turned to genuine joy as recognition dawned on her that he wasn't there to cause harm. Her white teeth and intelligent green eyes portrayed an image of confidence and innocence at the same time, making him want nothing more than to take her in his arms and reassure her. She had obviously been through a horrible ordeal and was only just now releasing the tension.

In her hands she gripped the wooden hilt of a double headed fire axe so hard her knuckles turned white. Sam didn't know whether to laugh or cry for the pitiful creature in front of him who held the axe close to her chest, more like a teddy bear than as a useful weapon.

"Whoa, we're on your side," he said. "We're here to offer our assistance, that's all."

She studied him as though searching for a reason to doubt, and then visibly relaxed. "Christ, am I glad to see you Mr. Reilly." She offered her hand. "My name's Alexis."

He accepted it. She had a relatively strong grip and looked him in his eyes. Like a woman who'd grown up with a heavy minded father or worked in a male dominated industry. He looked past her at the empty grand staircase. "This is my friend Tom Bower."

She smiled at them both. Dimples formed at her cheeks, surrounded by light freckles. "Nice to meet you both."

Sam looked at the vacant promenade. "Where is everyone?"

"I have no idea. I was kind of hoping you might be able to tell me?"

"You mean you don't know?" he asked.

"Not a clue. I just woke up and found myself all on my own."

"Really?" Sam asked. He crossed his arms and wondered if she had a reason to lie. "You went to bed one night and woke up by yourself?"

"That's pretty much what happened," she paused, as though she'd only just heard how crazy the statement sounded. "Well, not quite like that."

"So, how did it happen?" he asked.

"I had been confined to my stateroom with severe seasickness. One of the Doctors aboard gave me an antiemetic which he told me occasionally had the side effect of quite severe drowsiness. I must have fallen into that category, because I slept solid for forty eight hours. When I woke up I tried room service. I had no luck and went out to grab someone's attention. Pretty soon I realized I was all on my own."

He wondered if she had any reason to lie. She had a beautiful and innocent face, but that didn't mean she wasn't responsible for whatever happened. He let her keep talking. "How long ago was that?"

"Four days. I've searched the ship—there's no one else on board."

"Are the lifeboats missing?" Sam asked.

"No."

"Any obvious sign of a near disaster. Something that would suggest why an entire passenger list and crew would willingly abandon the ship?"

"No. Everything appears to be working normally. There aren't even any lifejackets missing. It's more like everyone just simply vanished."

"You're certain?" Sam asked. "Is there anywhere else they could be trapped?"

She gritted her teeth. "The crew quarters on the lower decks. You can only access them by elevators which require crew or entertainer's ID cards."

"It's a possibility." Sam depressed the transmitter on the portable radio. "Elise. When you find the security room, see if you can get us access to the crew and entertainer's decks."

"Veyron and I are on it," Elise replied over the radio. "We'll let you know when we have access."

"Elise?" Alexis asked.

"She works with us. Kind of a computer geek. Lovely, but nerdy. You know the type?" Sam looked at Alexis, trying to work out whether she too fit into that description of people. "She'll break the code and access the lower compartments fast and then we might find some answers."

Alexis nodded her head as though she knew the type very well. "Do you know where the security room is? There are security cameras all over the ship, but I haven't been able to find where their data is monitored and stored."

"Yes. We contacted the owners of the *Antarctic Solace* before we came and got them to send us a digital copy of the ship's schematics. Its three levels below us. We should be able to access it from where we came."

"The other side of the yellow door?"

"Yeah, why?" he asked.

"That would explain why someone went to great lengths to build a solid door, where a fire escape previously existed."

"Which means someone was intentionally responsible for whatever happened here."

"I think so." She looked at him, almost as though she was examining him — trying to decide if he could be trusted or not. "Where have you come from?"

"Ellsworth Land, Antarctica. We were on a mission to rescue some scientists whose ship had been trapped by the frozen ice."

"Did you find them?"

"No. We're still looking though. That crazy weather put a hold on our search for the past three days."

"Three days?" She looked confused. "I timed the storm, expecting to die at any moment. It lasted just fifty five minutes!"

"No. You're definitely mistaken," Sam said. "I was stuck less than five miles inland in an abandoned ice station while a vicious Antarctic blizzard demolished the coast."

"It's true," Tom said. "I had to come rescue his ass before he froze to death."

"But that's insane!" She looked both confused and angry, as though he and Tom were trying intentionally to obscure her memory. "I made breakfast two hours ago and ate it on the deck in perfect sunshine before the storm erupted!"

Sam looked at Alexis, trying to judge her response. "That's impossible. There hasn't been sunshine for three days. Instead there have been 140 knot winds raging. It only ceased an hour ago."

CHAPTER 12

A LEXIS TOOK A LARGE SIP from her strong coffee. She insisted on having a drink before explaining to the two strangers how she ended up in her current predicament. It felt like an interrogation the way they pummeled her with questions and queried the veracity of her answers.

"Do you want something to eat?" she asked.

"No thank you, ma'am," Sam said. "I just want to get to the bottom of what's happened here."

Tom smiled like he figured he was done getting any answers from her. "I'm going to meet up with Elise and see if we can find the Security Hub. That way we'll gain access to the crew and entertainer's decks and hopefully she'll find the security footage which will show us exactly what happened here."

"Okay, be careful," Sam said. "Let me know the second you find anything."

Tom nodded and disappeared through the broken yellow door. Alexis finished her story about how she'd been seasick and then woke up to find herself as the only person aboard the ship in the middle of the ocean.

Sam stared at her. "And since then you've been making the most of it?"

"Yes. I've been exercising, trying to keep fit. Mostly biding my time waiting for someone to rescue me, from wherever I am."

"You don't know where you are?" he asked.

"Not a clue. How could I?" She gritted her teeth. "I left port in Argentina eight days ago. I became sea sick four hours into the journey and spent the next three days confined to my stateroom. So I have no idea where I am."

"You're in the Weddell Sea, Antarctica."

"The Waddell Sea. Are you kidding me?" she asked. "The waters have been perfectly still. I thought it was renowned for having dangerous, large swells?"

"It is. Of course, I've already told you this entire area had thirty foot swells for the past three days, but we've already agreed to disagree on that account, so you can make your own judgment."

She stared at him. Her emerald eyes locked in a determined challenge. "You look like you already have."

"Have what?" he asked.

"Made your judgments," she said. "You think I'm crazy, don't you?"

"I haven't decided whether you're crazy or not. In fact, I haven't ruled out that you orchestrated the entire event."

She spilled her coffee. "You think I abducted all these people?"

"I have no idea what happened to everyone on board. I'm simply saying you're the only person we've found on board a perfectly sound cruise ship off the coast of Antarctica—and you weren't exactly trying to find help, were you?"

"Are you kidding me?" She swore. "We're in the middle of the Southern Ocean! What the hell was I supposed to do?"

"You could have called for help." His tone came across harsh and he quickly made a smile. It looked kind and warm, and practiced—he wanted her to feel that he was on her side and simply frustrated because he couldn't find answers.

"Well, it's not like we get a lot of cell phone coverage out here."

He laughed. "I didn't mean by phone. You could have gone to the bridge. They'd have a satellite connection, GPS, radio. Something that could have told you where you were and how to get help."

"I did. Only it didn't provide me with any answers. Only more questions."

"You woke up and found yourself on a deserted cruise ship in the middle of the Southern Ocean, and the bridge only gives you more questions?"

"Yeah. None of the instruments were working."

"Are you sure you just couldn't work out how to use them?" he asked.

"Certain."

"Do you sail?" he persisted.

"No. But I'm a reasonably intelligent person. I can usually work things out. And this was different. The GPS failed to locate any satellites, the digital logbook had been deleted, and the radio . . ." she took a deep breath in, sighed and then continued. "The radio provided nothing but static. Behind which, was the most eerie, and yet mesmerizing tune I've ever heard."

Sam started to tap his fingers on the side of the doorframe. Slow at first, then fast, and then evenly.

Her eyes widened at the sound. "You heard it, too?"

"Yes."

She looked somewhere between frightened and curious. Like the child stuck at home alone for the first time listening to a strange sound in an empty room, and terrified to open the door to investigate in case it should turn out to be an evil clown. "What was it?"

He squirmed as though unsure how much to say. "It took me two days' worth of frustration to recall where I'd heard it before. I had to write down the musical score before it hit me."

"You rewrote the musical score to the sound behind the

static?"

"I was stuck in an ice station. I had the time to waste. It turned out I'd studied the song in high school music—that's why it felt so familiar to me."

"You studied music?" she laughed.

"It was one of my fun subjects. I mainly took sciences, but I liked piano and thought a music subject would even it out. As it was, it came in useful to me this time."

"And what was the song?"

"It was composed by a Hungarian pianist named Rezső Seress while living in Paris in 1933. He titled the work, Vége a Világnak—Does the name mean anything to you?"

"Not a thing." She smiled. It was coquettish and endearing, but practiced rather than real. She wanted him to become endeared to her. "I like music but never had a good ear for it. It sounded so melancholy yet beautiful. Do you know what the song was about?"

"The English translation meant, *The World is Ending*." He paused to let the words sink in and then continued. "Written during the Great Depression and rise of Fascism in his native Hungary, Seress used it to emphasize the despair of the people and ended in a quiet prayer about people's sins. Incidentally, a poet by the name of László Jávor later wrote his own lyrics to the song, titled *Szomorú Vasárnap,* or *Sad Sunday* in which the protagonist wants to commit suicide following his lover's death."

Her sweet smile contorted at the new information. "So why was it playing in the background?"

"I don't have a clue. The Aurora Australis which are common this far south cause high altitude ionization and wreak havoc on electrical and radio waves. For some reason, the frequency of that sound appears to render it undistorted."

"But why would anyone on an Antarctic research station want to listen to such gloomy music on repeat?"

Sam laughed. "Funny you should mention that."

"Why?"

"During the Second World War an Urban Legend developed that people would listen to the song and then commit suicide. In Great Britain, the BBC became so concerned the song would affect the morale of the people during the war effort that the song became banned."

"So, people listened to the song and then killed themselves?"

"Yeah, most of them just jumped to their deaths. Of course, it was during one of humanity's darker hours, so perhaps there was always going to be a higher than average statistic of suicides. They just coincided with the release of such a dreary song." Sam shrugged his shoulders and then looked at the ship's railing. "Still. You can't help deny it's a hell of a coincidence, isn't it?"

She shook her head. "You think everyone jumped ship because they listened to a stupid song?"

"No." Sam laughed and opened the door to the deck. "I have no idea where everyone's gone, but I intend to find out."

"Where are you going?"

"To the bridge of course — to get some answers."

CHAPTER 13

S AM WALKED INTO THE BRIDGE of the *Antarctic Solace*. He noticed the broken door lock splintered in pieces on the floor. Otherwise the inside appeared perfectly normal. He looked at Alexis. She had a slight grin on her face—*so she had broken in to get answers.*

At the main navigation station he found the compass pointed correctly to the north. He switched on the Navionics computer. An image of the *Antarctic Solace* superimposed in the calm waters of the Weddell Sea appeared a moment later.

"There you go," he said.

She stared blankly at it. "I don't know what to say."

"It wasn't there a few days ago, was it?" he asked.

"No, it definitely wasn't."

Sam pressed the icon for the ship's log. It came up instantly. The ship had left Argentina ten days ago. It traveled at an average speed of fifteen knots for the first two of those days. Then the ship and any information about it disappeared from the log until it reappeared in the system at 0830—the same time he noted the storm had passed.

"That's strange. It appears the ship's log shares your apparent amnesia."

She smiled. It was genuine. No longer coquettish or practiced. It took him by surprise—it made her even more beautiful than he'd first thought. "I told you I wasn't crazy!

Now do you believe me?"

"Sure, but I still don't have any idea what's going on here." He turned the marine radio on and switched to channel 16. *"Maria Helena,* this is Sam Reilly aboard the *Antarctic Solace.* How do you read me?"

"Loud and clear." He recognized Matthew's voice over the clear radio. "Did you find out what's happened?"

"No. It would appear the crew and passengers have all disappeared."

"Everyone?"

"All except for one passenger. I'll bring her across shortly and we'll work out our next move."

Sam placed the radio's microphone back in its cradle and walked towards the broken door.

"I don't know, maybe you were right with your first theory."

"What theory was that?"

"That everyone on board listened to Rezső Seress's stupid Hungarian suicide song and simultaneously decided to jump ship."

She laughed. "You can't possibly believe . . ."

"I'm kidding. There'll be a perfectly reasonable explanation soon enough. Elise will get the CCTV results and it will all make sense."

He walked through the door.

"Where are you going?" she asked.

"To see if Elise can tell me where you've been for the past eight days."

CHAPTER 14

ALEXIS FOLLOWED SAM THROUGH THE door. She could hear the soft sound of feet on steel stairs where a young woman was running to meet them. Sam stopped in front of her at the top step and let the person come to him.

The woman stopped five short of the top step. She had an exquisitely beautiful face, framed by a plain gray beanie with the intricate plaits of her dark hair only just visible hanging through its edges, and a pair of impenetrable aviator sunglasses. Her complexion was golden and she guessed came from a mixed ancestry, most likely somewhere between the Mediterranean and Asia. She wore a light blue turtleneck that showed the muscular curves of her lithe and athletic figure and dark blue denim pants that rested over black zip-up military boots. She either didn't feel the cold or hadn't bothered to put her ski jacket on before leaving the warmth of the internal section of the cruise ship.

Sam had described her as nerdy!

Alexis felt an instant pang of guilt at her jealousy of the younger woman who was already in Sam's life. It was irrational and she found herself hoping the woman was too young for him. Alexis had always detested the emotion. It was the worst of them all and poorly placed given her present situation — the last thing she needed or wanted in her life was another man.

A slight pang of guilt tugged at her as she realized that his description of Elise as the most intelligent nerd he'd ever met was replaced by the image of a young and stunningly attractive woman.

The woman was breathing fast like she'd been running hard. She then smiled at Sam. Alexis thought it was coy and teasing. "You're going to want to see what the CCTV shows."

"You had some luck with the security tapes?" Sam asked.

"Sure did!" She grinned. "You're not going to like it, though."

Sam looked at Alexis. "Elise, meet Alexis — she's been stranded here on her own after she woke up to find instead of missing the boat, she was the only one who managed to catch it."

Elise ignored the poor play on words and looked at Alexis. "Pleased to meet you. I bet you've had a pretty shitty week."

Alexis smiled politely. "You have no idea."

"What did you find on the tapes?" Sam asked.

"You know that stupid song you made me listen to?" Elise said.

"The Hungarian Suicide Song?"

Elise lifted her sunglasses as though she wanted to better see his face in response to the news. "That's the one."

"Let me guess, the *Antarctic Solace* was playing the song over its loud speakers?" Sam asked.

"That's right." Elise smiled condescendingly; her bright purple eyes glowed like the Devil. "And then, immediately after it played, everyone casually jumped overboard."

"That's impossible," Sam said.

Elise smiled like someone who'd just checkmated the grandmaster. "I know that, but you watch the tapes and tell me it didn't happen."

CHAPTER 15

S AM WALKED INTO THE SECURITY room with Alexis and Elise. Tom was by himself sitting at the desk reviewing earlier footage from the cruise.

"Hey Tom," Sam said. "Where's Veyron?"

"He's gone up to the bridge to run a check to see if the engines are still functioning," Tom said, without looking up. "The Weddell Sea could turn into ice any day now and we thought it might be prudent to get a little further away from the coast before that happens."

"When did he leave?" Sam asked.

"About ten minutes ago, why?"

"We've just come from the bridge. I would have thought we would have run into each other, that's all." Sam sat down and looked at the main computer monitor. "All right, Elise. Let's see this recording."

Elise pressed play and the digital security recording started. Sam watched as the tape showed what appeared to be a normal day aboard the *Antarctic Solace*. The recording was taken from inside the main entertainment deck, which included a number of closed boutique shops and a view of the port outside deck. The passengers and crew were progressing through their day the way one would expect, with the former looking like they were on vacation while the latter worked constantly.

"How long does this go on for?" he asked.

"About an hour," Elise replied.

"Okay, fast-forward until a few minutes before the evacuation."

Elise stopped fast-forwarding and the recording played at its normal speed. Sam listened to the now familiar melody of the Hungarian suicide song. He then watched as the passengers lined up two in a file and slowly walked towards the ship's balustrade. When the music stopped, each person took a step forward. They slowly continued until each person went up and over the deck.

The recording lasted another minute after the last person disappeared and then stopped as though someone had intentionally paused the recording.

"That's it?" Sam asked.

"Yes." Elise replied. "Do you still think no one jumped after hearing that stupid song?"

"I know what I saw, but videos can lie. How much do you trust this video?"

"What you saw happened. That much hasn't been tampered with, but I can tell you now that we're not seeing the whole picture."

"Someone's done some clever editing," Alexis suggested.

"It would appear so," Elise agreed.

Sam stared at the final image. "So you're saying none of those people climbed overboard?"

"No, that much happened." Elise tapped on the keyboard. "Everyone in this recording is real and the event that you just watched, including them climbing overboard happened. Everything before and afterwards has been intentionally deleted and made to look as though the digital log simply broke at that point."

"But you believe someone adjusted it?"

"I'm certain of it. Whoever is responsible has gone to great lengths to build a picture that appears unadulterated and leads us down a very different path than the truth."

CHAPTER 16

"IS THERE ANOTHER VIEW? ONE that looks down at the water where they landed?" Alexis asked. "Maybe they survived."

"The Weddell Sea is only just above freezing," Tom said. "Anyone who entered the water would be dead within minutes from hypothermia."

"If they entered the water, at all that is." Alexis shuffled forwards in her chair. "Can I see the earlier part of the recording?"

"Sure," Elise replied. "But there's not much to show. Just hours of normal cruise ship life."

"All the same, I'd like to see it."

Elise slid the time stamp back two hours and pressed play. Everything looked completely normal inside the cruise ship. The boutique shops were open and people wondered in and out, people spoke to the on shore excursion concierge about sea kayaking near the Ross Ice Shelf, others gambled while in the background a young man played 50s classics on the ebony grand piano.

They watched for about ten minutes.

"It all looks normal to me," Sam said.

"All right," Alexis said. "Fast-forward another twenty minutes."

Elise did so and the video continued to play. This time a

young man with a red baseball cap stood outside a shop that offered an assortment of books and memorabilia from the Antarctic continent. He scribbled a message on a yellow piece of paper and placed it on the door handle. The words were just legible from that distance — *back in five minutes.*

They watched the familiar scene of passengers coming and going across the main promenade. Each one was wearing clothing befitting an expedition to the South Pole. They were a mixed group of young adventurers and older scientists.

Another shop closed for the afternoon, followed by a small café. A different person wrote another message on a yellow piece of paper and left it on the front door. They watched as the crew numbers dwindled on the promenade.

"Is it just me or do the staff keep disappearing?" Alexis asked.

"That would be normal for the afternoon on board a cruise ship like this. The promenade would settle down while passengers ate dinner and then the shops would reopen."

"But they're not closing down for dinner," Alexis said. "They're removing the trained staff!"

"What do you mean?"

"Check the time stamp. It's three o'clock — the place shouldn't be closing down for the afternoon." Alexis looked at the yellow card. "Can you see what the last one said?"

Elise paused and then increased the size of the image. It read, *back in five minutes.*

"I knew there was something wrong with those fucking yellow cards when I first saw them days ago!"

"You don't like people taking a toilet break?" Sam asked.

Alexis ignored the comment. "Okay Elise, can you please rewind to five minutes earlier than the earliest screen."

"Okay, sure."

The promenade was full again. Everyone looked happy. There was a general enthusiastic vibe to the entire place. Most people on board would have paid a fortune for the opportunity to visit Antarctica and were making the most of every minute. A man with a red baseball cap walked towards one of the boutiques. It offered to sell books and memorabilia on Antarctica. He stopped for a moment outside and started to write on a yellow piece of paper.

Elise stopped the video. "You've seen this section before."

"Okay, I think I know what's going on here," Alexis said. "And I think we're all in danger."

"What is it?" Sam asked.

"That man never walked into the shop. All he did was write on a yellow card that he'd be back in five minutes and then locked the front door."

"Maybe he's the security guy who does the locking up?" Tom pointed out. "I mean, if you can convince the rest of the passengers to jump ship, why go to the trouble of locking the crew and entertainers up?"

"Maybe whatever they've done to convince the passengers to jump ship wouldn't be possible if the crew were there to instruct them not to?" Alexis said.

"That's a possibility," Sam agreed.

Elise stopped the recording completely. The face of the man in the baseball cap remained on the computer screen for a moment and then disappeared. "It's all just a theory until I can break the code to these security recordings and see exactly what happened."

"Hang on," Alexis said. "Can you get that exact image back?"

Elise rolled her eyes. "Sure, but my time would be better used if I returned to hacking the older security records until I find the deleted parts of this time period."

"This won't take long," Alexis said. "I was certain there was something familiar about that man — and I just worked out what it was."

Elise brought the image back.

"There it is!" Alexis said.

"What?" everyone said in unison.

"He's wearing a Harvard Medallion on his right hand—it denotes the highest achievement in science. There's been fewer than fifteen of those given out in Harvard's history!"

"So, what does that prove?"

"Don't you see? There's no way someone who scored the highest marks in decades at Harvard is going to find themselves working as a sales assistant on a cruise ship. It's the same guy, I'm sure it is. He's been going around locking all the doors, and removing the staff."

"Maybe he had a good job and he lost it?" Tom suggested.

"No way!" Alexis said. "A guy like that doesn't lose a good job. Do you realize that more people have become the President of the U.S.A than receive a Harvard Medallion in science?"

"Anyway, how could you tell he was the same as the other guys? Their faces were obscured and each time the person wore completely different clothes?" Elise asked.

"Because I saw the ring on his left finger, each time."

"How could you be certain it's a Harvard Medallion?" Sam asked.

Alexis held out her right hand. On her fourth digit a plain ring with a golden medallion over the Harvard crest glowed orange. "Because I have one of those rings."

CHAPTER 17

SAM SHUFFLED IN HIS CHAIR. "Okay, so whatever happened here wasn't an accident. Someone orchestrated it. Elise, can your facial recognition software get a good enough image of his face to identify him?" Sam asked.

"Shouldn't be a problem."

Elise slowed the security recording until she could flick frame by frame. She stopped on an image of the man's face.

She then typed: *Harvard Medallion Recipients.*

"Hey, there's only ever been eleven people in the history of Harvard who met the criteria for its Medallion." She scrolled down; her eyes scanning the list of names. "Whoa! Alexis, you're not lying. You were a recipient."

"Why, Elise–" Alexis paused as she withheld a small smile. "Did you doubt my word?"

"Not for a minute."

Harvard Medallion recipient? She's smart. Sam made a note to find out what she does now for work once he had more time.

"Good," Sam said. "That leaves just ten names to identify. I don't suppose you know any of the other recipients?"

"No luck. I was the first in about ten years."

"Okay, it's back to you, Elise."

"Just a second."

A series of names flashed up on her laptop. Next to each

name was a likelihood of a match, represented as a percentage. There were a total of forty names left taking into account a possible change of hairstyle, color, facial hair and aging. Elise added the additional Boolean operator to the search query: *AND* — Attended Harvard University. Five names were left. She then added one more Boolean operator: *Not* – Deceased. Results: zero.

"Hmm. That's no good."

"What's wrong?"

"It says everyone who matches this image and attended Harvard is deceased."

"Could he have stolen the Harvard Medallion ring?"

"Yes, but it seems strange to steal one and wear it when you're committing a crime. More likely to think he'd always worn it and simply didn't think to remove it," Alexis said.

"Or that he was so confident he wouldn't get caught that he didn't bother removing it," Tom suggested.

"All right," Sam said. "Maybe you're over thinking this. Can't you just check a match with his facial recognition and winner of the Harvard Medallion?"

"Sure," Elise said. "But we already know anyone who looks like him and went to Harvard is now deceased."

"No we don't. We just know anyone the computer thinks looks like him and went to Harvard is dead. I know your software is good. Now I want to see the images with my own eyes."

Elise nodded. Then typed the elements of the search fields into her laptop and pressed enter. A moment later only one name came out.

Sam leaned over her shoulder and read the single name that came up — *Randy Olsen*. He stared at the picture. "That's our guy. A little younger back then, but definitely the same person."

Elise clicked on *Current Status.* A new page of information opened up. "There's just one problem."

"Now what?" Sam asked.

"It says here Randy Olsen died in a boating accident ten years ago. His body was never found. In his obituary, it's noted he was pitched to be the leading mind in quantum physics in the future."

"Oh great," Alexis said. "Just when you think things can't get any stranger, we find out our main suspect is a guy who's been dead for the last ten years."

CHAPTER 18

"ALL RIGHT ELISE, BACK TO the priorities." Sam said. "How are you going to find and retrieve the lost section of tapes so we can see where the passengers were taken?"

Elise sighed. "I have a program working on it now. It might take a while. Whoever deleted the original sections went to great lengths to make it appear normal."

"If they were deleted, how can you retrieve them?" Alexis asked.

"It has to do with how a hard drive is built. You never really get to completely delete anything. When you click delete, all you're really doing is removing the link to access the data," Elise explained. "The trick is whoever's responsible for this has placed about a million fake data locations for my program to search as well. It will take time, but I will get it eventually."

"Good," Sam said. "That's one thing; now on to the next. How can we access the crew and entertainer's levels?"

"It's going to take too long to break the code to the elevator to the lower levels. The elevator system is managed on a separate system."

"Meaning?"

"I can't hack the elevator from in here."

"Is there another way down?"

"No. Per the schematics, the crew and entertainment's level is below the waterline and accessible by three single elevators.

One at each end of the ship and one at the middle."

Sam picked up the security phone sitting on the desk. "Can you find me the number for the bridge?"

Elise typed the name into her laptop, which was synchronized with the security computer. A moment later a number was displayed on the screen. "Dial 99."

Sam dialed the number and the phone started to ring.

"Hello," Veyron answered. His voice sounded irritated, like a typical engineer he didn't appreciate being rushed or interrupted.

"Veyron. How are we looking?" Sam asked.

"Everything looks to be in functioning order. I'll need access to the lower decks to get the screws turning again."

Sam sighed. "Why?"

"They've been locked. It's a normal procedure for a ship at anchor or at port. The system suggests nothing's wrong with the propellers—just that someone's locked them."

"Let me guess. The locking section is inside the engine bay which is only accessible through the crew and entertainer's level?"

"Now you're getting it." Veyron sounded like he was cheering up. "How did Elise go? Has she got the code for the elevators yet?"

"No luck. She says it might take some time. The system is stored separately to the main security room." Sam gritted his teeth. "Veyron, any chance you can break into it the old fashioned way?"

"With brute force?"

"Yeah."

"Sure I can, but it will take me a few days without any heavy machinery. I've looked at the elevators, they're built to be watertight."

"All right. You'd better make a start on it until we come up with a better plan. We're going to need those screws turning if we're to move the *Antarctic Solace* out of the Weddell Sea before it gets frozen in permanently."

"Okay, will do."

Sam hung up the phone.

Elise stared at him, feigning a hurt expression. "I didn't say I can't hack into it."

"You didn't?"

"No. I said I can't do it from here. There must be a separate storage section for the security cards. It's not attached to the security center, but I'll find it."

"Can you see inside down there?"

"No. Per the owners of the *Antarctic Solace,* the crew and entertainers opted to have all security cameras removed from their deck due to concerns for privacy."

"So we're looking at the possibility the entire passenger list have been trapped down there?" Alexis asked.

"No," Sam said emphatically. "You can't hide two hundred people on a boat without making a sound. If they were trapped below we would have heard them by now."

The security phone rang. Sam answered the phone and placed it on speaker. "What have you got, Veyron?"

"I just remembered," Veyron said. "The owners of the *Antarctic Solace* or someone from her onshore team should have the security codes. Get the codes and you can input them into a security card and gain access."

"But we don't have blank cards?" Tom said.

"Yeah we do. There's a whole bunch in the second drawer on your left, Tom. I checked before."

"Thanks Veyron. Have you got their number?" Sam asked.

"Yeah. I'll give them a call and let you know once we have access."

"Thanks."

The phone line went dead.

"You want me to keep working on the elevators — see if I can beat the owners of the *Antarctic Solace* in finding the security code?" Elise asked.

"No. Leave it to Veyron to work out. How long will it take you to find the deleted security tapes?"

"Could take an hour. Might be days if they were clever enough."

"Is there anything you need to do? Or is it just your computer program working?"

"Just my computer program. What do you need?"

"I want you back on board the *Maria Helena* — we have to find out where the scientists of the Pegasus station went. While you're appropriating the satellites overhead, you'd better include in your search any ships or landmasses with an extra couple hundred people on board. We now have two groups to rescue and I intend to do so before the entire Weddell Sea freezes over and we become the third group who need rescuing."

"Sure, Sam," Elise said.

Alexis put her hand to her mouth. "The scientists from the Pegasus station are missing?"

Sam looked at her for a moment. She appeared unusually concerned after the news of the lost Pegasus scientists. "Yeah, that's who we came down here to rescue. They sent a mayday call fifteen days ago. Apparently their ship had become stuck in ice when a large iceberg, the size of a small island, floated into the peninsula. They were unequipped to survive the upcoming winter on board their ship, which was now frozen in the ice, and returned to the Pegasus station."

"But you never made it because you found the *Antarctic Solace* in trouble instead?" Alexis asked.

"No," Sam said. "We made it to the Pegasus station, but no one was home. That's when the storm hit. Tom and I waited inside for two days. When the storm finished this morning we came straight back to our own ship, the *Maria Helena,* and discovered the *Antarctic Solace* in trouble and came to investigate."

"Are you talking about the French science station, Pegasus?"

"Yes. They had a French flag out the front of their ice station, but I couldn't tell you where they had come from or what they were doing there." Sam sighed. "In fact, I have no idea what they were doing there—the place looked like it had never been lived in despite clothing, food and boots all still being there."

Alexis took a deep breath. "I can tell you why it looked unlived in."

"Why?"

"Because it wasn't their ice station."

"What do you mean? They gave us the coordinates fifteen days ago. We lost communication with them after the second radio transmission, but they were able to provide their GPS location."

Alexis's ordinarily soft and innocent façade took on an authoritative stance that took Sam by surprise. "Whoever it was you spoke to, it wasn't the scientists from the Pegasus station—that's for sure."

"What makes you say that?" Sam asked.

"Because the real Pegasus station is situated in East Antarctica, two hundred miles Southeast of McMurdo Sound—nowhere near the Weddell Sea."

"Perhaps they set up a second camp on this side of the Antarctic Ridge?"

"Definitely not. Their secret research for CERN was in East Antarctica."

Sam stared at her; a wry smile opened in his otherwise stern face. "How could you possibly know what they were doing there?"

Alexis crossed her arms. "Because I sent them."

CHAPTER 19

"YOU SENT THEM?" SAM ASKED.

"I'm a physicist at the Conseil Européen pour la Recherche Nucléaire in Geneva, known as CERN," Alexis said. "Last year, a group of researchers discovered that the Antarctic was full of ancient ice tunnels. Most likely caused by ancient meltwater which eroded the weakest parts of the ice over millennia—some of these are said to be in excess of a hundred and fifty miles long."

"Okay, so what interest does a quantum physicist have in ice tunnels?"

"None. I don't care at all about them." Alexis turned serious again. "Most of my research involves accelerating tiny particles and then colliding them together at unimaginable speeds."

"The Hadron collider," Sam said.

"She's my little baby. Without her, all of my work would have remained in the field of theoretic physics. Unfortunately, my current research requires something a little larger—about ten times as large."

"You're looking at building a new particle accelerator inside ancient ice tubes?"

"That's it."

"What were you researching, specifically?"

"It's a long story, quite complicated—you wouldn't understand."

"Try me."

"Have you heard of the Higg's Boson—erroneously dubbed the God Particle?"

"Yeah, didn't they prove it didn't exist?"

"No. They proved it exists, just that they can't reproduce it or control it because it's too unstable. My research suggests we could build more of them. I have a theory for how we could store them and if my research can one day prove it, we'll have enough power to finally send people out into space. We're talking about a totally different jump in the way we transport people. The sort of leap the human race got when they discovered the internal combustion engine."

Sam shook his head. "So that's what this is all about."

"You think someone's attacked the men from the Pegasus station and abducted every other person on board the *Antarctic Solace,* leaving me isolated, because of my research?"

"It makes sense, doesn't it?" Sam said. "Why else would someone go to such extreme lengths to get your attention?"

"But that's crazy. We're talking about research that will take a lifetime to move from pure theoretical physics to practical uses. The particle I'm talking about is so unstable it will be decades before we can even consider handling it for research."

"Even so, you must admit the coincidence that some physicists have gone missing the same week an entire passenger list that includes you, the head of CERN, also disappears is too unlikely for mere chance. And now we find out the only connection is a man who was once set to be the next leading quantum physicist."

"No one knew what we were doing," Alexis said. "It's impossible to think the whole thing's connected."

"But you sent a team down here to build a new particle accelerator!"

"No. I sent a team down here to investigate the feasibility of such a project. It would take years to get approval to build such a thing and all the countries who share Antarctica would have to agree. Then it would need to be built. We're talking at least a decade if we were lucky before we had a working particle accelerator."

"How many people know about your project?"

"Not many and of those, most think I was purely considering it for future development projects. Almost nobody knows why I really wanted to build such a large collider."

"All the same, the coincidence seems uncanny. Telling even a small handful of people a project is 'super-secret' is enough to ensure a leak."

"Do you have the GPS coordinates of the real Pegasus station?"

"Of course." She looked up the details on her smartphone and showed him.

Sam typed the GPS into his laptop. "The entire area is covered with cloud cover. It's been there about five days by the look of it."

"We need to get to them."

"I agree, but how long would it take?" Sam asked.

"If your ship could put us in at McMurdo Bay it's under two hundred miles inland over relatively flat surfaces. What snow craft do you have?"

"I have a two person hovercraft. It will do the return trip in under three days."

"Good. When can we leave?"

"Now — and you're coming with me."

CHAPTER 20

S AM STEPPED ABOARD THE *MARIA Helena* with Tom, Elise and Alexis. He introduced Alexis to Matthew and Genevieve and filled them in on their plan to check out the real location of the science station, Pegasus. Genevieve brought out a warm lunch — roasted lamb with rosemary and vegetables.

Elise switched on her second laptop while they ate. She quickly established contact with the satellites overhead and appropriated their functions to search the surrounding areas. Her laptop hummed as it confirmed a secure connection. "Okay, I'm in — Alexis, what's the coordinates of the real Pegasus?"

Alexis opened her smartphone and clicked on an App titled secure documents. Inside she quickly swiped left with her thumb until she found what she was looking for — a document titled Pegasus. She clicked to open it and then handed her phone to Elise. "Here."

"Thanks." Elise looked at it for a second and then handed the phone back to Alexis. She then typed the exact latitude and longitude into her computer down to their sixth decimal place and pressed enter.

The view on her computer screen showed a blurred image of Antarctica. East and West Antarctica is divided by the Trans Antarctic Ridge; the west being smaller and full of undulating ice and rock mountains, while the east was larger and almost entirely flat with deep ice. A moment later the image increased in size until it displayed only west Antarctica. By the time the process had magnified for the fifth time the entire screen went gray.

"What happened?" Sam asked.

"Sorry, Sam." Elise clicked the negative button on her keyboard once, zooming out again. "Looks like there's one hell of a storm cloud over Alexis's science station."

"Any chance we can get a view from yesterday?" Sam asked.

"Sure. These satellites take a digital image every twenty-four hours."

"Good. Do it."

Elise brought the image up again. "Same storm yesterday. I'm going to keep going back until I find you a clean image of Pegasus."

"Thanks," Sam said. "Is it just me or does it seem like everywhere we want to look gets covered by a storm cloud? The same thing happened when we first tried to find the Pegasus after their original call for help."

"So now our dead physicist has the power to change the weather!" Alexis griped.

Elise stopped at day fifteen. "Here we go. This was the image taken on the day someone from the Pegasus station made a call for help. Looks like you might be right, Alexis—someone has intentionally blocked our view of this station."

"People generally only like to obscure one's view of things they want to keep hidden. I think it's time we make a visit to the real Pegasus station."

"Do you want me to come?" Tom asked.

"Yes, but I need you on board the *Antarctic Solace.* It will need to be moved out of the Waddell Sea if we don't want it to become frozen in the ice."

"What about you?" Tom asked.

"I'm still hoping the scientists are trapped by the strange weather formation, intentional or not. We should be able to get in there undetected using the hovercraft. We can be in and out in under a day."

"There's one more thing you're both forgetting to consider," Elise said.

"What's that?" Sam and Tom said in unison.

Elise grinned. "Are you going to open the armory?"

CHAPTER 21

A LEXIS WATCHED AS MATTHEW, THE *Maria Helena*'s skipper, unlocked the door to the armory. She followed him and the rest of the gang through the steel door. Inside were more than a dozen rows of stainless steel storage cabinets on wheels. The sort you have to slide to access the rows behind. Sam pressed a button on the wall and five separate storage cabinets automatically slid to the middle of the room — revealing a cache of military grade weapons ranging from assault rifles to large machineguns that needed to be mounted to fire and rocket launchers.

"Holy shit!" Alexis swore. "I thought you were a civilian vessel? What are you planning on doing, overthrowing Antarctica?"

"You'd be surprised by the kind of people we sometimes meet," Sam said. "And I don't want my team taking any chances."

Who are these people I've been rescued by?

Elise stepped forward and picked up an Israeli 9mm open-bolt Uzi submachinegun from a foam cradle. She held it up to her shoulder and looked through its sight. It was dead straight. She retracted the bolt and checked the firing mechanism. Satisfied the weapon would fire if needed she picked up a box of 32 round magazines and grinned. "Can't go past an Uzi — durable, reliable and effective. Okay, I'm ready to get back to work."

Alexis took a deep breath as Elise removed the last vestiges of doubt in her mind that she was anything but a computer geek.

Tom moved the next three stainless steel shelves until a new weapons tray opened up. This one held seven types of shotguns. He ran his hand along the handles of three of them before picking up a twelve gauge Remington 1100 Tactical Shotgun. Lined it up to his shoulder and looked through its sight. Satisfied, he opened and checked the firing mechanism was intact. He then picked up two boxes of magazines loaded with eight rounds of 2 ¾ inch ammo. "Suit yourself, but I'll take this one."

Sam picked up a Glock 17 and held it in his hand looking through the end of its sighting mechanism. It was obviously plastic and looked light and flimsy, more like a toy gun than a deadly weapon to Alexis. "This will do perfectly."

Alexis smiled. "Well, it's nice to see one of you doesn't carry a weapon like it's an endorsement of your male appendage. That looks like a nice civilized weapon."

Sam checked the safety was on and then handed it to her. "I'm glad you think so, because I picked it out for you. Have you fired a handgun before?"

"No. Never," Alexis lied.

"Okay, I'll show you–" Sam started but never got to finish.

Alexis removed the magazine and then stripped the weapon, checking that each component was intact and functioning smoothly. She then reassembled the weapon and attached the magazine. She withheld the tiniest of coy smiles. "I was raised on a farm in Oregon — and you thought I'd never used a handgun before?"

"Well that's good." Sam stood there in front of her grinning like the fool she'd made of him. He shook his head in wonder and picked up an Uzi and a M40A5 Sniper Rifle with bipod and suppressor. "All right, let's get back to work."

Alexis walked out the armory door—unsure if she felt safer or more concerned by the weapons her rescuers armed themselves with.

Matthew locked the massive armory door. Then looked at the outside wall where a Browning M2 .50 caliber heavy machine gun and a SMAW II Serpent Rocket launcher sat on two boxes of military ordinance he'd brought outside the armory. "Are we forgetting something?"

Tom looked at the heavy weapons. "Good point, we don't know who's after Alexis, but we know they mean business and operate like professionals. No doubt about it, they'll be armed and they'll return for her on the *Antarctic Solace*. This time, we'll be ready."

"I don't mean to sound self-centered," Alexis said. "But if they're after me, shouldn't we forget the *Antarctic Solace*. I mean, wouldn't it be easier to defend the *Maria Helena*?"

Matthew grinned. "I wouldn't worry ma'am; the *Maria Helena* is armed better than most battleships and with some uniquely advanced weaponry systems. We'll be very lucky if they come after you while you're aboard."

CHAPTER 22

ALEXIS WANTED TO LAUGH AT the sight of Tom and Genevieve carrying the 128 pound heavy machinegun and tripod while Elise carried the rocket launcher, resting it casually over her lithe and muscular shoulder as she stepped down towards the runabout as though it were the most natural of all things for a computer nerd to be carrying. Trailing behind, Matthew whistled as he wheeled a cart of Serpent Rockets.

Who are these people?

"Elise." Sam stopped her from descending the ladder onto the runabout. "I need you to do something for me before you go."

"Sure, what do you need?" Elise replied.

Sam's eyes turned to avoid Alexis's gaze. "I'll tell you inside."

"Okay, I'll just be a second."

Matthew stopped pushing his cart and reached for Elise's rocket launcher. "Here, give me that. Go sort Sam's IT stuff out and I'll finish loading the runabout. I don't want to waste any more time than we have to."

"Thanks Matthew."

Alexis caught Elise's eye as she followed Sam inside the *Maria Helena*'s bridge. She looked like she was going to say something to her, and then turned and entered the ship's structure. Alexis couldn't tell if she was simply in a rush or trying to hide something. Alexis thought of following her. No one had told her that some places of the *Maria Helena* were out of bounds. Even so, the thought made her feel like she was interfering.

Instead, she waited outside feeling oddly conscious of the fact she had nothing of any use to contribute. Matthew completed his trip to the runabout, along with Tom and Genevieve, and then stopped to rest several feet from her. She watched as Tom and Genevieve remained on the runabout, chatting like old friends.

Then she noticed something. There was something about the way they interacted which made them look like more than just colleagues. Nothing obvious—a hand offered for assistance climbing onto the Zodiac held for a millisecond longer than it should have been; a glance at each other's eyes that seemed slightly too attentive for a coworker.

Genevieve caught her eyes, stared at her for a second, and then looked away—as though Genevieve knew precisely what she was thinking.

Does anyone like me on this boat?

Her heart raced as she reconsidered the cook's gaze, and thought about a second explanation—*what if they simply don't trust me?*

Alexis moved down the decking towards Matthew and leaned on the balustrade next to him, staring out at the icy waters. "What's your story, Matthew?"

"I don't have much of a story ma'am." He smiled kindly at her. "I come to work pretty much every day of the year and give my best to the project and the team."

"You don't ever go home?"

"This is my home, work, and entire life." Matthew smiled warmly as he spoke.

He seemed happy enough to her, but not driven in the same

way as the others who were part of Sam Reilly's team. Unlike Elise, Tom, Veyron and even Genevieve who all looked like they were constantly on the adventure of a lifetime, Matthew simply looked like he was working a nine to five career. He appeared neither pleased nor displeased by his earlier choices of vocation, and simply continued on his original way of life. *Perhaps he's been around so much longer he's merely more competent than the rest of them?*

"How did you end up working aboard the *Maria Helena* and involved with Deep Sea Projects?" she asked.

"I've been on this ship the longest, actually." He looked pleased that she'd taken an interest and then paused to see if she was really interested in his story. When she didn't say anything to stop him, he continued. "The *Maria Helena* was the first ship I commanded after completing my internship with Global Shipping."

"I thought this was Sam's brainchild?"

"No. His father, James Reilly owned this ship. He used it primarily for deep sea salvage operations. When Sam's old man was trying to entice Sam to return to the family business he told Sam he could choose the type of work he wanted to use the ship for—just so long as it paid for itself. James was quite clear he didn't want to give Sam a ship out of charity. He had to make it work. What that work was, was entirely up to Sam."

"So, Sam is connected to THAT Reilly?"

"You mean the shipping tycoon?"

Alexis nodded, "Yeah."

"That's him. He's probably one of the richest men in the history of shipping."

"Am I right that it was Sam's grandfather who started Global Shipping?"

"Yes, but it was Sam's father who made it the success it is today. I think James had hoped Sam would continue with his legacy."

"Sam doesn't want to be CEO one day?" she asked.

"Not even slightly." The question made Matthew laugh. "Can you imagine Sam sitting behind a desk?"

"No. I suppose not."

"Sam's father loves the sea, but he loves money even more. We're all good at something and James Reilly knows how to make money multiply. Sam of course, is the polar opposite."

"Really?" Alexis was surprised. "Sam doesn't like money?"

"Nothing quite so sinister," Matthew reassured her with placating hands. "Sam's just different on the subject of money. James wants to take billions and turn them into trillions. Sam was born into money. He's never had want of anything in his life, but instead of turning out greedy like so many other rich kids, he's dedicated his life to helping others. He joined the military, like so many others, after *Nine Eleven* because he wanted to do his part to serve his country. Since he got out, he's used this ship on countless missions to help people from around the world in areas he's passionate about, such as environmental conservation, humanitarian aid, and disaster relief."

"I've heard he's also made a small fortune of his own finding lost treasure, like a pirate?"

Matthew very nearly blushed. "The *Maria Helena*'s running costs aren't small and Sam has kept his promise to his father to fund Deep Sea Projects out of his own work."

"You trust him very much, don't you?" she asked.

"Of course I do. I wouldn't work for him if I didn't. No one would. The type of work the *Maria Helena*'s exposed to requires a high degree of trust." He smiled at her. "You too appear to have placed a large amount of trust in a man you only just met a few hours ago."

"I wasn't really given much of a choice, was I?"

"It's all right. He's that sort of man. Some people are good at public speaking; others have a natural head for mathematics;

James turns money into more money — Sam is a born leader; he's the real deal. He's a good guy, extremely competent in the work he does, and people naturally trust him with their lives."

"Thanks." Somehow Matthew had come to understand what she was thinking — *could she really trust a man who she'd just met, with her life?*

Elise and Sam walked out onto the deck surrounding the bridge four levels above them. A casual glance showed the two were setting up an external radio or satellite connection.

"They look pretty close," Alexis said out loud.

"Who?" Matthew asked.

"Elise and Sam."

Matthew leaned back and looked at Elise outside his bridge. "They are close. Go back a long way. Been through a lot together, and I don't know what Sam would have done without her."

"That's obvious. He barely tries to hide his feelings." Alexis didn't even know why it irked her that Sam should like another woman. Particularly a woman he'd known longer and was younger and prettier.

Matthew stood up. "I have to get back to work. I'd better plan the route between here and McMurdo Bay, if we're going to leave soon."

She wondered if he was brushing her off because she was asking sensitive questions about Elise and Sam. Either way, she wasn't going to get an answer from him, so she ignored it. "Okay. Thanks, again."

Alexis watched Tom and Genevieve working together tying down the armaments that threatened to sink the Zodiac under their weight. They were efficient and professional, but there was definitely something more to their relationship, too. She was almost certain they were romantically entangled. She made a mental note to ask Sam about it later. She trusted her own instinct. For some reason, she had always been able to tell when people were honest; what they were thinking, and who she could trust. It was because of that additional sense, she was willing and confident to entrust her life in Sam Reilly's hands — a man she'd met only hours previously.

It's the one area of my life that I naturally just get right. The last statement wasn't entirely accurate though. She used to look at women who were having relationship troubles and think, of course they picked the wrong guy. They were such fools.

Except she had been the greatest fool of them all, hadn't she?

CHAPTER 23

S AM ENDED THE CALL TO the Secretary of Defense.
Elise then broke the connection, which she'd woven
through a complex series of proxy servers that would take the
best hacker hours to unravel—by which time Sam hoped the
Maria Helena would be nowhere near the original place of the
call.

Elise closed her laptop. "What did she say?"

"That if Randy Olsen's still alive and behind this, we need
to be worried."

"Why? What's so important about him, and why should we
be frightened about a man who faked his own death?"

"She didn't say." Sam shook his head. "Just that she'd send
help immediately—and that we're to secure the *Antarctic Solace*
at all costs."

Elise secured her laptop inside her slim backpack. She then
slid her arms through the shoulder straps and tightened them
until it molded with the natural contours of her back. "Do you
still think it's a good idea to go to the Pegasus station?"

"No."

Elise removed her computer glasses and folded them into a
case. She slid that case into the side pocket of her laptop bag
and smiled at him. It was patronizing and he'd seen it before.
"But you're going anyway, aren't you?"

"Yes."

"Tom's going to be pissed."

"I know." Sam knew it, too. "But if we can reach them in time, we might just save their lives."

"You should be bringing Tom instead. Alexis's not going to be much use to you if this thing goes bad."

"No. I want him on the *Antarctic Solace*." Sam was emphatic. "I'm still working on the principle that no one else knows where the Pegasus science station is — for now. If we can beat whoever's responsible for all of this to the Pegasus station, then we can have the scientists out within a matter of hours. Then we hold up on board the *Antarctic Solace* until reinforcements arrive."

Elise stood up to leave. One of the things Sam had always liked about her was the fact she made a decision quickly and kept to it. In this instance, she'd decided she wasn't going to change his mind, so moved onto the next step — reducing the risk, which meant it was time he left.

She stood on her toes, wrapped her arms around him and gave him a big hug. "Don't do anything stupid while you're away. Tom and I will remain on board the *Antarctic Solace,* so that leaves only Alexis to stop you from being yourself and doing something that's likely to get you killed."

"Don't worry, I'll behave. I'll be careful and won't take any unnecessary risks — even if I have to," Sam lied. "You just concentrate on getting me the missing parts to the security tape and gaining access to the crew's levels of the *Antarctic Solace*."

"I will, Sam."

He caught Alexis's eye as she approached. She looked slightly upset but said nothing. Sam broke the hug and squeezed Elise's right hand.

"You should go."

"Okay," Elise said and she turned to leave. On the side of her right thigh, over the top of her skin tight leggings, Sam noticed she wore an Uzi like another girl might wear a pair of designer shoes.

Elise looked at Alexis who walked towards them. "Take care he doesn't do something stupid, will you?"

"I'll try my best."

CHAPTER 24

T HE ZODIAC DISCONNECTED FROM THE *Maria Helena.* It was no more than a dozen yards away before Matthew waved goodbye and increased power to the *Maria Helena's* twin propellers and steered a course for McMurdo Bay. Inside the bridge, Alexis found herself holding onto a side handle trying not to fall backwards under the increased pressure.

Sam looked at her. He had a warm smile that put her at ease. "What do you think of her?"

"Who?" Alexis knew damn well who he was talking about, but she wanted him to be clear about it.

"Elise. Isn't she really something?"

Alexis grimaced. "I think she's a bit young for you, don't you think?"

"Hey, I'm only thirty five!" Sam said. "And it's not like that, anyway."

"Really?" She didn't believe him for a minute. "You two look very close. I saw you embrace her when she left, yet I failed to see you share the same sentiment with Tom?"

"We are very close. We've been through a lot together. It's a long story. I love her, but not the way you're thinking."

"She's easy on the eye." Alexis looked skeptical. "Much less nerdy than I was expecting. How do you love her?"

"She's more like my kid sister, or my adopted, overly intelligent child."

"How old is she?"

"We think she's in her early twenties, but it's hard to tell."

"You don't know?"

"No."

"But she works for you? Come on, you must have her records on file?"

"Elise? No, she doesn't work for me."

"But you said . . ."

"I know what I said. The fact of the matter is Elise comes and spends time on board the *Maria Helena* because she feels like it. And in my line of work, there are periods of prolonged boredom filled with periods of craziness. We're currently going through a long spell of craziness—so Elise stays around for the adventure. She doesn't need the money—she just likes to see what happens next, I guess."

"What's her last name?"

"She doesn't have one. Heck, I doubt very much if Elise is her first name, for that matter."

"Does she have a passport?"

"Sure she does," Sam said. "She just creates a new one, along with an entire past life, every time we enter a country."

"Do you know what happened in her previous life?"

"How did she come to be living a life with no past, you mean?"

Alexis sat down in a chair. "Yes."

"Her parents died and the government wanted her to do some work she wasn't interested in—either because it didn't stimulate her or because she didn't believe it was the right thing. Either way, you can't make a person like Elise do something she doesn't want."

"She worked for the government?"

Sam nodded. "Something like that."

"I thought they could make anyone do what they wanted if

it was in the interest of national security."

"Not Elise. She just walked away."

Alexis persisted. "And they didn't try and stop her?"

"I'm sure they did, but it wouldn't have helped. Elise is way too smart to get caught. As one of the greatest hackers of her generation, she just deleted every trace of her old life and created a new one."

"How did you find her?"

"I didn't. She tracked me down and when she did, I asked for her help. She's spent the last few months aboard the *Maria Helena*."

"She must be pretty smart."

"Let me put it this way, she's probably as smart as the rest of my crew combined and I only work with the brightest people in this industry."

CHAPTER 25

T HE *MARIA HELENA* DROPPED ANCHOR in the McMurdo
Sound. To the west Mount Erebus, the active volcano,
stood silently dominating Ross Island at nearly twelve and a
half thousand feet. Half a mile to the south, the sea confronted
the Ross Ice Shelf, an impenetrable wall of ice. Just back from it
a tourist ship with the words *Frozen Magic* written in purple
lettering on her hull, rested at anchor. She was the only other
vessel still inside McMurdo Sound so close to the oncoming
winter, and along with the *Maria Helena* took the enormous risk
of becoming locked in the freezing sea. To the south-east the
transantarctic ranges filled the horizon with their imposing and
majestic heights. They provided a strange contrast to every
other high altitude mountain scenery in the world, because in
Antarctica, where snow is ubiquitous, the high peaks were the
only places barren of snow.

The water in the bay was icy still and crystal clear; the
morning light fixed in a permanent dull gray, which they'd
become accustomed to seeing. Sam breathed the fresh air
which seemed infinitely pure and unaffected by the manmade
pollution that now seemed more than a world away. A sound
like the crack of thunder disrupted the otherwise serene
environment, as the *Maria Helena*'s earlier bow wave caused a
piece of ice the size of a five story building to break free of the
Ross Ice Shelf and crash into the otherwise tranquil waters of
the McMurdo sound.

Sam loaded a bag of food and medical supplies into the hovercraft. He checked that the additional fuel tanks, strapped to every spare place on board were filled completely and each intact. Even with the hovercraft's recently installed long range fuel tanks an additional fourteen fuel containers would be required to reach the Pegasus station. Once there, Alexis assured him the science station would have plenty of fuel for the return trip. The hovercraft would be tested to its limits for endurance on this trip. He confirmed the antifreeze had been added to each container to prevent any deadly ice crystals from forming. "That's our cue. Time to go, Alexis."

Alexis slid inside the small hovercraft into the passenger compartment that Sam had occupied less than twenty four hours earlier, when Tom had rescued him. "I'm good to go."

Matthew placed his hand on Sam's shoulder. "I'm giving you three days. Find the Pegasus and get back here. I hope you appreciate we're in deep trouble here. Someone's gone to great lengths to kidnap those passengers, and if the Secretary of Defense is telling you to be frightened, for once I suggest you listen to her."

"I'm with you on this, Matthew." Sam grinned. He'd never learned that some things were out of reach. "Whoever's responsible for this don't know where the Pegasus is, but they'll be out there. I'm hedging my bet that we can find the scientists before Randy Olsen's men find us."

"You know you're on your own if something goes wrong?"

"That's not true. Alexis's with me — and she grew up in Oregon, so she's a pretty good shot. And we've got the radio."

"Lot of good that's going to do for you. What if we have another ionization storm and the radio goes dead?"

"We've got rocket flares." Sam held up a bag of four red flares. The type that are launched by a rocket and send a red flash several hundred feet in the air, akin to the flash of fireworks at an altitude anyone onboard the *Maria Helena* would see. "If you see it, you know it means we lost the race and we need help."

"What if you're already on the other side of the mountains?"

"Then, we've already lost everything," Sam replied.

"How do you expect Genevieve and I to come to your assistance?"

"Take the Sikorsky," Sam suggested, looking at the helicopter.

"I thought something in its engine was still frozen?"

"Veyron wrapped her for freezing condition and installed a heater while Tom and I were stuck in the fake Pegasus station. She's been slowly thawing over the past three days."

Matthew shook his head. "Why don't you take the Sikorsky instead of the hovercraft?"

"Because I checked on her systems an hour ago and there's a couple of parts I can't confirm aren't frozen, so I don't want to risk it—unless I have to."

"Unless we have to, you mean?"

"Sure," Sam replied, with his usual noncommittal insouciance.

"It doesn't matter anyway. Unless you forgot, I'm one of the best skippers you'll ever meet, but I can't fly a helicopter."

"That doesn't matter."

"Who do you expect me to get to fly the chopper if you get yourself stuck?" Matthew looked at Genevieve, who was smiling, wickedly. "You can fly? Where the hell did you learn?"

Genevieve nodded. "Don't ask where I learned, but yes, I can fly that thing if it thaws in time."

"All right then, Sam, go and come back as quick as you can. Good luck."

"I'll see you in less than three days."

Sam closed the door, sealing himself and Alexis inside the hovercraft. He pressed the start button and the twin six foot fans which ran directly behind them started to turn. Within a minute they reached full speed and whined more like the blades of a helicopter as they produced the air current required to create lift. Confident enough air pressure had been developed, Sam adjusted the gear lever in order to split a fifty: fifty ratio of that air current through the ducting gearbox. The impeller below them suddenly roared into life with the flow of the powerful air current, which then became trapped in the hovercraft's flexible skirt—causing the entire amphibious craft to raise five feet into the air on top of the trapped air cushion.

"Are you ready, Alexis?" he asked. His eyes fixed on the flat platform to the aft of the *Maria Helena*.

"Good to go."

"You'd better hold on." Sam waited until he saw her hands grip a holding point in front of her. "This might be a little rough."

Sam then adjusted the gear lever, so that all remaining thrust was expelled through the rear propellers, and increased speed to full. The hovercraft leaped forward, running off the flat aft deck of the *Maria Helena* and into the ice cold water of the McMurdo Sound.

CHAPTER 26

S AM SPED PAST ROSS ISLAND, across McMurdo Sound heading east towards Taylor Valley. The hovercraft skimmed across the surface of the cold and still waters at speeds above 70 miles per hour. If they were lucky, and the weather held, they would enter the dry Taylor Valley and from there they would cut across the Taylor Glacier and into East Antarctica where they raced time to reach the scientists from the Pegasus station.

Their speed would be drastically reduced once they entered the valleys. It was a twenty four hour run each direction if they were lucky, leaving a full day for the inevitable delays and complications. If Taylor Valley had become inaccessible, they would need to revert to the Wright and Victoria valleys, which were further away, to cross the Transantarctic Ranges.

Sam watched the majestic scenery through the windshield, which approached them with monotonous apathy no matter how fast he drove. He looked at Alexis, curled up in a ball in the passenger's seat. She was hugging herself through her cold weather jacket and had already fallen into a light sleep.

He set the hovercraft on autopilot and pointed the nose to a waypoint just before the entrance to the Taylor Valley. It would still take a number of hours to reach, even at the speeds he was doing. Sam then picked up a heavy blanket and covered Alexis to her shoulders. It was just enough warmth to send her into a deep sleep. She smiled at the warmth, sending big dimples to her freckled cheeks; her thick brown curly hair nestled like a pillow as her head sank into the seat.

Sam figured she'd been on edge for a number of days after her ordeal aboard the *Antarctic Solace*. He envied the sound sleep that she was now having, but figured she probably needed it more than he did. It made her look more innocent as she slept.

Sam couldn't help but notice that she was beautiful. Something about her current position made him want nothing more than to take her in his arms and just hold her tight; reassure her that everything was now going to be okay.

Alexis turned and leaned against him. Sam restrained his natural desire to embrace her. He caught the scent of her perfume. It was subtle, but intensely feminine. The more he looked at her the more he realized she was painstakingly beautiful. Not in the glamor magazine type of way and not in the overtly skinny or athletic kind of way, but instead in the homegrown natural beauty of a down to earth, stunning woman. He was also a sucker for beautiful eyes, and her green eyes took his breath away. If she was a physicist at CERN by the age of thirty-eight, it meant she was exceedingly intelligent. He stared at her as she buried her beautiful face into his shoulder. He tried to slide away, but she moved closer until she was close enough he could feel her warm breath on his neck. She was everything he desired—and exactly what he didn't need right now.

He suddenly felt guilty for admiring her while she slept, and instead turned to work on the navigational routes through the McMurdo dry valleys.

Three hours later the still waters of the McMurdo Sound reached the rocky beach that led to the entrance of the Taylor Valley. He slowed the hovercraft and increased power to the impeller, creating more lift to mitigate the deep rifts and openings in the mountainside. He then shoved the hovercraft forwards and began the steep climb out of the water.

It took forty minutes to reach the peak before descending

into the Taylor Valley. Sam had an immediate misgiving about his ability to maneuver the hovercraft if the wind gusted through the valley.

On the right side of the valley entrance the remnants of what was once a large glacier still made its exceedingly slow journey towards the sea. It was ancient ice, compressed by thousands upon thousands of years of snowfall which had squeezed all the air bubbles out, leaving an extremely dense mass of ice. Like any body of deep water, this ice absorbed the red, orange, yellow, and green wavelengths of light—leaving in its place the shorter wavelengths of the most splendid blue Sam had ever seen.

The hovercraft dropped off a ravine larger than Sam had realized—the engines whined as the cushion of trapped air in the skirt beneath them became free from the confines of earth, causing them to land with a soft jolt. More like landing on a semi-inflated jumping castle than the shock absorbers of a car. He continued to drive through the Taylor Valley. In front of him the mountains extended on each side of him like the jaws of a monster; rising so high that even the snow failed to reach their peaks.

Next to him, Alexis startled after the sudden movement. Not quite awake, she took his left arm in hers and held his hand; her delicate fingers interlocking with his. Sam knew he should let go of her hand and somehow find a way to send her back to her side of the hovercraft, but at the same time, didn't want the experience to ever end.

She opened her eyes and looked up at him; they were dark green like jade with a multitude of sparkles. He felt her squeeze his hand in hers. *Did she just mean to do that?* She then let go of his hand and rolled back to her side of the hovercraft.

"Good morning," he said.

"How long have I been out for?" she asked without making any mention of the fact she'd been lying in his arms.

"About three hours. We're descending into the Taylor Valley now."

After crossing a land filled with snow and ice, the hovercraft reached the floor of the Taylor Valley—a barren land, and driest, windiest desert on earth.

CHAPTER 27

S AM ADJUSTED THE FIRST GEAR lever to his left, cutting power to the main propellers which generated forwards propulsion. The hovercraft immediately slowed along the barren valley floor. He then used his right hand to reduce the revolutions of the impeller which was the downward facing propeller used to generate lift. Thirty seconds later the hovercraft slowed to a complete stop and sank gently to the ground.

Alexis sat upright. Her eyes wide with sudden concentration. "What is it?"

Sam grinned as he reached for his orange exposure suit. "I thought it was time to get out and stretch my legs."

Alexis stared at the arid landscape; bitter in its hostility. "You want to get out here? The outside temperature is minus 65 degrees Fahrenheit!"

"All the same, I need to get out and refill the fuel tanks." Sam began sliding each of his legs into the thick exposure suit, which more closely resembled a spacesuit than snow clothing. "Do you want to wait here, in the warmth?"

She smiled. It was full of wonder, like the scientist she was, and it expressed her interest in this rare phenomenon. "And miss seeing this place, first hand, are you kidding me?"

Sam finished zipping up his exposure suit. He wore a thick woolen beany and then strapped the hood of the suit over the top as an additional shield from the elements. Over his eyes, the only aspect still vulnerable to the extreme conditions, he wore thick snow goggles which formed a perfect seal. His entire outfit was cumbersome but imperative to protect him from the katabatic winds that raced down over the ice at the edges of the valley, potentially ripping through the hostile valley floor at speeds as fast as 220 miles per hour.

He waited until Alexis had fully donned her purple exposure suit and then said, "Ready?"

"I'm good to go," she replied.

Sam released the opening hatch and climbed out through the top of the hovercraft. Standing on the stainless steel grate which protected the massive impeller, he had an unhindered view of the entire Taylor Valley in all its splendor.

Like the other dry valleys that make up the legendary McMurdo Dry Valleys, the Taylor Valley was an Antarctic anomaly. While most of the continent was covered in a thick layer of ice, the dry, frigid valleys were almost entirely ice-free. Sam examined his unique surrounding environment. An arid expanse of mostly dirt, small rocks, and big boulders littered the valley floor. A single frozen lake stood like a mirage on the horizon and Sam couldn't tell if it was made entirely of salt or ice. There were five jagged trenches—ancient remnants of streams that no longer flowed, and now scarred the valley floor.

Giant ventifacts lined the valley; some as large as the hovercraft. The oddly shaped, smooth formations of the stones were caused by the erosive action of wind and grit sandblasting the valley over the millennia. Sam took a deep breath. The intensely dry, cold air stung his throat. The entire valley gave him the impression he was visiting Mars rather than Antarctica, and with the exception of the fact he could breathe—both environments were just as inhospitable to human flesh.

He felt Alexis's hand on his arm. Sam looked up; the only

part of her face visible were her green eyes, which radiated wonder. "It's beautiful, isn't it?"

"Yes. Even though it's lethal."

"Oh, it's deadly, all right," she agreed. "We should probably do what we need to and get inside before the weather changes."

Sam nodded and then removed the first fuel jerry can from its cradle. He carried it to the back of the hovercraft where the fuel cap was located. Undid the jerry can's cap as well as the hovercraft's fuel tank cover and began pouring.

"Why doesn't that freeze?" Alexis asked.

"I used an antifreeze additive before we left the *Maria Helena*."

"Good thinking. How many of these jerry cans do you think we'll need?"

Sam finished pouring the first one. "Three more."

"I'll start fetching them for you. I don't want to be stuck outside the vehicle if a windstorm erupts."

"I agree. This place is cold enough without adding its sandblasting wind-chill."

Sam started on the second fuel tank. "So, Professor, explain to me the anomaly of the valley?"

"Are you asking me why it doesn't snow in the valley?"

"Yeah. I mean, it's certainly cold enough, isn't it?"

Alexis changed her voice, as though she was suddenly accustomed to lecturing a student. "They're caused by the katabatic winds—do you know what those are?"

Sam matched her erudite tone as he responded. "A wind that carries cold air, which is therefore of a higher density, from a higher elevation down a slope under the force of gravity."

"That's right. So you were listening at school?"

Although he couldn't quite see Alexis's face through her protective clothing Sam imagined she was grinning at him with that teasing smile he was fondly getting used to seeing. "Just a little bit."

"The wind can reach extreme speeds in excess of 220 miles per hour, heating as it descends, and evaporating all water, ice and snow. This valley in particular will receive the equivalent of only 10 cm average of water each year in the form of snow."

Sam poured the third fuel tank. "So, why doesn't the snow eventually form water?"

"That's easy," she replied.

"Go on."

"The Taylor as well as the other dry valleys are nestled between the Transantarctic Mountains, which serve as a barrier, largely blocking them from the East Antarctic Ice Sheet. You will have noticed a few small glaciers creep through the gaps, but any ice that breaks off those quickly sublimates — transitioning from a solid state to a vapor without passing through the intermediate liquid phase because of the arid atmosphere."

"You really are a nerd!" Sam congratulated her.

"Hey, I thought you liked me?"

"I never said I didn't like nerds," he teased.

"Didn't you?"

"No." Sam stopped pouring. "I'll have the last jerry can, please."

She handed it to him and he began to pour the final container. He quickly filled the tank with the final container and firmly locked the fuel lid. He then placed the jerry can back inside its cradle and tightened the strap.

Alexis tapped him on the shoulder and pointed up at the peak of the mountain closest to McMurdo Sound, where they had just come from. "Just in the nick of time."

Sam looked up. A small tuft of snow rolled over the tip of the mountain. Known as a rain shadow effect, it was often caused by air rolling off the polar plateau being forced over the

Transantarctic Mountains; which then cools it, condenses and deposits its moisture as snow which dips down over the ice at the edges of the valley peaks.

Such a formation precedes any number of meteorological events around the world. But in the dry valley of Taylor, it meant one thing only — an extreme wind was coming. The type capable of sending sand, gravel, and grit through the valley at such speeds it would tear holes through the hovercraft and kill them both.

Sam checked the last strap was secure. "Get in the hovercraft!"

He waited until Alexis was inside and followed her, quickly securing the hatch behind him. Sam then immediately went through the process of restarting both the impeller and aft propeller engines.

The engines whined as the thick rubbery skirt inflated, raising the hovercraft five feet on to the new cushion of air. Worried about the effects of the extreme cold, he glanced at the few engine gauges. They were still within normal parameters, which meant they hadn't cracked a seal yet. Not that it mattered if they had, he couldn't wait the storm out — he had to go now. Sam threw the left hand throttle down to full, sending maximum power to the aft twin propellers. The hovercraft lurched forward towards the mirage in the horizon — at full speed.

"You'll never outrun it!" Alexis said.

"Got a better plan?"

"As a matter of fact, I do."

CHAPTER 28

"**H**EAD FOR THE LAKE!" ALEXIS shouted.

"How far do you make it?" Sam asked.

"No more than two miles."

Sam swerved to the left to avoid falling into a large crevasse without reducing speed. "What's there?"

"An ice cave. The remnants of a glacier that once ran through the mountain. It's now retreated leaving a hollowed tunnel like a scar beneath the mountain."

"That'll do, but can we reach it?"

"I have no idea — how fast can this thing go?"

Sam looked at the speedometer. On the completely level surface of the valley's floor the hovercraft had reached its maximum speed and wouldn't gain a mile no matter what he did to coerce the dual engines. "Eighty-four miles per hour!"

"It'll be close."

The violent wind screamed from behind them, sending dust and grit running through the valley at a lethal velocity. The small stone particles mostly bounced off the hovercraft's hardened rubber skirt as the anemometer registered gusts above a hundred miles per hour.

"It might be too close." Sam glanced at the speedometer. The speed of the hovercraft had increased to a hundred and two miles per hour; running with the wind like a sailboat. Several small stones smashed into dust particles as they were pelted into a solid boulder. "Keep a look out for any other caves, we might not get a chance to reach the one you're talking about while we're still alive."

Alexis flipped through detailed maps of the Taylor Valley. "I'm on it!"

Small stones showered the rubber skirt and hovercraft's aluminum shell like a machinegun. Sam considered his chances of pulling in behind even a small boulder, but something told him he needed to keep driving to reach the cave if they were going to survive the storm.

A rock no larger than a dime shot through the aluminum backing and ricocheted through the windshield like a bullet.

Sam swore. Then swerved right and aimed for a small opening in the glacier. "What about this one?"

"I have no idea where it goes," she replied. Her voice loud enough to be heard through the storm. "It's not on the map."

"I don't care."

"It might not be stable," she pointed out.

"We're not going to be stable much longer. If that wind picks up any more speed those rocks are going to rip right through our hull." Sam steered towards an opening just slightly larger than the hovercraft. "Outside in the wind tunnel we won't last more than a few minutes before one of those stones takes off our heads — I'm willing to take my chances inside the glacier. How about you?"

Alexis nodded.

The hovercraft made a loud crunching sound as its inertia allowed it to scrape through the remnants of ancient glacial ice that would have otherwise prevented them from entering.

The loud clamor from outside dulled to a gentle roar. Sam switched on the headlights. The cavern opened up to an area large enough to drive a semitrailer. The walls glowed with the deep blue of the dense glacial ice that was both mesmerizing and terrifying in its beauty.

"I think we're safe," Sam said.

Alexis smiled. The joy of coming close with death only to discover she'd survived, radiated from her face. Sam noticed it served to somehow make her face even more beautiful.

"We're good, Sam." She gripped his hand in her own and squeezed it. "Thank you."

"You're welcome." Sam switched off the engines and the hovercraft settled onto the icy cavern floor. "How long do you expect this wind and sand storm to carry on?"

"Not long," she replied. "They're normally short lived, localized weather events. Should blow over within the hour."

CHAPTER 29

F OUR HOURS LATER, THE LIGHT no longer reached the Taylor Valley and still the wind storm had not decreased its force—if anything it worsened.

"We may as well get comfortable," Sam said. "We may be here a while. Tell me about the Pegasus science station."

Alexis shuffled in her seat. "What do you want to know?"

"Why it's so important someone might have gone to the length to abduct an entire cruise ship to somehow reach it?"

"I have no idea. Their research is important, but only in the long term, not in the present. Not for decades. It's research that has to be done, but nothing that-someone's going to kill for."

"What exactly were they researching?"

"Glacial tunnels."

"Lava tubes?"

"No. Glacial tunnels," Alexis said. "In 2014 a team of British scientists discovered an 820 foot high tunnel stretching hundreds of miles, hidden in the base of Filchner-Ronne Ice Shelf in West Antarctica. They were most likely formed by meltwater—the water released from melting ice that then flowed underneath the ice sheet, overland, and into the ocean."

"What did you want to study with it?"

"Nothing. There's a lot more ice in East Antarctica. If there were ice tunnels in West Antarctica, there were definitely some in East Antarctica." Alexis shuffled in her seat. "Then, in 2015 researchers using ground penetrating radar while flying over East Antarctica found two seafloor channels underneath the floating ice shelf of Totten Glacier."

"And you want to build inside one of them?" Sam asked.

"Exactly. I want to build the world's largest particle accelerator." She sighed. "Of course, even if I find the perfect conditions to do so, it will become a legal nightmare to gain approval to build it."

"Because of the Antarctic Treaty System?"

"Precisely. It came about because Antarctica is the only continent without a native human population. For the purposes of the treaty system, Antarctica is defined as all of the land and ice shelves south of 60°S latitude. The treaty, entering into force in 1961 set aside Antarctica as a scientific preserve, establishes freedom of scientific investigation and bans military activity on that continent. The treaty was the first arms control agreement established during the Cold War.

"To utilize such a place for your research, all members of the treaty would have to sign."

"Yes."

"So you were heading to the Pegasus station to review their research?"

"No," she was quick to respond.

"Then what were you doing aboard the *Antarctic Solace?*" he asked.

She shuffled uncomfortably in her seat. "It's a long story."

"Really?"

"Yes."

"Why?" he persisted.

"I don't think I'm ready to talk about it."

"That's okay. We might be freezing here all night. Let me know when you feel up to speaking about what got us into this mess."

"It's not that."

"You could have just told me you wanted to see the killer whales." He looked at her face, waiting for some sort of sign that she was going to fold and reply honestly.

"All right." She crossed her arms. "If you must know, I was on my honeymoon."

CHAPTER 30

ALEXIS WATCHED SAM'S FACE CHANGE. His happy go lucky, and playful demeanor was replaced with a sudden seriousness. His intensely blue eyes, the same color as the glacial ice, and just as mesmerizing had now taken on a despondent light. There was something else there, too. *Was he disappointed to hear I was married?* She almost felt guilty for misleading him. She was still trying to work out what happened before and why she was even holding his hand. She knew she started it, but he didn't make any effort to remove her hand from his, either.

Sam sat up, his posture suddenly rigid and uncomfortable. "I'm so sorry. You must be worried sick about your husband."

A glint of smile crossed her lips. "Don't be. We never got married."

He returned her smile. "You didn't?"

"No."

"What happened?" he persisted.

Life had offered her some unique challenges recently. Alexis wondered how things had changed so dramatically in such a short time. This was supposed to be the best time of her life. Normally, Alexis wouldn't have indulged herself in such wasteful thoughts of negativity. But, the last two weeks had changed so much that she couldn't help but let her mind drift into the ridiculousness of it all. It was supposed to be her honeymoon with Daniel.

Daniel!

Her thoughts returned to the man whom she was meant to marry. The man who she'd so easily and totally forgotten about until that moment.

She gritted her teeth and began talking about some deeply private issues in her life to a man who'd been a complete stranger to her three days earlier. "His name was Daniel — and I was supposed to marry him less than two weeks ago; this trip was meant to be our honeymoon."

"What happened?"

She sighed. "The night before our wedding day, when some stupid superstition suggests a woman shouldn't see her betrothed I discovered the reason for such a fallacy."

He looked at her attentively. "Why; what happened?"

Why am I telling this man my secret?

She took a deep breath and let go. After all, she could have been killed twice since that night. "I walked in to find my fiancé having sex with a stripper."

Sam looked blankly at her with incomprehension, but remained silent.

"We all make mistakes," Alexis said. "Perhaps it was only a onetime thing. Like on a Buck's night after he'd gotten so drunk and carried away with his guy friends that he'd made a mistake. I probably could have forgiven him for that. Only it wasn't his Buck's night, and the stripper hadn't stripped since she was a Freshman trying to pay for her college tuition fees — she was my best friend, Imogen."

"Holy shit!" Sam swore. "What did you do when you caught them?"

"A lot less than you'd expect. I cancelled the wedding with a simple text message to the guests. I tried to keep it as short as possible. Something along the lines of, *My apologies dear friends. Having discovered my betrothed in bed with a stripper tonight, I'm afraid I won't be attending the wedding. Please enjoy the food and wine on my behalf. By the way, I thought men normally waited until they were married to start affairs?"*

"And then what did you do?"

"I switched off my cell phone. I had no intention of reading the myriad of sympathetic responses, or worse still, angry and vengeful replies. Instead, I grabbed my travel bag and cruise ship tickets, and started my honeymoon a day early."

"You must have been so angry."

She recalled that night as though she were still there. She'd boarded the *Antarctic Solace.* Relaxed in the Jacuzzi inside her decadent honeymoon suite, and drank overly priced cocktails that had been delivered to her door. Afterwards she lay down on the oversized bed and closed her eyes. The first image to spring to her mind was that of Daniel and Imogen naked together, on her bed.

Thank you, Imogen.

She then fell into the deepest and most relaxed sleep she'd had in years.

"Sorry, what did you ask, Sam?"

"I said, you must have been so angry."

"No." She grinned sheepishly. "I know that's what I was supposed to be, but I wasn't. Not for an instant. Outwardly, I had taken it stoically and simply said that I would take the cruise without him and that he would be the one finding a new apartment, but inwardly I was jumping for joy with relief."

"You didn't like Daniel?"

"No. I liked him very much. Heck I even loved him, but I would have forever been far from in love with him."

"You nearly married a man you liked very much, but weren't in love with?"

"It sounds so childish, doesn't it?" She put her hand on his, without even considering why she wanted to. "I should have been happy with what I had. Daniel was a nice guy. There was nothing wrong with him. But it wasn't the fairytale you hear of when you're a little girl."

Sam squeezed her hand sympathetically. "I understand. If the person you're with isn't the type of person you dreamed about, why are you risking everything to spend the rest of your lives together?"

"Exactly!" Somehow the man next to her seemed to understand her more after three days than Daniel had in seven years. "Do you mind if I tell you how it happened?"

"Sure."

"We met at a conference on quantum physics. Despite its cool name, our industry has few particularly interesting people. By all means, I worked with some of the most intelligent people on the planet, but that made them no more interesting or fun to be around."

Sam laughed. It was warm and genuine; and she liked the sound of it. "You paint a great picture for which profession to enter if I want to meet a girl."

She continued. "Of the small group of eligible men around my age, Daniel was by far the most logical choice. He was more than averagely attractive. He respected me as his scientific superior. Despite the fact that I was one of the leading professors in an industry consumed by male egos, Daniel appeared to be the one amongst them who simply accepted me as the prodigal genius I am."

"Aren't you confident?"

"Have you ever met someone under the age of sixty who'd managed to reach the pinnacle of CERN's upper echelon of academics?"

"No, but then again, you're the first Professor I've met who worked at CERN."

"With the exception of Daniel's one or more infidelities, he had treated me well. He had similar, albeit rather boring interests, worked in the same unique industry, and certainly appeared to love me. After six years of dating he proposed, and without finding any obvious reason to object, I simply agreed; because that's what you're supposed to do. But as the days lead towards our wedding day, all I kept thinking was—I'm going to be married to Daniel for the rest of my life! And I kept asking, is this as good as it gets?"

"So after that you ended up here?"

"As the *Antarctic Solace* sailed south I felt good. Instead of being somber I reveled in the freedom and strength of my decision. The one I knew I needed to make and Daniel helped me to make it, without any risk of that future emotion of torment—regret. So I drank freely; danced, sang, and simply enjoyed my new life." She sighed. "And then we sailed past the fortieth latitude and felt sicker than I ever have before."

"Which is how you ended up confined to your stateroom?"

"Yes. And how I survived being taken prisoner, if that's what's really happened."

Sam looked at her seriously. "I just realized something."

"What?"

"You said your husband was very good at particle physics. Was he as good as you?"

"No. He was my subordinate."

"But he was intelligent enough to understand what you were researching?"

"Yes. Why?"

"It might sound far-fetched given everything that's happened, but do you think he could have been trying to take your research?"

"You mean, is Daniel responsible for this?" She thought about it for a moment. "No way. It's not his style. He can be Machiavellian and as deceitful as the next academic fighting to produce the next big thing in particle physics, but there's no way he'd have the gumption to orchestrate anything like this. Why do you ask?"

Sam looked at her, reassuringly. "Because we're looking for a criminal who's capable of stealing your research, and you just said less than a handful of people on the planet could even understand what you're doing let alone be capable of reproducing it."

"We're not looking for Daniel. That's for sure."

CHAPTER 31

S AM FOUND HIMSELF FEELING MORE attracted to Alexis the more she spoke. He wanted to embrace her, comfort, and love her. The thought filled him with irrational guilt, as though he wanted to cheat on Aliana. It was absurd. Aliana had recently broken up with him. They were well matched and he loved her, but their lives had been set on very different paths, which would never quite align.

Why should I feel guilty for wanting to be with this woman?

"We should get some sleep," Sam said. He shuffled in his chair until he was relatively comfortable. "Then we'll be ready to make a full day of it as soon as the sun comes up. You can take the single bunk behind us and I'll sleep here."

She looked at the narrow bunkbed that ran perpendicular to the two hovercraft seats. "Don't be so immature, we should both sleep there. We should conserve our warmth. We're probably going to freeze to death anyway."

Sam laughed. Outside in the Taylor Valley, where the wind had reduced the ambient temperature to eighty degrees Fahrenheit below zero, he knew there was a possibility of the two of them freezing to death. Inside the ice cavern the temperature was a balmy ten degrees below freezing—there was no way the two would freeze to death in a single night. "No, it's fine. You sleep there, and I'll be comfortable enough here. I've slept in worse places."

"No. I'm smaller than you, if you're set on being so chivalrous, you take the bunk and I'll stay in the chair." She looked at him. Her green eyes, like a myriad of stars forming a constellation in a faraway galaxy, made him acutely aware of her hand on his. "It was nice having someone to talk to. Do you know you're the only person who I've ever been honest with about Daniel?"

"I'm glad I could help."

Sam had become so engrossed with her story he hadn't noticed until that moment that her hand had found its way into his. By the time he felt her delicate hand squeeze his own he looked up and found her face was right next to his. Her eyes were closed. She was vulnerable and he knew he shouldn't act on it. He meant to stop it, but he didn't. Instead, her warm breath was on his lips. He gave in to desire and gently kissed her lips. "Everything's going to be okay."

She didn't respond or say anything. Instantly, he wished he hadn't kissed her. Alexis looked at him. Her face was a confused image of pensive guilt and deep yearning. Sam imagined her weighing up everything which had happened over the past two weeks and deciding if it was morally wrong for the first time in her life to simply do what she wanted, not what was expected of her. A moment later her body relaxed as though her naturally cautious behavior relented to desire.

Her freckled dimples closed as she opened her lips and kissed him. Gentle at first. Teasing his lips and progressively kissing him harder, until they were both passionate. Sam knew it was a mistake; he knew it was wrong given what she'd just told him. He hadn't meant to, and yet it felt so very good he never wanted it to stop.

She pulled away, like she was unsure of herself. Sam felt instantly regretful of taking advantage of her. He stared at her beautiful face. No more than a few inches away from him. It was entirely unreadable and at the same time infinitely full of expression.

"I'm sorry," he said. "That was inappropriate. I've made you uncomfortable."

In complete silence she slipped off her thick woolen jumper. She still wore a tight fitting light blue skivvy, but it accentuated her shapely figure instead of hiding it, and flamed his need. Without saying a word, she climbed over the center console and straddled him with her thighs firm against his hips.

She stared at him; her green eyes seductively close. Her lips once more close enough he could feel the warmth of her breath on his. The hovercraft was cramped and their two bodies blended together. She smiled lasciviously as his abject desire could no longer be concealed. She paused, so close that he wanted to scream.

Her lips taunted him.

Alexis then twisted her arm behind her back, unclasped her bra and removed her skivvy. Her breasts were large and her figure voluptuous and feminine. Her cream colored skin was soft and unblemished. The little hairs on her arms stood erect and her body gave the slightest of startled shivers in complaint of the sudden loss of heat.

She wrapped her naked arms around him and whispered, "No, this would be considered inappropriate."

CHAPTER 32

S AM WAS THE FIRST TO wake. Distinctly aware Alexis was still lying with her head cradled on his chest and in his arms, wearing only her light blue skivvy, he tried his best not to move. He was worried that he'd wake her and she'd leave his arms. Her perfume was the next thing he noticed. It was subtle and intensely feminine. Something about it brought back memories of the night before. It had been an amazing, wonderful experience, but there was something else he felt, too. It wasn't quite guilt, but maybe loss? Why should he feel this way? Alexis was an astonishingly beautiful and intelligent woman who any man would find it hard not to adore, so why should he feel something was missing?

Because she wasn't Aliana. The answer stung him with its subtle truth.

Was he still in love with Aliana?

Sam already knew the answer to that question. Now wasn't the time for self-pity. Besides, Alexis was still in his arms. The thought made him feel guiltier. Alexis had already been through enough trouble with men. He checked his wristwatch. It was five thirty a.m. and the faintest of lights reached the opening to the valley. He should have made the effort to check on the wind.

He gently ran his fingers through her hair and watched her breathe. Some people snored when they slept. Others tossed and turned uncomfortably. Very few people ever looked peaceful, and fewer still remained beautiful. Alexis was one of them who managed both.

At six thirty a.m. Alexis woke up. "Don't you ever sleep?"

"Sometimes," Sam replied. "But I got distracted by you and once I was awake and you were in my arms, I was more interested in running my hands through your hair."

"Oh, that's sweet." She kissed his lips lightly.

"It would probably sound less so if I told you your snoring woke me up."

"Really?"

"Afraid so."

"I don't normally snore. Then again, I don't normally sleep inside a hovercraft parked in an ice cave."

Sam smiled. "I'm glad you woke me anyway. Your face is one of the nicest things I've woken up to in a long time."

She dismissed the compliment. "Has the wind settled yet?"

He climbed out of the confined space of the bunk bed into the driver's seat and slid his thick jumper over his head. "I haven't looked outside. Let's go see."

He flicked on the headlights.

She climbed out onto the seat next to him. She'd already managed to slip her jumper and thermals on before leaving the bed. In front of them the faint light shined on the valley through the opening in the ice cave. Unlike when they'd entered the cave and the valley was made almost dark by the sand and grit being blown through, it looked perfectly clear.

Alexis zipped up the sides of her thick snow boots. "The weather looks good. If we leave right away we should reach the Pegasus station by afternoon.

CHAPTER 33

T OM WALKED INTO THE MAIN eatery of the *Antarctic Solace* where Elise had set up a new computer hub and workstation. Veyron had modified a section of the restaurant to provide excellent protection against attackers while maintaining good all round visualization of the ship's main promenade. Veyron and Elise were both arguing over something on Elise's computer.

"What's going on?" Tom asked.

Veyron shook his head. "We're in trouble, again."

"We're not in trouble," Elise challenged him. "So long as I can sort this out within the next day or two, everything will be fine."

"Why, what's wrong?" Tom poured himself a mug of black coffee. "I've been away for an hour setting up the makeshift machinegun turret above the bridge. How much trouble could we have gotten into?"

"Veyron tried the engines," Elise said, as though that explained everything.

Tom looked at Veyron. "I thought you said everything was working?"

Veyron shook his head. "Yeah, that's what I thought."

"You were wrong?" Tom almost sounded happy at the thought of catching Veyron out for once. "What's broken?"

"Nothing," Veyron replied. "Per the computer controls in

the bridge they are working perfectly fine."

"So what's wrong then?" Tom persisted.

"The computers are! Nothing's physically working on the diesel engines and now we're floating ducks in a sea that's about to freeze over for the oncoming winter. The computers say everything's working perfectly fine, but the second I try starting the engines, I get nothing." Veyron's face took on a new surly nature. "And do you want to know the best part?"

"What?"

"Guess where the access sites to the engine rooms are?"

Elise was grinning, but remained silent. Veyron was a double Doctorial graduate with one PhD in Submarines and a second in Mechatronics. He was fifty-five years old and the only person on board the *Maria Helena* who came close to her fundamental intellect, and now he'd made a mistake. Tom thought she looked as though the news that Veyron had made a mistake and was now paying for it was worth any amount of inconvenience.

"So, where are the engine room access sites?" Tom asked.

"Inside the crew levels."

"Oh, good news there," Tom said. "I just spoke to Gerald and he says he's got a copy of the security codes."

"Who's Gerald?" Elise said.

Tom took a drink of coffee. "He works in security for the cruise ship company that owns the *Antarctic Solace*."

Elise shook her head. "Sorry, and he has the security codes — to what?"

"Everything," Tom replied. "The backup digital security tapes, the elevators, the crew living quarters — everything. He told me he had them in a spreadsheet on a memory stick in his drawer in case there's ever an emergency where people need to gain immediate access."

"So, where's he been for the past few days?" Veyron asked. "Why are we only just now hearing of this?"

"He said he's been on vacation and returned to the office last night, or this morning our time?" Tom looked at Elise's face, beaming with relief. "I thought you might be happy."

"You've got the codes?" Elise said.

"Should have," Tom replied. "Gerald said he'd email them to me straight away."

Elise pushed her laptop towards Tom. "Log in here and download them now."

Tom quickly typed in his details, found the email and downloaded the spreadsheet. He clicked print and the entire list of codes to the ship was printed on a single page.

Elise picked the page up, read the first couple lines and said, "All right gentlemen, it's time to get some answers."

CHAPTER 34

THERE WERE TWO ELEVATORS IN the middle of the Antarctic Solace and one at each end of the ship. Tom entered one of the main elevator doors in the middle of the ship with Veyron. It was modern with a full length mirror extending to the floor on the inside and a recent digital photo of both the Arctic and Antarctic landscape. A security camera in the far corner still displayed its red light indicating it was recording. Both men held Israeli built Uzis. Each of them carried an additional four magazines, each one loaded with thirty two 9mm rounds.

Of the two men in the mirror, Tom looked taller and despite his muscles he appeared thinner. Veyron, on the other hand, appeared shorter, but not much at six foot three inches; he was also obviously heavier. Once a successful heavyweight boxer, Veyron would now be considered overweight. Beneath the excess body fat he still maintained extraordinary strength and agility. Despite Tom's military training, he correctly guessed Veyron would be the one who was more dangerous in a fight.

Elise handed them both a security card with the code imbedded into a microchip inside. "These cards should grant you access to every location on board this ship."

"Everything?" Tom asked.

"Anything on the list Gerald provided you with from the Captain's quarters, right down to the cleaner's storeroom."

"You're not coming with us?" Veyron asked, holding his Uzi

cheerfully.

"No. I'll keep an eye on you from the computer station." Elise had a wry smile. "Besides, you don't want to leave the entire topside of the *Antarctic Solace* unmanned if THEY return, do you?"

"Good point." Tom looked at her. "Are you going to be okay?"

"Are you kidding me?" Elise replied. "I'll be fine."

"We'll start at the bottom level," Veyron said. "From the engine room we'll work our way up so we don't miss anyone. Elise, you're certain you've put the other two elevators out of action?"

"Certain. I've disconnected power to them. They're not going up or down anytime soon."

"Good," Veyron said. "And you can stop the doors from opening on any of the main passenger levels?"

"It's already done, Veyron." Elise reached for the Uzi attached to her right thigh. "The only place anyone's getting from the crew decks to the passenger decks is through the doors of these two elevators on this level. And I'll be watching from this level—don't worry, I don't want a loose rat running through this ship any more than you do."

"Good," Veyron said. "Then I think we're ready, Tom."

Elise noticed the red light on in the elevator's security camera. "Has that always been on?"

"I don't know," Tom said. "I just noticed it when we opened the elevator doors. Why?"

"It means I should be able to access the camera and visualize the elevator. I have access to every other camera that's currently active," Elise said. "But I don't have access to that camera."

"So, what's it doing there?" Tom asked.

Veyron removed the safety from his Uzi. "It means someone else is watching us."

CHAPTER 35

T HE ELEVATOR DESCENDED PAST THE second deck, where the main living quarters for crew and entertainers were. It then carried on down to the lowest deck. Per the ship's schematics this level opened to the engine room. The plan was to clear out the lowest level first and then work their way back up.

Tom looked at Veyron. "Are you ready?"

"No, but I don't have any other choices, so let's get this over and done with."

Tom switched the safety to off and held his trigger finger at the ready. "All right, here we go."

The elevator came to a stop at the lowest floor. The engine room was located two stories below the ship's waterline. A terrifying thought as the elevator doors remained closed. Veyron hit the door release button and the doors opened — to a completely dark room.

"Well that's perfect!" Veyron said.

Tom switched on the flashlight at the end of his Uzi. The light barely reached the end of the room and there were more shadows than areas able to be seen. "Hey, if anyone's down here, my name's Tom and this is Veyron. We're the good guys. We're here to help."

The sound of his voice echoed in the massive engine room, but otherwise there was no response. He looked at Veyron.

"I don't think they're interested," Veyron said.

Tom swept his Uzi around the room so the light shined across it. "You have any ideas?"

"Yeah, this!" Veyron stepped out of the elevator. Shined the light from the end of his Uzi around until he found what he was looking for and then fired two, three round bursts, into the bilge water. "If anyone's here, I strongly suggest you come out now before I light up this entire damned engine room."

Silence.

"Jesus, Veyron!" Tom said, "Now they know we're here!"

"Don't worry, they already knew we were here. Remember the red light from the elevator camera? Someone's been watching us."

Tom shined his flashlight around the room. He felt exposed in the dark with his own flashlight forming a beacon to shoot at. A large brass miner's lamp hung from the edge of the elevator. "What the hell is that?"

Veyron stepped closer and picked it up. "It's a carbide lamp. Circa 1910 at a guess, but what the hell it's doing down here, I have no idea."

"Would it be bright enough to light up this room?"

"Something this size could light up a good portion of it."

Veyron opened the water nozzle until tiny drops of water mixed with the carbide inside, causing a chemical reaction that released the highly flammable gas, acetylene. He flicked the striker at the back of the device a couple times. A tiny piece of flint struck the spark wheel and ignited the acetylene gas. The entire thing burned with a warm glow. He adjusted the flow of water until an adequate balance between flame and lighting was achieved.

The warm light filtered through the engine room. Not quite prominent enough to reach the back of the room, but it went a long way to making them feel less vulnerable to an ambush.

"Hey, what do you think of that?" Veyron said, placing the

glowing light on the floor in front of him. A proud grin forming on his otherwise serious face.

"Great, but I think I just spotted the main light switch." Tom looked at the wooden switch. It appeared old and ornate. Underneath, was a circular metal device like a light dimmer. Next to it a label: *Engine Room. Main Lighting.*

Veyron followed him. He looked worried. Something was definitely wrong about the whole situation. His hands gripped the Uzi's handle, and Tom could see he was preparing for the imminent ambush. "Well don't just wait there staring at it, turn the damn thing on and let's see what we've got."

Tom flicked the switch.

The sound of flint striking several spark wheels went, click, click, click. A tiny glow of light resonated throughout the ceiling. Veyron stepped behind him and adjusted the metal turn wheel. The sound of water hissing as it turned into gas resonated throughout the room. Moments later, the warm lights lit the room.

Tom felt instantly sick. He gripped the hilt of his Uzi for reassurance. Something was very wrong about the entire place. The warm lights flickered throughout the ceiling. Water could be heard dripping in the distance. And Tom couldn't help but feel like he'd just entered some kind of disturbing nightmare envisioned by one of Steven King's more outlandish imaginings.

The entire room could now be seen. The shadows dwindled away and the massive diesel engines and their outer mechanical workings were all that remained.

Somehow he saw the room for what it was — something evil.

"What the hell is that?" Tom asked.

"That's a carbide lighting system," Veyron said. "It appears whoever installed it has set it up to light the entire level."

"But why is it here?"

"For lighting, of course." Veyron grinned. "Carbide lighting was used in rural and urban areas of the United States which were not served by electrification. Its use began shortly after 1900 and continued past the 1950s. Calcium carbide pellets were placed in a container outside the home, with water piped to the container and allowed to drip on the pellets releasing acetylene. This gas was piped to lighting fixtures inside the house, where it was burned, creating a very bright flame. The house I grew up in still used carbide lighting. It's awfully reminiscent for me. You know, it was inexpensive, but prone to gas leaks and dreadful explosions."

"That's really fascinating, Veyron . . ." Tom interrupted him. "But, what's it doing in the state of the art engine room of a modern cruise ship?"

"Back up lighting, in case the power goes out?" Veyron suggested, although he clearly didn't believe it.

"But this is a modern cruise ship. There must be any number of better electrical based options, such as LED headlamps to be used in an emergency power outage?"

"I have no idea, but it seems to me that whoever brought these down here was expecting to have a prolonged period without electricity sometime in the near future."

CHAPTER 36

T OM RAPIDLY PERFORMED A RECONNAISSANCE of the now
well-lit engine room. Veyron, behind him, covered him
with his weapon as Tom searched the rest of the room. Tom
moved around the room in a counterclockwise direction.
Clearing each section and confirming no one was hiding before
moving on. Two locked doors were found at opposite ends of
the room. Per the schematics, each one led to the level above.

He turned to Veyron. "All right, the engine room's clear —
let's get the hell out of here."

"Okay. You want to go stairs or elevator?"

"Stairs. Easier to secure."

Tom scanned the room and then approached the door at the
end of the room. His eyes stopped at the elevator door, which
after remaining open for the past ten minutes, suddenly closed.
"Shit, the elevator."

He ran towards it. Pressed the open door button and then
watched as the elevator ascended without them. He banged on
the up button, and watched as the elevator numbers glowed
until it stopped at the second level.

Tom hit the up button again.

Instead of descending, the numbered lights continued to
raise until it stopped. The number six remained glowing.

"Shit!" Tom swore. He hit the transmitter on his portable
radio. "Elise, you've got company!"

"I'm on it!" Elise replied. Her voice calm and confident.

Veyron swiped his card on the elevator door and pressed the up button again. The light flashed red: *Access Denied.* "What the hell? I thought Elise said she gave us access to every door on the ship."

Tom stared at the elevator numbers. Six was still glowing which meant the elevator hadn't moved from the level Elise was guarding. "I don't know what to say, but Elise is in trouble."

Veyron depressed his radio transmitter. "Elise, what have you got?"

"Nothing," she replied. "I tracked the elevator from the second basement level up to the sixth passenger level. It's stopped but the doors have remained shut."

"Don't let whoever the hell is on the other side of that door out!" Tom said. "We're coming back up to help."

"I have the M2 heavy machinegun fixed on the door," Elise said loudly enough for Tom and whoever was inside the elevator to hear. "If anyone tries to come out those doors they're going to be made into pureed flesh pretty quick."

"That-a-girl!" Veyron knocked Tom on his shoulder. "Let's find our own way out of this mess. Elise can look after herself."

"Elevator door's opening!" Elise yelled. "I have an M2 heavy machine gun pointed at you. Get your hands up, now!"

Tom pressed the up button again.

"What the fuck?" Elise swore.

The sound of machine gun fire echoed down the elevator shaft. Three bursts and about fifty rounds fired. Tom felt the vibrations of metal piercing metal in the door below where his hand rested.

"What just happened?" Tom asked Elise in a panic.

He never heard her reply. Instead a large explosion rocked the elevator shaft, echoing throughout the engine room.

Veyron listened intently and then grabbed Tom. "Get away from the door — Now!"

A moment later, the door smashed open as the elevator came crashing through the floor. Tom fought through the smoke and debris. He looked inside the destroyed elevator.

"Elise, are you all right?" Tom caught his breath. "What the hell just happened?"

Silence.

Veyron tried his own radio and then stopped. "It's pointless."

"Why?"

"The radios have been jammed again by that depressing music — *Gloomy Sunday.*"

CHAPTER 37

TOM WATCHED AS THE RED glow of the second elevator started to ascend. He tried his access card again, but received the same message: *Access Denied.* The engine room security codes must not have been included in the list Gerald had sent him. The elevator stopped on the second crew level.

"We've got to get to her!" Tom yelled.

"Of course we do." Veyron grinned viciously. "And to do that, we need to get to the crew level above. Come on, we'll take the stairs."

Tom kicked at the locked door, throwing the full weight of his two hundred and forty pounds of solid muscle into it. The door barely moved. The two men tried kicking it together. Nothing happened. The door was designed to stop flooding water from ascending to the levels above—there was no way they could kick it open.

"You have any ideas?" Tom asked.

Veyron returned to the elevator and picked up the carbine lamp. "As a matter of fact, I do."

CHAPTER 38

E LISE BROUGHT THE BROWNING M2 machinegun out of the crook of her shoulder, where it had butted in while she shot. Close to sixty 50 caliber used shell casings were scattered on the floor to the right of her. The weapon smelled of burnt gunpowder and smoke still wafted from the firing mechanism. She grinned. The weapon had fired smoothly and accurately.

She left the Browning on its tripod on the floor and stood up. With her right hand she took hold of the Uzi and approached the second elevator. Something exploded when she fired on the first elevator, but there was no explosion with the second. Still, she wasn't taking any chances. She'd fired a number of rounds into the closed door of the second elevator before it had the chance to open.

She watched carefully. Standing in a firing position, she aimed her Uzi at the door, which looked like Swiss cheese. The door opened and she stared inside. The back wall of the elevator was scattered with bullet holes. There was only one thing remaining in the otherwise empty elevator. It took her a moment to recognize it.

A large teddy bear.

It was one of those novelty-sized, soft and cuddly toys. Its wide eyes stared at her with an expression of affection. The bear's round tummy was shredded by bullets, but otherwise it was entirely intact. It had a big grin made out of black stitching to match its eyes. The thing had probably been an intimate gift for one of the crew or entertainers below. Around its neck a yellow sign was attached by a small silver chain.

Elise recognized the card immediately. It was written in the same lazy scrawl she'd seen throughout the rest of the shopfronts. The card read: *I'm sorry. Do you want to play? I'll be back in five minutes.*

She noticed a small camera at the back of the bear's head. It had fallen off during the shooting, but the light still glowed red. Elise picked it up. "I'm sorry, I don't play with toys. I'll be waiting for you, in five minutes time."

Elise then swiped her own card on the elevator door and pressed descend. She watched as the elevator lights showed it descend until it stopped at the second crew member's level. She depressed the transmitter to her radio. "I'm all right guys. I just sent a teddy bear packing."

There was no response.

She waited a full minute and then depressed the transmitter again without speaking. The radio was full of static. Mostly white noise. When she listened long enough she heard the depressing music. She let go of the transmitter — someone had blocked the radio channel again.

Elise sat down at her security station and looked at her computer. Someone had restarted the power to the two other elevators on board. The ones she'd disconnected earlier so she would only face an enemy from one location at a time. Both elevators were stopped on level two. She glanced through the images taken from the 205 security cameras on board the *Antarctic Solace.*

According to her computer, none of them had identified any movement. She felt reassured she was still alone on the sixth level. She typed on her keyboard and quickly executed a search of any movement in the past ten minutes.

Her eyes stopped at the one entry.

The aft elevator moved from the second level up to the sixth. There it remained for a total of three minutes. At the same time, the cameras on the sixth floor suffered a power outage, before the elevator returned to the second level.

The question was — *did someone return with it?*

Elise thought about it for a minute. Someone was playing with them, and she didn't like it. She considered the most secure place for her to take command of the situation.

She gripped her Uzi for comfort. If someone had taken the aft elevator up to greet her, she was ready to play.

A moment later, she heard the sound of a large explosion below.

CHAPTER 39

"**J**ESUS CHRIST!" TOM SWORE. "DO you think you used enough acetylene?"

Veyron looked at the now demolished door. "Hey, it opened the door, didn't it?"

Tom nodded and walked through the new opening. His Remington shotgun led the way through the smoke and debris. It was kind of empowering to know their enemy already expected them and so there was no reason to attempt to go in quietly.

The smoke cleared and Tom could see the entire room well enough. It was narrow and had a series of ladders reaching to the ceiling far above. Unlike the other decks which had all been slightly less than a story high, the distance between the engine room and the crew deck was close to thirty feet to house the massive diesel engines.

Veyron looked up to the opening near the ceiling. "You climb up first and I'll cover that door in case anyone has other plans."

"Sure." Tom slid the strap of the Remington over his shoulder and began climbing.

There were three ladders. All of them were surrounded by a semi-circle of grated steel to stop the climber falling. Each ladder was then divided by a small landing partition so that the climber could only ever fall a maximum of ten feet.

He climbed quickly. Hand over hand, he took three rungs at a time and reached the highest platform in just under a minute. He then unslung his shotgun and aimed it at the steel hatch. If anyone tried to come in while Veyron climbed they'd never know what hit them.

"All right, Veyron," he called out. "Your turn."

Veyron smiled and climbed up behind him. The platform was barely adequate to accommodate the two grown men.

"Is the door locked?" Veyron whispered.

"No."

"Then I suggest we go through it."

CHAPTER 40

T OM TURNED THE HANDLE AND slowly opened the hatch. It opened to a long passageway. The lights were turned off along it, but in the distance the lights were on in the large living area for the crew and entertainers. The sound of a television being played came from the room ahead. It was some cheap daytime sitcom. Tom couldn't hear the sound of anyone. He shined his flashlight in the other direction. It finished only a few feet away at the aft elevator.

"Should we be concerned about the elevator?" Tom asked.

"No. Elise cut the power to the aft and forward elevators. Nothing's going in or out."

Tom nodded and then stepped out into the corridor. The lights were bright at the end of the hall making it easy to become focused on what's ahead and forget about the doors before it. Tom had to consciously remind himself to check each door before moving further along.

He swiped his card and then entered the first door. It was one of the sleeping quarters for the crew. A picture frame next to the bed showed a young man in a sailor's uniform holding hands with a pretty brunette in a red skirt. It suggested the room belonged to a crewman. It took a few moments to rule out anyone hiding inside and then they continued.

They checked at least a dozen more before reaching the main living space. The sound of the television increased. It wasn't like the scene had changed and now was playing louder. Instead, it seemed like someone had consciously adjusted the volume until it became a blaring distraction.

Tom fired a single shot from the Remington. The powerful twelve gauge spray created a large opening in the wall at the back. "That was a warning shot. If you don't come out in the next five seconds I'm going to assume you're one of the attackers and the next shot I won't miss."

Silence.

Tom pumped the shotgun. "If you're in here, I strongly urge you to come out with your hands up."

"There's a few of us in here. We're all well-armed so I suggest you take my friend's advice and come out now."

More silence.

"It appears our friends aren't interested in the easy way," Tom said.

"No. It would appear not." Veyron signaled with his hands that he would go to the other side of the large room and then the two would approach from the opposite side of it.

Tom nodded and watched as Veyron took his position. The common living area was basically a big square room. On one side an eatery and the other a big television with at least twenty Lazy Boy reclining chairs.

The eatery was empty, but the back of someone's head could be seen in each of the reclining chairs. Tom signaled to Veyron that there were people in the chairs. Veyron acknowledged and the held up the number three on his right hand.

Veyron then dropped each finger one at a time.

Three. Two. One.

Both men approached with their weapons ready to fire.

"Show's over!" Tom said. "Who wants to start with the explaining?"

No response.

Tom took aim and fired at the television. It exploded into a hole in the wall behind it. "I said, show's over. Now I want some answers."

Still no response.

Veyron grabbed the first person on his shoulder. "Hey, we said — show's over!"

The man didn't even flinch. His eyes were open, but they stared vacantly at the destroyed television. Tom glanced at the rest of them. No one moved. They looked like a bunch of zombies. Each one with their eyes open, taking slow, shallow breaths and entirely unaware of their surroundings.

Tom noticed a sealed plastic bag hanging next to the chair of the first person. It dripped fluid into the man's left arm via an intravenous needle. Every person in the room had the same bag attached to them. He picked up the fluid bag and read the name: *Normal saline.* Additive: *Morphine and Midazolam.*

He recognized the strong analgesic, Morphine, but had no idea what the other drug was used for. "What's Midazolam?"

"It's a potent sedative and also a very powerful amnesic agent."

"Meaning?"

"Someone went to great lengths to make these people forget something."

CHAPTER 41

T OM TOOK A PICTURE OF the group of twenty people who were badly drugged out of their minds in case one of the zombies were replaced by the person responsible while they were away. It took him and Veyron another half hour to complete checking the entire deck.

"The place is empty," Veyron said.

"Sure, but someone must be out there. You don't think those people drugged themselves, do you?"

"No. Not to mention how they fed themselves?"

"Good point." Tom picked up one of the drugged persons arms. The drug-filled liquid still flowed into the man's vein. He slid the clamp shut.

"No, let it flow." Veyron slid the clamp open until small drops of the liquid entered the man's veins. "The last thing we need right now is to have someone waking up on us all hysterical until we make sure Elise is all right and work out what we're going to do with them."

"Good point." Tom stared at the man more closely. Most likely in his late twenties, he appeared clean shaven. His arms and legs looked like they had normal muscle tone. "These people haven't been confined to their beds for the past ten days."

"You think they've been working in the day, only to be sedated for bed?"

Tom grinned as realization finally dawned on him. "Look at these people, what do you see?"

"I see a bunch of drugged zombies."

"What else do you see?"

"Most are men." Veyron sighed as he took in the entire group of people at a glance. His scientific mind reaching for objective facts. "There are two women amongst the eighteen men. They are all well cared for with no signs of malnutrition, bedsores, mouth ulcers or any other aliments common to people permanently bed-bound. Each person here is wearing a uniform . . ." He stopped mid-sentence. "Damnit, they're all maintenance staff and engineers!"

"Exactly!"

"Someone's been making them work," Tom said. "And then sedating them in the evening."

"After being given opium based morphine regularly they most likely would have developed an affinity if not an addiction to the drug. Like any other addict, they could be coaxed to perform tasks before being given any more of it."

"The question is — what task have they been performing for the past ten days?"

CHAPTER 42

T OM LEFT THE ENGINEERS IN their chairs, staring blankly at the wall. He and Veyron, now confident both the engine room and staffing deck were otherwise empty, returned to the middle elevator. He swiped the access card Elise had made for him and pressed the up button. The doors opened and he and Veyron stepped inside.

The back of the elevator had more than fifty bullet holes scattered in a tight grouping. Sitting in a chair at the center of the elevator a man-sized teddy bear sat grinning at them. A large hole where its tummy belonged bled polyester stuffing.

Veyron bent down and examined it. "This was Elise's would be attacker?"

Tom pressed level six. "It looks like it never stood a chance. I just hope it didn't come with any friends."

The elevator stopped on level six. Veyron held the doors shut. "Elise, it's us—don't shoot!"

"Us who?" Elise replied.

"Veyron, Tom and the remains of a teddy bear!" Tom said in a clear voice.

"All right, come on out."

Veyron took his hand off the hold button and the elevator doors opened.

Elise grinned and lowered her Uzi. "Well it took you two long enough!"

Tom smiled at her. "You all right up here?"

"Fine. How about you guys? I heard a loud bang."

"Sorry," Tom replied. "That was Veyron playing with chemistry. What happened here? We saw you had a run in with a teddy bear."

"Yeah, whoever sent it was playing with me specifically."

"Did you kill him?"

"No. I don't even know if it was a HIM. Whoever it was sent the teddy as a decoy so they could access this level from the aft elevator."

"I thought you disconnected the power to the aft and forward elevators?" Veyron said.

"I did." Elise shook her head. "It appears whoever we're dealing with reconnected it so they could go snooping on what we're doing up here."

"What about the cameras?" Tom asked.

"I think that stupid song somehow blocked them for a few minutes."

"Gloomy Sunday?" Veyron asked.

Elise shrugged her shoulders. "Yeah, somehow they've worked out a way to make it superimpose the radio channels and some digital devices. The radios could be done easily enough, but I have no idea how they blocked the cameras. What I do know is that the cameras returned to normal immediately after the song stopped playing."

"Weird," Tom said.

"Sure is," she said. "Everything about this ship is strange. What did you find down below?"

"More questions without any answers," Tom answered.

"What did you find?" she persisted.

Tom poured himself a mug of hot coffee. "An engine room wired with carbide gas lighting and a crew room with twenty of the ship's engineers."

"What did the twenty people have to say?"

"Nothing," Tom said. "They'd all been drugged."

"That's crazy." Elise shook her head. "Someone downstairs is responsible for all this. Whoever came up before went back down again. That's for certain. Any chance you missed someone?"

"No. The living quarters are basic downstairs. There's not enough room to hide a cat let alone a person. I'm confident those twenty people are the only people below decks."

Elise smiled. "And I'm confident no one is on the passengers' decks, which means one of those twenty drugged people must be the person we're after."

"So, how do we differentiate?"

Elise crossed her arms. "Let's bring them all here—I have a few ideas how we can determine who's faking it and who's not."

CHAPTER 43

T OM STARED AT THE PICTURE of the twenty supposedly
drugged people in their recliner chairs he'd taken twenty
minutes before and then back at the people themselves. They
were all the same. No one had switched places or moved.

If one of them is faking it, they're doing a really good job at it.

"Who do you want to start with?" Tom asked.

"This one." Veyron reached for the handles behind the one
closest to the end of the rows of chairs and began moving it.

"Why?"

Veyron heaved as he pushed the heavy man on the recliner.
"No reason. He's closest to me, that's all. Besides, just look at
him — he's the biggest out of the lot. We're going to have to
make a separate trip for each one. No reason to risk it now. If
we get sloppy and take one each we're more likely to get
attacked, but with the odds two against one, whoever we're
looking for will have no choice but to wait."

"Until what?"

"A better chance to escape — and our job is to make sure that
never happens."

"Just stop a minute, will you?" Tom said.

"Sure, what is it?"

"You just reminded me." Tom held his Remington shotgun
to the person's head.

"Everything okay?"

Tom smiled reassuringly. "Fine. We should search each person before we move them. If they're faking it, they probably have a weapon."

"Good thinking." Veyron padded the man down in front of him. Starting at the guy's head he worked all the way down to his feet. He checked the clothing and removed the guy's shoes. He used zip ties to secure both ankles together and one to tie each wrist to the chair. Veyron checked his work. "I'd say that'd make it pretty hard for him to escape. Feel better?"

"Much."

"Good. Because we've got another nineteen of these to go."

Tom pressed the up button on the elevator. The door opened and he stepped inside with Veyron and their patient. He started at the man, his eyes darting between the man's wrists and face.

Veyron looked at him. "What?"

"I don't know. Something about this whole thing gives me the creeps. It's like we're waiting for one of these zombies to lash out at us."

"Which is why we've made it so they can't."

The elevator stopped on the sixth deck and the doors opened. Veyron heaved to push the recliner with his sleeping giant out. "Where do you want to line them up, Elise?"

"Over here." Elise pointed to the end of the dining room where the tables and chairs had all been removed to make a clearing. She stopped when she saw the sleeping giant of a man. "Whoa, who's the big guy?"

"No idea. His shirt has the name Mitchel stitched into it. Of course, the clothes look tight, they might not even be his."

"Christ, I hope he's not our troublemaker," Elise said. "We'd need the rocket launcher just to stop the bastard."

Veyron patted the man on his shoulders. "He's big, but he'll go down with a bullet same as anyone else."

Tom looked at Elise. "Any chance your computer system has

missed something?"

"Like what?"

"Like a person running around, secretly avoiding every security camera?"

"No. There was one event where something blocked a few of the cameras while you were down stairs, but I'm confident my system is working."

"So then . . . how did these people get like this?"

"You mean, where did the person go who did this to them?"

"Yes."

"The *Antarctic Solace* has been searched. There are twenty-three people aboard. You, Veyron and I — and those twenty people there in front of us." She took a deep breath in and slowly exhaled. "One of those people is responsible for abducting all the missing people on board, drugging the rest of them, and for leaving me a teddy bear in the elevator."

"But why would he or she drug themselves?" Tom asked.

"To avoid getting caught," she replied. "Once they discovered we had the upper hand and were approaching, he or she quickly joined the rest of the drug affected zombies to cover their tracks."

"But they were all drugged."

Elise shrugged. "It's a pretty good alibi, isn't it?"

"Now what?"

"Now we have to work out which one wants to play."

CHAPTER 44

E LISE TESTED THAT THE MAN'S massive arms and legs were well tied and then read the additive label for the bag of saline. She picked up her phone and made a call to a Doctor who was the head of Intensive Care at St. George Hospital, London. She went through the doses and checked the maximum amount possible without killing a person. She then thanked the man and hung up.

Elise opened the intravenous clamp and increased the drip rate of the sedative. She looked up and saw Tom's face. "So long as these people remain sedated I can look after them on my own until the cavalry joins us."

"I thought you wanted to find out who was faking it?" Tom asked.

"I do. But no reason to have them conscious for that."

"What do you plan to do?"

"I've spoken to a friend of mine." Elise put medical gloves on and attached a tourniquet to the guy's other arm. "He tells me most cruise ships carry the facilities to test blood for drugs and alcohol. Date rape and illicit drug use while partying can be a problem. Most ships are well equipped with the facilities to test blood."

Tom nodded, glad he'd never gone through that sort of party scene when he was younger. He watched as Elise picked up a needle from the drawer of a small medical cart and felt for a vein. She waited until it swelled with the backflow of venous blood and then anchored it with her thumb. A moment later she inserted the needle. Blood flushed into the little chamber of the needle. He stared vacantly at the blood. He'd never had a problem with blood, but the sight of it being drained from a person who was tied and unconscious seemed wrong.

Elise looked up at him. "Can you pass me that black vacutainer, please?"

"Sure, what is it?" Tom asked.

"It's that little sample tube with a black lid sitting on the top of the medical cart. It has an additive that will stop this blood from clotting until I can take it down to the ship's medical center, and test it for drugs and alcohol."

Tom handed it to her. "How did you learn all this stuff?"

She took the vacutainer and said, "Youtube."

Tom laughed. "No. Really, how?"

"Youtube."

"You learned how to take someone's blood from an online video?"

"What can I say? I've always been a quick learner."

"You're a freak, you know that?"

"I've been called worse."

It took three hours to complete the multiple journeys required to move all twenty sedated persons. Tom, Elise and Veyron stared at them all lined up in four rows of five chairs. They were positioned at the end of the main restaurant facing the computer hub Elise had set up. That way she would be able to watch if any of them tried to move. Any one of them could be the person responsible for the attacks. More frightening was the thought it might not just be one person, there could be multiple people in the group who were responsible.

Tom tried to see if any of them were fidgeting, blinking, or showing any other signs of having difficulties holding still. "It seems strange to think one of those zombies is still awake, waiting, planning their escape."

"A scarier thought is all of them could be responsible," Elise said.

Veyron smiled cheerfully. "No, a scarier thought is none of them is responsible and the rat is still loose aboard the *Antarctic Solace.*"

"No. There's no way we have a loose rat." Elise pointed to her open laptop on the desk beside them. "The cameras would have picked up the movement and my program would have notified me. There are more than two hundred CCTV cameras recording every aspect of this ship.

"Do we know for certain those bags even contain sedatives?" Tom asked.

"Yes." Elise spoke in her usual air of confidence. "One person might be able to fake it, but not twenty."

"When will we know about the blood samples?" Tom asked.

"A couple hours and I'll have the results on my laptop," Elise replied. "I also have my computer running a program to see if any of these faces were recognized in the earlier security recordings. It will then cross reference what they were doing before the attacks in order to determine who really works for the *Antarctic Solace.*"

Veyron stood up to leave. "All right, now that's done—I need to get down to the engine room to start the diesels if we're going to avoid spending the winter trapped in the ice."

Elise opened an App in her computer tablet and began scrolling through the schematics of the lower decks. She looked up at Veyron. "Go."

"What do you need me to do?" Tom asked.

"According to the *Antarctic Solace*'s shore side security team, there's a redundancy data hub downstairs. I want to go check it out. Maybe it will provide the answers that have been erased on the other security tapes."

"You want me to go retrieve it?"

"No," Elise said. "You stay here and guard these people, will you? I'll go and get it. I know what I'm looking for."

"You want to go down there on your own?"

She grinned. "Of course. Why not? The only people on board this ship are now sedated right here in front of us."

CHAPTER 45

E LISE DESCENDED TO THE SECOND level where Tom and Veyron had discovered the twenty people lying like drugged out zombies in recliner chairs. The elevator doors opened and she entered the crew and entertainer's deck. An eerie silence pervaded the dark hall. Elise shined a flashlight along the wall until she found the light switch. It struck her as odd that Veyron and Tom hadn't bothered to switch the lights on when they moved all the zombies upstairs.

She followed the hall until about midway, passing the first three side passages before taking the fourth to the right. She reached the first access hatch to a maintenance area which housed much of the electrical wiring and communication conduits. Elise unlocked the hatch with a key the on shore security IT staff informed her could be found in the ship's main security office on level three. She removed the hatch and then slipped inside. She carefully maneuvered her way through the narrow series of maintenance conduits and passageways which formed the labyrinth between the lower crew and the passenger decks. She lithely shuffled and crawled through the tiny maze of electronics without checking her computer tablet for the schematics. Her memory was photographic; always had been, so she had no need to check that she was taking the right routes.

At the end of the fourth shaft she reached it—a large, immaculate, stainless steel cabinet. Numerous wires and fiber optic cables streamed into it. Elise took a second key from a small chain and carefully inserted it into the lock. It turned freely and she opened the cabinet door.

Elise grinned as she stared at the *Antarctic Solace*'s backup digital storage device. A five terabyte external hard drive capable of housing every image, video and sound recording absorbed by the ship's two hundred plus security cameras for the past twelve months. Elise unscrewed the device from its alcove and quickly backtracked through the tunnels to the main crew lounge again.

Tom looked up at her when she walked out of the elevator and on to the sixth deck. "How did it go?"

She smiled and plugged the five terabyte external hard drive into her laptop. "Good. It's time to find out what this is all about."

CHAPTER 46

E LISE'S POWERFUL LAPTOP WORKED TO process the enormous amount of data it was being fed. She brought up a search query and entered the main passenger entertainment security footage, followed by the time and date range commencing the hour before and after the other CCTV recording had been tampered with.

The computer then began sieving through millions of hours of data recordings until it downloaded the one she was after. It was taken from a single camera on the port side of level six and looked outwards towards the ocean.

She pressed play and the digital video started.

It began the same as the other ones she'd watched where people casually walked along the promenade and decking. Some of the people walked slowly, talking to friends and family while drinking something alcoholic; others had a brisk pace, as though they had somewhere to be. Nothing appeared out of the ordinary for a cruise ship.

Then the alarm began its signal. A two minute continuous ringing from the ship's bell sounded like a fire alarm that should have woken the dead. When it stopped, the calm voice of the Captain was heard over the ship's loudspeakers.

"This is an emergency. I regret to inform you the *Antarctic Solace* has struck an iceberg and is taking on water rapidly. There is no need for concern and you will not need lifejackets because another tourist ship is on its way and will be here within five minutes. I must please ask everyone to move to the sixth level in preparation for departure from this ship. Do not bring your belongings — the *Antarctic Solace* will reimburse you for your losses."

Elise looked at Tom. "Told you there was a perfectly logical explanation why everyone happily jumped ship."

"Sure, but where did they go?"

Elise watched as the deck on the sixth level filled with orderly rows of people preparing to disembark. Minutes later a ship arrived and docked alongside the *Antarctic Solace.* Elise pressed pause on the video so she could read the name on the side of the vessel. "*Frozen magic*— that's what we're after. Find that ship and we find the missing people."

She pressed play again and watched each row of passengers confidently jump over the railing onto a cushioned landing on the deck of the *Frozen Magic.*

Elise stopped the tape. "Well that answers it! They slowly removed each staff member until the ship was filled with passengers only. No one to tell them they hadn't hit an iceberg. Then, they made the simple ruse and convinced everyone to happily leave the ship. At that stage Alexis was still feeling the sedative effect of the antiemetic given to her the day before and consequently slept through the entire event."

"Okay," Tom said. "The question now is where did the *Frozen Magic* take them, and why?"

Elise typed the name into her computer and pressed search. It came back with zero tour companies in Antarctica with a ship named *Frozen Magic.* She opened the search to any ship large enough to accommodate two hundred people within the Antarctic waters. This time the results showed a medium to large icebreaker employed in Antarctica over the past five years. But there were no notes about who employed its services. The vessel was privately owned by a resident of St.

Kitts in the Caribbean.

"That's interesting," Elise said.

"What?"

"St. Kitts is notorious for selling citizenship at a high price to people who want a second passport as a backup or want to set up a business without the U.S. being involved."

"I'm sure it's perfectly legal."

"And I'm sure there's a reason an icebreaker is owned by a resident of St. Kitts."

Tom stared at the vessel. "So where is it now?"

Elise searched for an IAS international ship tracking beacon. It came up empty. "That's strange, a vessel that large must be displaying an IAS response under international shipping law."

"Can you find it some other way?"

"Sure. Let's check some satellite images." Elise typed several queries into a database of current and recent satellite photographs taken over Antarctica. The search finished within seconds and showed the image of a single ice breaker in McMurdo Sound. Next to it was the *Maria Helena.* Elise swallowed. "Get me Sam on the radio!"

Tom looked at her face. "Why, what's wrong?"

"Sam and Alexis are heading straight into a trap!"

CHAPTER 47

S AM STOPPED THE HOVERCRAFT AT the highest point of the Taylor Glacier before descending into East Antarctica. He switched the engines off and climbed out as the machine sank onto hard ice. He looked ahead where leveled ice and snow drifted as far as he could see until it blurred with the horizon.

"East Antarctica!" Alexis said. "The most vacant land on earth."

"Can we see it from here?"

"I should be able to." Alexis scanned the horizon using a pair of military grade binoculars. She stopped after about forty seconds and handed him the binoculars. "Found it—Pegasus."

He took them and looked through. Still thirty miles away, the science station looked like no more than a small rabbit mound covered in snow. "You're certain?"

"Absolutely."

He picked up the radio. "*Maria Helena*—we're approaching the location. There's no cloud cover. Can we please get satellite confirmation there are no hostiles in the area?"

No response.

Sam increased the volume and frequency; then tried again. This time the only response was static and an almost inaudible white noise. He lifted the speaker right to his ear and then grinned. "It's that fucking song again—Gloomy Sunday!"

"What do you want to do about it?"

"Not much we can," Sam said. "We have a small window if we're to rescue them. All we can do is be careful and go quickly."

"So we'll keep going?"

Sam shrugged. "I didn't come all this way to stop because the radios are still being jammed by some stupid song."

With the decision made to carry on, Sam and Alexis climbed back inside the hovercraft. Within minutes Sam began descending the glacier. It was slow and tedious work, dangerously navigating the labyrinth of glacial fissures, ice troughs, and unstable snow. Seracs, often as tall as fifty feet sometimes overhung their path like giant axes.

Sam chose his route carefully to minimize the risk, but it was slow work. By midafternoon they reached the ice plains of East Antarctica. Sam opened up the throttle and the main propellers reached their maximum speed, sending the hovercraft gliding across the near perfectly flat ice surface at a rate of eighty miles per hour.

It took less than half an hour then to reach the Pegasus station. Sam slowed the hovercraft. Out front of the Antarctic station an orange Japanese-built Ohara Snow Tractor faced back towards them. Parked out front of the station and covered in snow, it looked like a once proud and now forlorn pet, forced to brave the elements while its owners stayed warm inside. Two flags stood proudly next to it — one French and one Swiss.

Sam looked at the Snow Tractor as he shut down the hovercraft's engines. "It looks like someone's still here."

Alexis reached for the Glock he'd given her. "Yeah, I just hope it's my guys."

CHAPTER 48

S AM CHECKED HIS UZI, THE smaller of the two weapons he'd
taken with him, but much easier to use in a confined space.
He removed the 32 round magazine, took it apart and pulled
the trigger. The firing mechanism worked smoothly. Confident
the icy conditions hadn't affected the weapon, he reassembled
it and stepped out of the hovercraft.

Pegasus was a portable, dome shaped igloo with internal
insulation. From the outside it stood four feet above the ice, but
Alexis had explained to him earlier that the scientists had dug
out the main living space and the dome was just the protective
shield, made out of aluminum, it reflected the cold.

Sam opened the unlocked door of the Ohara Snow Tractor.
"I'm Sam Reilly. I'm here to help. Anyone inside?"

No response.

He signaled to Alexis. "Keep an eye on the door to Pegasus."

Alexis drew the Glock he'd given her. "Go. I've got it
covered."

Sam quietly entered the large snow machine, built
specifically for the harsh environment of Antarctica. It was cold
inside, and he immediately doubted anyone had been inside
recently. Even so, his basic training kicked in and told him not
to leave himself exposed from two directions.

He flicked the lights on and carefully searched the Snow
Tractor, which was capable of carrying up to twenty people

inside. There were four individual compartments. Each one consisted of a range of scientific equipment for researching ice tunnels. Radar screens, seismographs, and ground penetrating sonar lined the walls. Sam opened each one individually until he reached the back of the machine.

Confident it was empty he climbed the steps at the front. Alexis looked at him. "It was empty. Any movement on your end?"

"No. Shall we knock on the door?"

"Sure."

Sam approached the entrance to the science station. The steps descending into the Pegasus were clear of snow, as though they'd been shoveled free of ice earlier today. He pointed to them. "Someone's definitely been home recently."

She shook her head. "Those steps have heating elements inside to avoid snow build up from blocking them inside."

"What are their names?" Sam asked.

"The scientists?"

"Yeah."

"Auben, Pier, Jean, Hugo, and Dominique," she replied.

Sam nodded. "Okay." He stepped down to the door and banged loudly. "Anyone in there? My name's Sam Reilly. I've come to help."

No response.

He opened the door slightly and banged louder. "Auben. Pier. Jean. Hugo. Dominque. Any of you in there?"

Still no response.

"They must be inside," Alexis said. "The snow tractor's the only means they have of getting out of here. If it's still here, so are they."

Sam nodded. He understood what she was saying. He opened the door slightly and stepped inside. The place looked disheveled. Tables were on their sides, beds were torn, and food scattered. Sam glanced at the aluminum insulated ceiling — it was riddled with bullet holes.

He stepped out again.

"What is it?" Alexis asked quietly. The urgency turning her calm voice sharp. "What did you see?"

Sam looked at her; his piercing blue eyes, cold and hard. His jaw rigid and taut. "They're all dead — every one of them."

CHAPTER 49

LEXIS STARED AT HIS FACE for a moment. She didn't need to ask what had happened. He had already told her everything she needed to know — they'd been murdered and it was her fault. She pushed through Sam's arms and tried to see inside.

"Wait!" He grabbed her.

She shook her head. "No. I have to see what I have done."

"You didn't do anything. It's not your fault."

"Of course it is! You said so yourself. The coincidences are too much. Someone wanted me dead because of my research, but I can't even imagine why."

Sam held her tight and stopped her from pushing through. Alexis tried to wriggle free but he held her with too much strength and she finally relented, relaxing into his comforting grip. "We'll find out why, and we'll fix this — I promise."

"Fix this?" She buried her head in his strong chest. "You can't fix this! No one can. Those people are already dead and there's nothing we can do about it."

"You're right. We can't. But we must now ensure they didn't die in vain. Someone must have had a pretty compelling reason to murder them and we need to find out what that was."

"Why?" Alexis asked. "Why did they do this? There's no reason. Why would anyone want to kill scientists who were simply looking for a place to build a particle accelerator?"

Sam shrugged. "Maybe it was what they were looking to make?"

"The Boson Higg's particles?" She shook her head. "No, that's not possible. No one knew about the project. Not even the scientists working here. All they knew was I'd heard about these ice tunnels and wanted to know the feasibility of building a particle accelerator inside."

She felt Sam's arms wrap warmly around her. Ordinarily she would have found it comforting, but right now, she wanted to feel the pain. Somehow she felt she deserved to suffer. "Maybe someone was upset about even the suggestion of building in Antarctica?"

"It's possible, but unlikely."

"Why?" he persisted.

"Because gaining approval would require a unanimous positive vote. If one party wasn't happy, they didn't need to go to the extreme lengths of killing everyone here simply to stop the research."

"Okay, so if they weren't killed because of what they knew when they arrived here, they must have been killed because of what they found."

Alexis took a deep breath. "You think they found something here which got them killed?"

"It's the only explanation I'm left with."

"But Antarctica's a giant landmass covered in ice." Alexis shook her head in disbelief. "There's nothing here of any real value. There's no oil, no precious stones, nothing. Why else do you think the countries of the world were so willing to sign the Antarctic Treaty System, accepting no country owns Antarctica?"

Sam looked at her. "I think it's time I go inside and see if I can find out."

"I'll come with you," she said.

"Are you sure?" He stared at her. "They were killed from

the air and left where they died."

"I have to."

"Okay."

Sam opened the door fully and stepped to the side so she could choose how much she wanted to see. It was one of the things she'd already learned to love about Sam. He was infinitely protective of her, but at the same time capable of letting her make her own decisions and not mollycoddling her. It was a terrible sight, but one she needed to see.

She stepped past him and entered. Pegasus was one large dome shaped room, with everything from food preparation, study, entertainment, through to sleeping arrangements being shared. A separate lavatory was built outside with its own enclosed space. Immediately, she could take everything in at a glance. The insulated ceiling had been peppered by hundreds of bullet holes. Everything inside was shredded. The dead scientists remained in the positions they had been in when they were killed. Alexis placed her hand over her mouth and said nothing.

Pier was the first one she saw. A recent Doctorial graduate in Physics, she had been impressed by his confronting thesis which challenged some of the accepted norms of particle physics. In the end he'd proved many of his own theories wrong. She had been impressed by the strength of his conviction despite multiple attacks from professors around the world; experts who didn't like to have their established theories challenged. In the end, she offered him a job at CERN.

And now he was dead.

Slumped back in his chair, his breakfast porridge looked like it had just been boiled. A spoon rested half out of the bowl, as though he'd been in the process of taking another bite when the bullets stopped him. Three bullet holes pierced his chest. Otherwise he looked no different from the last time she'd seen him nearly eight months earlier. His long, dark brown hair almost covered his eyes with large waves. His mouth was open, in aghast shock and misunderstanding—as though he couldn't comprehend how his life had so suddenly been taken from him. His unseeing eyes stared vacantly at her in accusation.

"I'm so sorry, Pier." She stepped past him and kept walking. "What the hell happened here, Sam?"

"At a guess, I'd say someone flew overhead and machine-gunned the entire place. The aluminum insulation was strong enough to protect them from the elements but did nothing against large caliber machinegun bullets. By the looks of things, they made several passes just to make sure they got everyone."

"You mean they might not have died immediately?" She put her hand back over her mouth. "They must have cowered somewhere only to realize they had nowhere to hide?"

"No. By the look of it, I'd say they all died on the first pass. Whoever's responsible flew by a few more times just to be certain."

"That's terrible."

She watched as Sam rifled through a series of paper notes. Next he switched on three laptop computers sitting on the main dining table, which also doubled up as a work station. None of them started.

He picked up the one closest to him and examined the six bullet holes. He poked his finger in the first one and then looked up at her. "Fifty calibers—they never stood a chance."

Alexis barely heard him as she concentrated on walking to the far end of the dome where five hammocks hung on a rack. She pulled each of them out and ran her hands along the sides of them where a zipper held some minor personal effects from each individual scientist.

Sam looked at her as she opened the third zipper. "What are you looking for?"

"Their personal effects."

226

"Why?"

"In a world made unsecure by digital thieves, most of these people kept their most private discoveries in paper journals."

Sam grinned. "Any luck?"

"Not yet."

Sam gathered the laptops. "If you don't get lucky, we'll take these back to the *Maria Helena*. Elise might still be able to access the hard drives for us."

Alexis started to flick through Pier's journal. She stopped after a few minutes, feeling guilty, like she was somehow intruding on the dead man's most private thoughts. She dismissed the guilt and continued reading — if there were clues about what they had found that brought this entire disaster it would be worth prying.

She picked a section two thirds of the way through and started skimming. The date at the top of the page was nearly a year old and she was about to skip further when something caught her attention.

What does Professor Alexis Schultz see in her fiancé? There's something I don't like about him. He's intelligent enough — nowhere near as bright as she is, but definitely smart enough to work at CERN without her recommendations.

So then, what is it that I don't like? Because his IQ, which must range somewhere above the top percentile is the only good thing he shares with her. The guy's a loser. He's slimy and unctuous and although I can't put my finger on why, I know he's just plain wrong for her. She deserves much better.

The next section of the journal seemed to return to a project that he was working on. Alexis quickly skimmed through the next sections to see if there was anything else Pier had written about her husband. His comments had made her curious. *Why*

would Pier have thought Daniel was wrong for me? He was a very effective scientist — by no means naturally brilliant, but definitely good at what he did. She thought about it some more and decided it wasn't important. Nothing more than the passing thought of a new Doctorial graduate who she'd recommended for a permanent position at CERN.

She shook her head at his comment. It was silly and ridiculous. The kid barely even knew her or Daniel — *even if he'd been right, Daniel was a loser and he'd been having an affair.* She continued flicking through pages of the journal. Berating herself for not moving to the end of the journal and working backwards. Naturally if they'd found anything it would be documented close to the end of the journal. Just before he died.

For some reason, she couldn't shake her curiosity — *what did Pier know about my fiancé that I didn't?* She skimmed three more pages before finding it.

I found Alexis's fiancé in her office again today. He was searching for something and I interrupted him. He was quick to give an explanation that he was finding something for Alexis, but he looked guilty as all hell. It wasn't until he left that I noticed he'd been taking photographs of her notes with his phone.

Should I tell her that her fiancé's a schmuck?

Even if I did — would I be doing so for her, or for me? No. Better to let her make her own mistakes. Who am I to advise her what she wants? If you love someone let her go free; if she returns she loves you. If not, she was never yours to begin with.

Alexis flicked through several more pages without finding another note regarding her fiancé. *What the hell was he looking for? There's no reason for Daniel to be combing through my stuff.* None of it made any sense. His work was completely different than hers. It was one of the reasons they worked as a couple. Most academics were possessive about ownership of research papers.

Two senior academics would never get married because they'd fight about their work. With Daniel and Alexis the two focused on entirely different areas of particle physics. Daniel studied new technologies to collide particles together, which further improved on the basic concepts of the Large Hadron Collider, while she focused specifically on new subatomic particles.

She shook her head. It was another mystery she'd never understand. She turned one more page and promised herself she'd start at the end and forget the nonsense about Daniel. Only on the next page there was another note that she should have ignored but couldn't.

I accepted a job in Antarctica today. I think it's for the best. If I stay here the situation with Professor Alexis Schultz and her fiancé will drive me crazy and I'll be forced to tell her the truth. That her fiancé is a schmuck who doesn't deserve to spend one minute with her, let alone a lifetime – and that I'm in love with her.

Alexis stopped. There were tears in her eyes.

"What is it?" Sam asked.

"Pier was in love with me – and that's what got him killed."

CHAPTER 50

S AM FELT HELPLESS AS HE watched Alexis cry. After everything she'd been through, it was only this instant that she finally let go and burst into tears. He'd tried to comfort her, but she made it abundantly clear there was nothing he could do for her or Pier, or any of them. She just needed to let herself grieve and then she could get back to work. That much he could understand. Sam had known grief when his brother died. It took time to grieve, and a certain part of it never stopped. But grieving was good — so long as you didn't let it overcome your life.

Somehow he was confident Alexis would be strong enough to understand that. He continued searching through the debris for any clue that could be used to discover why the scientists from Pegasus were killed. He checked each of the deceased for notes or anything that could explain the bizarre scene.

His eyes glanced at Alexis. There were tear marks along the freckles of her cheeks, but they had stopped flowing and were now dry. Her green eyes, glossy as though the tears could start at any moment, were focused on the journal again.

"There's one thing I don't understand, Alexis."

She put the journal down and looked up at him. "Really, because I've got at least a dozen questions with no possible answers."

He didn't take the bait and instead asked her directly. "Why didn't they hide their crimes?"

"What do you mean? Hide their crimes from whom?" she asked.

"If you killed five leading scientists because of what they'd discovered, what's the last thing you'd want to do?"

"Get caught."

"Yeah I wouldn't want to get caught either. But no. Instead I was thinking I wouldn't want anyone to find out a crime had been committed because that would start people investigating—and that would lead to someone discovering what I killed to keep hidden in the first place!" Sam took a deep breath. "So then, why didn't they bury the bodies so they were simply presumed lost?"

"You're right. They could have easily buried them in the snow and no one would ever find the bodies. Not in a hundred years. By which time, it would be irrelevant."

"That's it!" Sam screamed the words.

"What is?"

"They didn't bother because it was the end of the summer. A search for the missing scientists wouldn't be possible until next summer, by which time their secret would be irrelevant. Whatever it is, they must be confident it will be over before next summer." Sam looked at bodies lying where they had been killed. "You have to get back to reading. We need to find out exactly what these people discovered before it's too late."

Alexis dipped her head and started reading again. "Okay, okay. No more personal stuff—if there's anything in here, I'll find it."

Sam picked up another journal. He skimmed through the pages and put it back down. It was mostly irrelevant. He went outside and climbed into the Snow Tractor. He turned the key and the main diesel engine fired up. Sam waited until the amp meter began showing power coming in from the alternator and then switched the GPS on.

The advanced global positioning system, based on triangulating satellites to determine exact positions was once considered something akin to science fiction. Modern advances and competition within the automaker industry had placed a similar system inside just about every modern car. And like all computers, they have a memory of where they've been.

Sam pressed recent locations and a list of fifteen GPS coordinates became highlighted. He pressed on the most recent one. He stared at the location as the GPS zoomed into the coordinates. Sam had been there before—it was the Taylor Valley.

What were they doing there?

Then the answer came to him. *Were they trying to run?*

He scrolled down to the previous coordinates. The location was closer to the coast, but still on the eastern side of the Trans Antarctic Ridge.

Sam stared at the image of the place. It looked vacant. *What did you find there?* He took a picture of the rest of the recent locations with his smartphone, but was willing to bet his year's salary that the second most recent location was the one that counted. He switched off the GPS and shut the diesel down and then stepped inside.

"I know where they've been recently," Sam said. "I just don't know what they found there."

Alexis looked up at him. The slightest of smiles formed on her beautiful face. "I do. And I think I know why they were murdered."

"Really, why?"

She sighed. "Do you remember me telling you the primary research objective for the Pegasus was to locate an ice tunnel large enough to feasibly house a Massive Hadron Collider?"

"Yeah."

"Well. It appears they found the perfect place to build one."

"Where?"

"On the eastern side of the Trans Antarctic Ridge," she said. "It was beneath the ice flats and less than a hundred miles from the coast. There was just one problem."

"And what was that?"

Alexis stood up and closed the journal. "Someone else had already built a Massive Hadron Collider inside."

CHAPTER 51

E LISE STARED AT THE RESULTS of the blood test. Every one of them had a large amount of both the narcotic morphine and the sedative midazolam in their system. The biggest guy had a slightly lower amount than the rest. *But was that because he'd intentionally dosed himself with a smaller amount, or because he was so damn big the medication had been diluted in his larger blood volume and worn off faster in his system?* It was just one more thing that didn't make any sense in an entire mangled mess of riddles and confusion. The radios were still jammed with the Hungarian song, *Gloomy Sunday* and so they couldn't get a message to Sam and Alexis that they were heading for trouble. She'd suggested moving the *Antarctic Solace* to McMurdo Sound so they could at least reach the *Maria Helena* and then Tom could take the helicopter out to retrieve them. But Veyron couldn't get the diesels to start, which meant the *Antarctic Solace* was stranded — and they were helpless.

"No good?" Tom asked.

"They all have drugs in their system. The big guy has a lower ratio of the drugs in his blood. It might have been intentional, or it could have been the side effect of being so damned big."

Tom opened another packet of cable ties. "No reason to wait until we find out which one it is. Let's attach a few more ties to his arms and wrists."

"Good idea."

"Any idea when our reinforcements are going to get here?"

Elise shook her head. "Satellite imaging showed they passed Cape Horn yesterday. At a guess I would say they'll be here by tonight. Do you know who the Secretary of Defense was sending?"

"No. Sam just said she'd make sure we had reinforcements and that we were to hold the ship, no-matter what happens."

She watched as Tom bound the giant's wrists and ankles with another set of cable ties. Elise kept her Uzi pointing at the man from a distance of eight feet. She figured if he broke free she'd need at least that much room between him and her to put him down with a burst of nine millimeter Parabellums. The elevator door opened and Veyron stepped out.

Elise turned her head to face him. "Any luck with those engines yet? I don't care what the Secretary of Defense advised us to do with the *Antarctic Solace* — I can't get through to Sam and I think it's time we move to McMurdo Sound."

"No. We're stuck here until reinforcements arrive."

"What do you mean? You couldn't fix it?"

"Not before the ice had well and truly bound the *Antarctic Solace* to the sea." Veyron grinned. "You're not going to believe this, but someone's completely reconfigured the *Antarctic Solace*'s main powerhouse!"

"The diesels are gone?"

"No. They're there all right. Only, they have been completely disconnected from the ship's main systems."

"Why?"

"Because now they're entirely free from all electronics."

"Don't they need electricity to start?" Elise asked.

"Not anymore!" Veyron clenched his jaw. "The entire thing has been retrofitted with hand operated starting mechanisms and although the steering is still hydraulic, instead of being power assisted, someone has increased the ratios of the gears so that the entire thing can be steered by hand.

"Why would anyone go to such trouble?" Tom interrupted.

"Unless . . ." Elise started to say.

Veyron sighed. "They knew an electromagnetic pulse was going to shut everything down!"

CHAPTER 52

A BLACK SHIP APPROACHED. ITS dark outline formed a menacing silhouette on the horizon. It was a battleship, but whose was impossible for Tom to identify from such a distance with plain eyesight. He reached for a pair of binoculars and stepped out onto the deck along to the bow to get a better view. Veyron trailed behind, eerily whistling the tune to Gloomy Sunday.

Tom looked at Veyron. "Do you have to?"

Veyron sighed. "I'm not saying I necessarily like the song, but there's no doubt about it—the melody becomes catchy."

Tom shook his head and focused the binoculars until the port side of the battleship came into view. It looked recently painted in matt black from the waterline to the top of its bridge, which looked as though it extended at least fifty feet in the air. Just forward of the bridge were two massive gun turrets, each with twin fourteen inch guns. Aft of the bridge triple boiler towers formed a triangle and released thick dark smoke high into the atmosphere, giving it an even more intimidating presence, like some evil monster in the night. He moved his line of sight towards the hull and stopped.

BB-35 was painted in bold letters and numbers.

"My God!" Tom swore. "It's the USS Texas!"

"You must be wrong," Veyron said. "The USS Texas is supposed to be in Texas as a permanent National Monument!

Besides, the thing's over a hundred years old—there's no reason for it to have come down this far, and certainly no way it would have survived the dangerous seas."

"Beats me what the hell it's doing down here, but it's definitely the Texas." Tom held out the binoculars. "Here, have a look for yourself."

Veyron snatched the binoculars from him and studied the battleship as it crept towards them at full steam. "That's either the USS Texas, or a very good replica, but only a madman would try to bring it down here."

Tom recalled the USS Texas BB-35 was the last of the Dreadnought era, steam-powered battleships in existence. Her twin coal boilers had been retrofitted with six oil burners in the late twenties to increase speed, but otherwise, she'd remained true to her original form. Two years ago the USS Texas had been moved from Texas, where she was permanently displayed as a National Monument and moved to dry dock under the auspice of ongoing maintenance. If it really was the same battleship, Tom guessed someone had spent that time returning her to a state of battle readiness—although why someone would go to the length of doing so without upgrading and modernizing the weapons systems flummoxed him.

It slowed and pulled up alongside the *Antarctic Solace* until the towered bridge dwarfed them by thirty feet. A multitude of hand fed machineguns lined its decks. American sailors manned every one of them as though waiting for an imminent attack. Smoke billowed from the three separate towers as the battleship's screw was thrown into reverse and the ship was brought to a standstill. Navy SEALs, armed with assault weapons, secured the ship, while several sailors tied off alongside the *Antarctic Solace.*

No one spoke and Tom just grinned as a single woman climbed down a rope ladder and on to the deck of the *Antarctic Solace.* She looked like she was in her early forties, but Tom knew she was closer to fifty. Wearing a military dress uniform littered with medals, her dark red hair was tied back in a bun without a single strand of hair out of place. She had an angular, almost permanent scowl to her face — yet there was something undefinably exquisite and beautiful about it also.

Tom grinned. "Madam Secretary. I'm surprised to see you here in person."

A smile opened and replaced her scowl. She was definitely beautiful. "Tom Bower, I babysat you when you were still trying to work out how to walk — I think you can call me Margaret out here."

"Okay, Ma'am."

Margaret ignored him and looked up at Veyron. "Hello, Veyron. I hope you've got things under control."

"Trying to, Ma'am."

Tom stared at the massive battleship. "Can I ask a question, Ma'am?"

"Shoot," she replied.

"What the hell is the USS Texas doing in the Antarctic?"

She smiled. "It's here on a hunting expedition."

"For what?"

"I'll explain shortly. First, tell me what you have here? Is the *Antarctic Solace* secure? How many people have you found aboard? And where the hell's Sam Reilly — he should have been the first to meet me here."

Tom sighed. "Sam's in East Antarctica at the moment trying to . . ."

"I thought I made it clear to him that his only priority was securing the *Antarctic Solace* until reinforcements arrived?"

"Yes, well . . ."

Margaret interrupted Tom before he could finish his sentence. "I'll deal with him later. Tell me what do you know so far? Is anyone else aboard?"

"Yes, Ma'am," Tom replied. "We found twenty people

inside—all of them prisoners of some sort. They appear drug affected and no one's awake yet. Elise is currently inside keeping an eye on them."

"But are they secure?"

"Definitely. They're all sedated, actually."

Margaret's scowl returned. "How many people do you have guarding them right now?"

"Just Elise—but she can take care of herself. Besides, like I said—we've done bloods. They all have high levels of drugs in their systems."

"Let me guess—with morphine, midazolam and trace amounts of LSD."

"Yes, how did you know?"

"Because Robert Cassidy experimented with just such a concoction to make people work for him. Opioid based drug addicts are the easiest people of all to control if you own the drugs."

"Who's Robert Cassidy?"

She ignored his question. "Do you have a picture of them?"

"Who?" Tom asked.

"The drug affected survivors!"

Tom handed the Secretary of Defense his smartphone with the picture of the twenty drug affected people. "This is all of them. We've done blood tests—they've all been sedated."

She turned to face one of the Navy SEALs behind her. "Major—I want your Delta and Echo teams to follow me immediately! We're about to have a hostage situation included in this royal fucking disaster!"

"What is it?" Tom asked.

"We need to get to them immediately!" Margaret spoke in short, curt words.

"Follow me." Tom started moving down the length of the ship. "Elise has them secured mid ship in the main dining area.

It's all right, they're all sedated and Elise is armed."

"No. It's not all right. They're not secure at all. They may all have drugs in their system — but one of them has been using for years and built up a tolerance to the drugs. One of them is conscious and in control of the situation."

"Who?" Tom asked.

Margaret pointed to the person in the picture at the end of the third row. "This one!"

CHAPTER 53

E LISE BLINKED AND THE BIG guy in the recliner chair moved again. It might have been another automatic reflex, or he was starting to wake up—then again, there was always the possibility he'd been awake all along. Either way, Elise wasn't going to wait to find out. She used her right thumb and flicked the three positioned ARS lever on her open-bolt Uzi two notches to the left, and it changed from safe to automatic mode. She watched as the giant moved both his hands. First they were twitches in his left hand, followed by his right. She wasn't even certain they were accidental or intentional movements. Each one started to look more like a spasm and the cable ties no longer seemed sufficient as he clenched his fists and tested their resistance.

Elise grinned. *So the blood tests were right, this was the person who was responsible.* He must have taken a smaller dose in the hope he could pretend to be one of the prisoners and not the captor.

"I know you're waking up. I suggest you open your eyes and talk to me."

The fidgeting stopped, but the man said nothing.

"Last chance," she said. "Open your eyes and talk to me."

Still nothing.

Elise gently squeezed the trigger with the required four pounds of pressure. A short burst of 9mm Perabellums was released.

Three bullets whipped past the big guys head. He opened his eyes instantly. "What the hell is wrong with you? What have you done to me? I did everything you asked—you said you'd let us go."

"Good morning," Elise said. "Decide to take some of the same stuff you were giving to your patients?"

"What?" He looked drowsy but instantly angry. "Who are you? What have you done to me?"

He tightened his grip and the muscles in his forearms bulged. For an instant, she thought he might actually snap the cable ties just by flexing. At a glance she guessed he was six foot four and somewhere in the vicinity of three hundred pounds. Some of his muscles had turned to fat, but there was no doubting the strength beneath it.

She stepped back, just in case he broke free. "My name's Elise. I'm here to rescue these people. What's your name?"

"Mark." His voice seemed unnaturally weak and feminine for a man his size. "I work in the engine room. They said they'd let me go after I finished the work. Well I finished the work, and I want to go home."

Elise studied him. For a big man Mark looked more like a frightened child. It could have been an act, albeit a very good one or he could be telling the truth. "Who held you hostage?"

Mark tightened his fists again, trying vainly to break free from the restraints. "I don't know. Really I don't. They came in during the middle of the night, woke us all up and made us work. Told us we could only go home once we'd completed the task."

"And what was the task?"

"They wanted us to reconfigure the diesel engines so they no longer required electricity to start. We were to install manual starting mechanisms and additional gearing to the steering so they no longer required powered assistance."

"Why?" Elise asked.

"They didn't say. They just said we could go home once it was complete." Mark shook his head. He looked like he was going to cry. "Elise. I just want to go home. Do you think you could please put the gun down?"

Elise looked at the other survivors. Every one of them remained precisely where she'd left them. "Sorry, Mark. There's a ship full of Navy SEALs docking alongside us right now. Once I have some help, I'll untie you and we can get to the bottom of this. I must ask you to remain patient a few minutes longer. Can you do that for me?"

Mark began to shift his arms violently. He looked like someone who'd mentally snapped. "No! No! Not you again — I don't want to talk to you lady. You're gonna hurt me again!"

"Hey Mark, relax!" Elise moved to the side of him, but his brown eyes kept staring straight ahead, directly where she'd just been standing, as though she hadn't moved. "Everything's going to be okay."

"No. No. Please don't hurt her!" Mark mumbled through the tears of a child. "I'll be good. I will do what you ask."

"Who are you talking to, Mark?" Elise scanned the room. "No one's asking you to do anything, Mark."

Mark turned to face her directly, and cried out in abject horror. "The little lady standing behind you!"

CHAPTER 54

I N FRONT OF HER, ELISE noticed one of the twenty survivors had disappeared. She was the smallest of the lot of them; a petite blonde woman who looked too small for her maintenance clothes. Elise hadn't given her any notice because the levels of drugs were so high in the woman's system Elise figured she would be unconscious for a few days still.

Elise moved quickly. She ducked and turned to face the woman. Bringing the Uzi up to fire simultaneously, her response was fast—but not fast enough. Elise felt the knife gently prick the side of her neck and then stop dead.

"It's resting on your carotid—so I suggest you don't move if you'd like to live." The female voice was barely more than a whisper, but confident.

"Okay. Who are you and what would you like me to do?" Elise asked.

"My name's Christine and I'm now in charge. And you're going to drop the Uzi."

"What's to stop you just killing me once I do that?"

"Nothing, but I don't see what other choice you have. If I let you go with a weapon like that you're bound to kill me. So we're at an impasse."

Elise shrugged. "Or I let you pierce my carotid and I turn and kill you instantly with the Uzi."

"That's another option too!" Christine's voice betrayed her

doubt. "But you'll have to choose fast—I don't feel thrilled by the idea of meeting a bunch of Navy SEALs."

"There's a third option, you haven't thought about."

"Yeah, what's that?" Christine asked.

"Mark!" Elise said. "He's the big guy whimpering like a baby by the way. He might snap his cable ties and take his chances that you won't sever my carotid when he tackles you. Perhaps he figures we're both going to die anyway, at least this way he'll get to live"

"Never. You'd die before he even got out of his chair and then I'd take your Uzi and finish Mark and the rest of them—now I'm finished with them."

"Maybe." Elise watched as Mark broke all the cable ties and stood up. "But I'd say it's our only chance of surviving. You're a big guy, Mark. I trust you."

"All right, no more games–"

Christine's voice was stopped short by the motion of Mark throwing his full three hundred pounds of bodyweight into her. The knife brushed along the side of Elise's neck but didn't have the force to damage her carotid artery.

Elise ducked and pivoted round to the right bringing the Uzi up straight towards Mark and Christine who were both on the floor. Christine was much faster than Mark to regain control and had already brought her small pen knife to rest in Mark's throat.

"Stand up!" Christine yelled. "Now."

"I'm so sorry," Mark said as he stood up.

Elise smiled kindly. "It's all right, Mark. You did great."

For a small woman, Christine had managed to pull Mark back so her arm could wrap around his neck. Only a little under half of her face was visible. "So, we're back where we started," Christine said. "Only now I have a hostage and a shield."

Elise grinned. "Not exactly." She then squeezed the trigger and put a grouping of three 9 mm parabellum bullets through

Christine's right eye.

The Secretary of Defense stepped into the room, followed by two teams of Navy SEALs. Christine's lifeless body dropped to the floor with a thud and Mark backed away immediately.

"My dear, Elise!" Margaret smiled like a proud mother. "I'm so glad to see all that time we spent training you in the CIA didn't go to complete waste—you can still shoot like a professional."

CHAPTER 55

T HE HOVERCRAFT SPED ALONG THE Taylor Valley at eighty
miles per hour. Sam had worked hard to convince Alexis
to wait until they had made it back to the *Maria Helena* and
Antarctic Solace for reinforcements before heading to the
Massive Hadron Collider. Somewhere inside they would find
answers to what happened to the passengers of the *Antarctic
Solace* and why the scientists of the Pegasus were now dead. He
wanted those answers as much as she did, but there was no
way he was going to let her get killed on a fool's errand hell
bent on revenge. They would have their revenge, but they
would do it on their terms, with a lot more firepower.

Alexis remained quiet in a solemn trance for most of the trip.
Sam didn't try to press her. She'd just found out that five of her
friends were now dead because she'd sent them here to
investigate ice tunnels.

Next to him, Alexis stopped reading a passage from Pier
which she'd read at least ten times before and closed the
journal. "What's Genevieve and Tom's story?"

"What story?" Sam asked.

"Why did their love work?" She sighed. "How did they get
their balance right? I was Pier's mentor and advisor for his
physics doctoral thesis. He was younger than me, and quite
attractive with boyish good looks. I was attracted to him and
he made me laugh, but I never would have dated him let alone

marry him, because we were in different places in life and no amount of time would have brought us together."

Sam paused. Unsure if she was somehow comparing her non-relationship with Pier and what happened in the ice cavern. Sam wasn't sure if she saw him as a fun break in her normally conservative life, or wanted more. Then he heard the names Alexis had spoken. "Did you say Genevieve and Tom?"

"Yeah."

"Why do you want to know about them?"

Alexis smiled. It was coy and quickly replaced with genuine surprise. "Don't you see the similarities?"

"No."

"They have a love for each other but their position keeps them apart. By your words, Genevieve is a jack of all trades on board the *Maria Helena,* whereas Tom is a pilot and in charge of deep sea operations."

Sam smiled. "You think Tom and Genevieve are romantically attached?"

"No, not at all." She grinned. "I know they are."

"You've got to be kidding me, right? Those two would make the least likely of couples."

"So you haven't noticed then. What are you, blind?"

"Trust me," Sam said. "Genevieve is a stunning woman, but she's not interested in men currently. I can tell you that for a fact."

"How could you possible know what she wants?" Alexis burst out with laughter. "Christ! She rejected you, didn't she?"

"She didn't just reject me, she rejected everyone. She's been through a lot and the last thing she wants or needs right now is Tom Bower."

"Why aren't you happy for him?" Alexis asked.

"No, I'd be happy. She's a great catch and he's a great guy, but that doesn't make it true."

"The fact she rejected you doesn't make it untrue."

Sam never got the chance to argue his case. Up ahead, a yellow aircraft with a single propeller came into view on the horizon. It flew towards them just above the Taylor Valley. It was flying slowly, and Sam had no way of telling what it was until it got closer.

"We'll need to have a raincheck on the debate." Sam looked for anywhere to hide in the barren valley. "It looks like we have company."

Alexis looked at the plane in the distance. "Any chance it's a rescue plane coming to look for us?"

Sam shook his head. "Not a chance. There's a rescue team at McMurdo Base and it uses a Sea King Helicopter."

"So we're in trouble."

"It would appear so. Let's hope it just wants to make a pass first to see who we are before it gets rid of us the same way it got rid of your friends back at the Pegasus."

The plane flew directly towards them. It was the first time Sam got a better look at its double wings. Sam pushed the throttle fully forward and tried to cajole the hovercraft to beat its maximum speed.

Alexis looked up as it approached. "Is that a biplane?"

"Yeah, a de Havilland Hornet Moth," Sam said. "Tom and I learned to fly on one of those."

The biplane passed them and then made a wide turn and circled back in front of them. For a moment Sam thought it was going to keep going and simply report on their position. It then circled back again, dipped to the left and descended into the Taylor Valley—and flew directly towards them.

"What the hell's it doing here?"

Sam watched as the biplane descended to mere feet off the valley's floor. "Beats the hell out of me, but right now it looks like its pilot wants to play a game of chicken."

"You've got to be kidding me!" Alexis held on to the

hovercraft's stabilizing handles. "What will happen if that things hits us?"

"I have no idea. It's probably light enough the damned thing will probably bounce off our inflated skirt." Sam looked at the pilot's eyes as he approached. The aircraft was coming in slow by modern aviation standards—probably about 75 knots at most.

"It's not turning and there's not a lot of room in the valley!"

"Jesus Christ!" Sam swerved the hovercraft to the left. A split second later the Tiger Moth increased its pitch and made a rapid climb. Sam hit the dashboard. "What the hell was that about?"

"I have no idea," Alexis said.

Sam moved the steering wheel to return the hovercraft to its original direction, but nothing happened. He stared at the dashboard. The lights behind the instruments were no longer lit and none of the electronics worked.

He'd already seen the stone ventifact protruding from the ground ahead. There was nothing Sam could do to avoid it.

"Brace!" he yelled.

The hovercraft hit the smooth boulder at eighty-four miles an hour. Part of its skirt gripped the stone hard as it flew over the stone—sending the hovercraft rolling like a cartwheel until it came to a harsh rest in the middle of the valley.

CHAPTER 56

S AM FELT A SMALL TRICKLE of something warm running down his forehead. He smelt the acrid whiff of blood first, before tasting the salty iron on his top lip. He shoved a handful of tissues on his forehead and was relieved to feel it was only a minor laceration. Sam's mind then turned to Alexis. He hadn't heard a sound from her yet.

He dropped the tissues and tried to find her within the dust filled cabin of the hovercraft. Sam reached down and felt her hand grip his. "Alexis! You alive?"

She squeezed his hand. "I'm alive. You?"

"I'll live." Sam climbed to the bedding compartment behind the driver's seat which was now upside down. He felt around and found his sniper rifle. "Let's get out of this thing before that biplane comes around for a second look."

Sam used the butt of the sniper rifle to break the glass panel in the side of the hovercraft and then climb out. Alexis followed a moment behind. Sam could already see the tiger moth approaching for a second fly over. It had circled around and was now descending into the Taylor Valley once more.

Alexis crouched behind the smooth boulder. "Will this thing protect us from whatever it is he's shooting at us?"

Sam removed the casing of his M40A5 sniper rifle. He opened the bipod and mounted the rifle before attaching the magnified scope. With his right eye he stared at the approaching yellow aircraft until a clear view of the pilot came into its crosshairs. "Well that depends."

"On what?"

Sam settled into a comfortable firing position. "On what they're firing."

Almost in response to his question, the pilot began spraying the hovercraft with a barrage of bullets from a hand held machinegun, which fell short by sixty or more feet. The distance was decreasing rapidly as the biplane approached. Sam breathed in and then slowly exhaled. Halfway through the process he paused, neither breathing in or out.

He squeezed the trigger.

Before the loud report from the sniper rifle was heard, Sam watched the pilot's head obliterate into a spray of blood and bone. The tiger moth dipped and descended to the ground in a steep and uncontrolled dive past them. Ten feet off the ground its elevator changed position and the aircraft naturally tried to climb, failed, and then crashed into the ground fifty feet behind them. It slid along the rough surface of the valley's floor before coming to rest with its wooden propeller being split into kindling as it struck the valley's wall. There was no explosion and the entire thing remained eerily silent.

"Now what?" Alexis asked.

Sam shrugged. "Now we shoot a flare into the sky and hope to hell that Genevieve can still fly the Sikorsky Night Hawk."

CHAPTER 57

I T TOOK AN HOUR FOR Genevieve to reach them with the Sikorsky Night Hawk and another two days for the *Maria Helena* to reach the *Antarctic Solace* inside the Weddell Sea. Sam had told Matthew that he didn't care if it destroyed the 44,000 horse power twin diesels he wanted to reach the *Antarctic Solace* as soon as physically possible.

When the *Antarctic Solace* came into view, Sam noticed a pitch black battleship moored alongside. Large plumes of dark smoke permeated the horizon where three boiler towers from the battleship released pressure. At that distance, he couldn't see a flag and hoped to hell it was one of his and not the enemy's. He used the binoculars to get a better view of the *Antarctic Solace*. Mounted machineguns were now manned at several locations along her upper decks. Sam studied the men on watch. They wore the desert uniforms of the US Marine Corps. On their right shoulders a small image of the American flag proudly identified them as U.S. soldiers.

Sam looked at Matthew. "Well, I have no idea who thought to bring the old smoking battleship, but it looks like the Secretary of Defense came through with the promised reinforcements."

"So it does," Matthew said. "Looking at the number of reinforcements it kinda makes you question what this is all about that makes it important to bring so many uniformed men all the way down here?"

"Bring us alongside the *Antarctic Solace* and let's find out," Sam said.

Matthew nodded and over the next ten minutes slowed the *Maria Helena* to a stop alongside the *Antarctic Solace*. Sam and Genevieve quickly ran the mooring lines and Sam stepped aboard.

A uniformed Marine shook his hand. "If you come with me Mr. Reilly, she's waiting for you on the bridge of the USS Texas."

Sam grinned. "The USS Texas? What the hell's a national monument doing down here?"

"She's hunting, sir."

"Hasn't she provided enough service to her country?"

The marine smiled, pleased Sam knew her history. "That she has, sir. But I'll let Madam Secretary explain why she was needed."

"The Secretary of Defense is here?" Sam asked.

"Yes, sir."

Sam took the next series of steps. "If she's come down in person, it can't be good news."

"No, sir."

Sam followed the marine on board the USS Texas. She'd changed since he'd last been on board. The deck was now cloaked in mat-black paint from her waterline to the top of the bridge. Her armaments were rebuilt and sailors manned the ubiquitous guns that surrounded her deck. Sam climbed the series of ladders to reach the bridge.

He stepped inside. The bridge was empty with one exception. The Marine closed the door and left without saying anything.

"Mr. Reilly!" Sam instantly recognized the almost permanent scowl of the only woman who ever truly owned him. "The next time I give you an order I expect you follow it explicitly."

Sam ignored the reprimand and smiled, genuinely pleased to see her. "Good morning, Madam Secretary."

Margret paused as though contemplating any further rebuke of his actions; then sat down having thought better of any further waste of her time. "As you can see, I've secured the *Antarctic Solace.*"

"That's good." Sam remained standing. "Is the Department of Defense looking at expanding its business to polar cruises?"

She smiled. Not quite a laugh, but definitely a positive reaction. "No. It appears you've stumbled on someone we've been searching for a long time."

"Who?"

"His name's Robert Cassidy," she said. "He was once the most brilliant scientist the Department of Defense ever employed — until he disappeared."

"We had a disagreement with what he was building?" Sam asked.

"Yeah, he lost interest in building what we wanted. Instead, he found a new project to work on. Something too dangerous for even us to muddy our hands with."

"Really?" Sam didn't believe her.

She grinned. "Okay, we were happy for him to build it. The problem was we had a disagreement over what we were going to use it for."

"I see."

"After a secret meeting with President Reagan he broke off all communications and disappeared completely."

Sam sighed. "When did you lose him?"

"1983 — Sometime early in the year I'm told."

Sam looked out past her and out into the crystal clear, icy waters of the Weddell Sea. "You lost him and his weapon in 1983 and you still think he's out there?"

"Who said it was a weapon?"

Sam frowned. "Why else would the DOD been interested?"

"Robert Cassidy didn't see its benefit as a weapon. We did. He threatened to leave. We told him wherever he went we would find him."

"So what happened?"

"We were wrong. He left and we've never seen him since." The Secretary of Defense sighed. "Since then we thought he might have gotten himself killed as he continued his research. Then we prayed he'd got himself killed. And then we had an incident in 1983 which nearly led to complete nuclear Armageddon that we believe he orchestrated. We hoped that event, at the very least, had got him killed."

"Go on."

"Since then small events have occurred which have made us wonder if he was still alive. Each time they were small enough that on their own, they meant little. But over time, if you collected all the pieces, you made a picture that proved undoubtedly that Robert Cassidy was still alive and that he's still working on his Project."

"And you think he has something to do with the disappearance of the crew of the *Antarctic Solace?*"

Her jaw tensed. "Yes. This is the closest chance we've had to capturing him in thirty years, and we won't fuck it up this time."

"Okay," Sam said, pleased to see some things got to her. "We'll get him."

"There's something else." She looked directly at him. "He's taking risks he's never taken before; he knows he's close to getting caught and there's only one explanation as to why he's become so brazen."

"He's nearly completed the Project?"

"Exactly," she confirmed.

"So, where do you think he is?"

"Why, he's at the same place where all the people from the

Antarctic Solace were taken."

Sam sighed. He hated it when she played espionage games, riddled with lies and obscurities when he wanted answers. "And where do you think that is, Margaret?"

The Secretary of Defense smiled. It was wicked and tormenting. He'd never addressed her by her name out of courtesy before, despite their close relationship. She then stared directly at him; her face rigid and unwavering. "Why, Robert Cassidy's taken them to *the Island,* of course." She slightly emphasized "*the Island*" as if it were something special that he should already know about.

CHAPTER 58

"**A** SECRET ISLAND?" SAM ASKED, skeptical. "You want me to believe the entire population of the cruise ship ended up on an island that doesn't exist on any maps?"

"Yes." The Secretary of Defense smiled. "Quite a coincidence really, isn't it? The island has no name, location or existence except for the fact that we financed its development in the sixties and lost it to Robert Cassidy in the eighties."

"So where should this island be?"

"It comes and goes. We've come close to finding its location a number of times over the years. The most recent of course, was in 1983. But I'm afraid since then, all signs of the god forsaken *Island* have disappeared completely."

"Are you telling me in an age of satellite imaging, we can't find an island?"

"Yes. But if it makes you feel any better, we didn't have GPS in 1983 so we were using spotter planes. It certainly made it easier for him to get away. He never would have succeeded if he'd tried these days."

"*The Island* moves?"

Margaret nodded. "I'm afraid so, Mr. Reilly. *The Island* was built into a large iceberg that broke away years ago. The iceberg has a large structure of volcanic rock. This allowed them to build inside it and then tow the island. The ice can be increased or decreased to serve its purpose of concealment. It remained in the northern hemisphere for years, but judging by the aerial photo you sent me of the ice structure you found blocking the entrance to the Weddell Sea, it would appear Robert worked out a way of moving it to the southern hemisphere. None of our scientists can imagine how it was done. Maybe they somehow froze the area below the rock to keep the entire thing from melting and sinking into the Pacific Ocean."

"Technically it's not really an island then, is it?" Sam said.

"No. Technically it's a floating island. It's made up of porous volcanic rock called pumice and lava tunnels. We found it buried inside an ice wall within the Arctic Circle. Originally, that's where Cassidy's scientists worked. One year, when the ice melted and it broke away, most likely as a result of one of Cassidy's experiments, we discovered it floated quite well. With the entire infrastructure needed already inside the island, a decision was made to keep it as an island for research and development."

"Broke away, where?"

Margaret smiled. "You see, we worked out that the island naturally floated being made of porous rock. Then we could flood the lava tunnels in order to sink the island if its location ever became known. You see some of the research happening on the island was the world's best. Governments from all nations, friendly and enemy, would kill to get access to the sort of information it was turning out."

"Could it move?"

"Not on its own. But a series of ships could theoretically tow it, but it would be slow. About ten years ago one of our nuclear submarines disappeared whilst in dry dock for maintenance. We believe Mr. Cassidy was behind that."

"Someone stole one of our nuclear subs and no one reported it missing?"

"It was intentionally documented as a mechanical fault leading to decommissioning."

"Why did he want a submarine?" Sam asked.

"Because underneath the island was a large cavern with air inside. The submarine could surface there and move people and equipment inside the island without anyone noticing from above."

"Okay, so we've been searching for this island for how many years now?"

"Since 1983."

"So why haven't we found it?"

"One of the many projects being performed on the island was a device that creates a fake cloud overhead."

"They create rainclouds?"

"No. They send out a signal that even the best of our satellites picks up and interprets as impenetrable cloud cover. The shape is often different and unless you knew the island was below you would never see it. Despite the simple fact that the sky above was clear."

"So why not search for a cloud the size and shape of the island?"

"Because the island is comparatively quite small."

"How small?"

"Five square miles. Think of the equivalent of a few modern aircraft carriers lined up together to make one giant raft. From the surface it looks like a beautiful island, but underneath it's a monstrous submarine. It's incapable of driving itself, but can be slowly towed by surface vessels."

"I have a theory . . . and you're not going to like it. What if Robert looked at his beautiful island and decided he just wanted to live by himself?"

"He was never by himself. He had a small population of scientists living aboard. Nearly a thousand people in total."

"You mean, at the height of the cold war, when people were frightened of what was to become of them, we built Robert

Cassidy his own private paradise?"

"Yes."

"How does he even feed that number of people?"

"If they're still alive, he's been bringing food in from somewhere. Which is why I think he stole one of our submarines—so he could use it to bring in food and supplies without being detected."

"Is it much larger below the waterline?"

"Yes. Like an iceberg—it's the areas you can't see that are often larger, and submerged. Cassidy's not stupid. The clouds that he creates change and at times are ten times the size of the island, whereas at other times they don't even cover the island."

"When that happens can't you pick it up by making an exact match on images taken on satellite passes?"

"No. The island itself keeps changing. The topside where you can see it is often covered in ice, but it doesn't have to be. There are large heating and cooling systems designed to cover the entire island within minutes."

"The blizzard that nearly killed me when I was searching for the Pegasus on Ellsworth Land—it was caused by the island, wasn't it?"

"Exactly."

"Now it makes sense!" Sam felt the fog of confusion lift.

"What does?"

"When I boarded the *Antarctic Solace,* Alexis was certain the blizzard had only raged for fifty five minutes, while Tom and I were certain it had carried on for nearly three days."

"Go on," she said.

"The cooling systems were facing us. That's why the storm didn't show up on any synoptic charts. It was a truly localized storm, because it was artificially created on the island."

"That would make sense."

"Then when the island moved, the direction of the blizzard changed momentarily and headed towards the *Antarctic Solace* — making it appear to only rage for fifty five minutes."

"Before the island opened its doors and flooded the lava tunnels, causing it to sink and disappear — which means the island is still nearby."

Sam shook his head in disbelief. "All right, tell me exactly, what was Cassidy's Project?"

CHAPTER 59

"THE PROJECT CAME ABOUT AS a secondary discovery during our initial tests involving high altitude nuclear explosions above the Pacific during an operation code-named Starfish Prime."

Sam tensed his jaw. "If I recall the story, Electro Magnetic Pulses were wreaking havoc from New Zealand in the southern hemisphere to Hawaii in the north in response to those tests—which disrupted electrical fuses and damaged communication systems for thousands of miles."

"That's right. Of course such a concept had tremendous potential. If we could strike the Soviet Union with an EMP capable of taking out their communication system, we could then eradicate them with a first strike nuclear attack without any fear of repercussions."

"There's a great thought," Sam said.

"Hey, you weren't around during the height of the Cold War. The Russians were trying similar experiments on their side of the planet. Mark my words, it was a race run on many platforms. If they'd won it, we wouldn't still be here today."

"So why didn't someone succeed?"

"The problem was the EMP didn't last long enough. Ultimately, we gave up on the project when we discovered it would never block the Soviet's communications long enough. That's where Robert Cassidy came in."

"Go on, what did he discover?" Sam persisted.

"After determining that a nuclear blast created an EMP, Cassidy discovered that he could create a radio wave on the back of the nuclear event that remained in the atmosphere for years. It could then be used to block communications and electronic signals." She looked tense. "It had something to do with disrupting the Van Allen Belt or creating a secondary radiation wave inside it."

"If a standard EMP disrupted electronics for five or so minutes, how long could one of these radio waves theoretically disrupt electronic signals?" Sam asked.

The Secretary of Defense grinned. "Indefinitely—modest projections showed the possibility of blocking the area above the Soviet Bloc for over a hundred years."

Sam stared at her amazed. "If he'd gone through with it no one would be living inside Russia currently. The refugees alone would have swamped the rest of Europe. And we would have won the Cold War."

"Exactly. Ronald Reagan tried to sell the plan to the Democratic Party whose members were broadly horrified at the prospect. He took the plan in secret to members of the Republican Party who helped him rise in the political ranks to eventually take Office as the President of the United States. He proved to be a very good President. Who would have believed his entire campaign was developed in secret by a group of men who wanted to elect a man with the tenacity to fund the Cassidy Project. To push through Congress a secret Bill to fund a project to enable them to initiate a first strike on the U.S.S.R. with no retaliation.

"It sounds like the project should have worked. The American people would never have gone for it, but the theory appears sound."

"It was," she confirmed.

"So what happened? How did we lose Robert Cassidy and

his project?"

The Secretary of Defense crossed her arms. "Able Archer 83 happened."

CHAPTER 60

"**W**HO WAS ABLE ARCHER?" SAM asked.

"Not who, but what. Able Archer 83 was the code name for the North Atlantic Treaty Organization exercise that took place on November the Second, 1983. To this day it was the largest orchestrated movement of nuclear bombers in the world. Historians argue it was the closest the world came to a nuclear holocaust since the Cuban Missile Crisis of 1962. The Soviet Union was certain the exercise was a ruse for actual nuclear war, and prepared their own nuclear rockets for firing."

"And what were we really doing?"

"Trying to find *the Island,* of course—before it was too late."

"Reagan nearly took us to World War Three because of *the Island?*"

"No, he nearly took us to World War Three because Robert Cassidy and what he'd nearly finished building. Able Archer spanned Western Europe, centered on the Supreme Headquarters Allied Powers in Europe known as SHAPE in Casteau, north of the city of Mons. Able Archer exercises simulated a period of conflict escalation, culminating in a simulated DEFCON 1 coordinated nuclear attack. The exercise also introduced a new, unique format of coded communication, radio silences, and the participation of heads of government."

"How could someone as intelligent as Reagan have misunderstood how risky such an exercise would have been?"

Margret shook her head even just remembering her first briefing on this bit of history when she became Secretary of Defense. "The realistic nature of the 1983 exercise, coupled with deteriorating relations between the United States and the Soviet Union and the anticipated arrival of Pershing II nuclear missiles in Europe, led some members of the Soviet military to believe that Able Archer 83 was a ruse of war, obscuring preparations for a genuine nuclear first strike. In response, the Soviets readied their nuclear forces and placed air units in East Germany and Poland on alert."

"So, why did Reagan go ahead with it?"

"Because he had to—it was the only way to find Robert Cassidy. The Russians were right about Able Archer 83 being a ruse; only it wasn't because we wanted to start a war, it was because we wanted to prevent one."

"What do you mean?" Sam felt like he was being strung along in a massive conspiracy.

"Late August 1983 a U.S. Congressman from Georgia attended a clandestine meeting in New York at the express request of Robert Cassidy. A Soviet agent was sent there under the direct orders of Mikhail Gorbachev to meet with the Congressman to discuss a new weapon that threatened to end everything." She paused and watched his reaction. "Robert Cassidy threatened both sides with sending either or both the American and Soviet countries back to the dark ages if they did not agree to a peaceful de-escalation and de-proliferation of nuclear weapons."

"He treated them both like naughty children?" Sam laughed. "How did that meeting go?"

"Both sides were pissed," she said. "It took time and Robert was persuasive. You have to remember, Cassidy may be a megalomaniac and he may be hell bent crazy on sending the world back to pre-electrical times, but there has never been a doubt that he was anything but a complete genius. From what we now understand Robert made some significant advancement towards de-escalation with this threat. Of course it was only the start. He'd convinced some relatively low key members from both sides of the Bearing Strait to agree, but now they had to return to their prospective Commanders and pass on the offer. The meeting was adjourned and a second meeting was set for September the fifteenth when the Congressman was set to return from a meeting in Seoul."

Sam pushed forward. "What happened at the second meeting? Why did it fail?"

"There never was a second meeting," she said.

"Why not?"

The Secretary of State took in a deep breath and slowly exhaled. "Because on September 1, 1983 United States Congressman, Larry McDonald, a representative from Georgia, was on Korean Air Lines Flight 007 from New York to Seoul, via Anchorage, Alaska."

Sam swore. "That Flight was shot down over the Sakhalin Island, wasn't it? I was only a kid, but I remember how angry my father had gotten. He was certain the Soviet Union was responsible."

"Yes."

"Do we know why?" he asked.

"To this day, we believe the Soviets genuinely believed it was a spy plane. We know a Soviet Su-15 interceptor, near Moneron Island west of Sakhalin in the Sea of Japan, shot it down under the auspice of Flight 007 flying through Soviet prohibited airspace. What we don't know is whether Konstantin Chernenko, who was already becoming concerned that Mikhail Gorbachev couldn't be trusted, had planned the attack after discovering Mikhail Gorbachev had sent one of his own men to have a secret meeting with Congressman Larry

McDonald. And what Robert Cassidy couldn't work out was whether the attack was perpetrated by the U.S. or the U.S.S.R — either way, he decided it was the final sign, he needed to disappear so he could finish what he started."

"He wants to send America and Russia into the Dark Ages?" Sam asked.

"No. He wants to send the entire planet into the dark ages. He wants to return us to the days of Eden when we were simple hunter gatherers. He thought he was working towards resetting the world to the way it was before electricity. He was a devoutly Christian man, who followed the Old Testament implicitly. He had originally become a scientist to challenge religion, but instead found the Old Testament to have all the answers. Why not send the entire world back to the dark ages — to a time without digital money, without computers, to an Eden where man simply had to work to gather food and live with nature?"

"And we let him get away?"

"Ronald Reagan was his greatest advocate, but after Korean Airlines Flight 007 was shot down, Robert Cassidy disappeared. In an attempt to locate the island before it was too late, Reagan authorized exercise Able Archer 83. It ended on November Eleven 1983 — and Robert Cassidy hasn't been seen since."

"So then what's stopped Cassidy from completing his Project?"

"Power, he needs more power to produce the sort of energy he requires to create a large enough radio-wave to effect the Van Allen Belt and send the entire world into the Dark Ages."

"What was he after?"

"He's looking at something more powerful than a nuclear bomb — he needs to utilize a thing called a Higgs Boson particle. And to do that, he needed someone with access to the Large Hadron Collider. That's why he took the passengers off the *Antarctic Solace,* he needed just one person from it who could build him what he wants."

"Alexis Schultz!" Sam's mind cleared suddenly from the fog of misperceptions.

"Yes!" Margaret looked surprised. "How did you know she was aboard the *Antarctic Solace?*"

"Because she was the only person left on board when I reached it seven days ago."

"Christ! She was there when you found it! Why didn't you say? Where is she now?"

Sam grinned. It wasn't every day he got to genuinely see the Secretary of State pleased about something. "On board the *Maria Helena,* why?"

"You left her alone?" She looked horrified.

"Yes, Genevieve's there. Why?"

The Secretary of State stood up to move. "Because right now she's probably the most dangerous person alive."

CHAPTER 61

G ENEVIEVE WAS DICING VEGETABLES IN the kitchen of the *Maria Helena*. She'd developed a unique range of skills in life, but cooking had come naturally to her even before she started her apprenticeship under a three hatted French sous chef. Tonight she wasn't cooking anything so difficult. Instead she was preparing a multitude of nutrient rich vegetables and diced bacon for minestrone soup. She'd already decided it was precisely what Sam and Alexis needed after the troubles of the past few days.

Okay, it was probably just what Sam needed. Alexis, she wasn't so sure about. Alexis was lying on the couch in the living room opposite the kitchen and continued to read and then re-read several well-handled pages of a dead man's journal. Over the course of the past hour Alexis had been insistent that she hear the thoughts of a troubled dead man who'd been in love. As far as Genevieve was concerned, Alexis looked as though her world had been crushed. It wasn't just the news that her colleagues had been murdered. Everything about her life had been reduced to a wreckage of lies and deceit culminating into a field of missed opportunities.

Genevieve finished with the food prep. She quickly cleaned and dried the nine inch carbon fiber cutting knife before placing it in the top drawer. The bacon and finely chopped onions fried in a pan while the pasta boiled in the broth. Genevieve added the vegetables and adjusted the gas flame until the saucepan stopped boiling. Ten minutes later she tasted the soup with a wooden spoon. It lacked salt, she decided, but was otherwise perfect.

She heard the door to the outside deck open. "Is that you, Matthew? Dinner's nearly ready, but I thought we'd wait until Sam, Veyron and Elise were back."

Genevieve listened, but there was no reply.

Alexis sat up and frowned. "I'm sorry, did you ask me something? I've been such a wreck lately, it's not like me."

"No. I thought I heard Matthew." Genevieve held out her hands in front of her to hush Alexis. Her instincts told her to listen hard—there were footsteps. They were quiet, but definitely inside the main cabin and they were coming towards them. She looked at Alexis and mouthed the words: "Hide. Now!"

Genevieve switched the gas burner underneath the pot of minestrone soup on to full. The flame hissed and began heating the liquid. She then turned to grab a knife or anything she could possibly use as a weapon—and was confronted by five frogmen.

They wore black dry-suits and military grade Viper S10 rebreathers. The sort of hard-surfaced, recirculating and fully enclosed breathing apparatus preferred by most navies. Their faces were concealed by reflective full faced dive masks. Each carried Heckler & Koch MP5s. She looked at the man closest to her. He had a single red band on his left shoulder and she wondered if he was in command. At a glance she noted the ambidextrous, four setting trigger position on his weapon was set towards the red number 30—meaning it was positioned to fire in fully automatic mode.

She turned and smiled. Her striking blue eyes and short cropped hair made her appear elfish and gentle. She feigned a coy and polite smile. "May I help you gentlemen?" Her words were soft and clear, and showed no sign of concern, as though she'd expected their company for dinner. Perhaps she'd assumed they were part of the U.S. Navy SEAL's teams.

The first frogman grabbed her without pausing to answer. She would have screamed if she were allowed, but a gloved hand smothered her mouth. Genevieve pretended to struggle for a moment and then let her muscles relax completely. She gave the appearance of being weak, vulnerable and docile. Like a woman brought to Antarctica only to cook and serve in a man's world.

"I'm afraid we're not here for dinner, darling," the man said. His left arm held her; wrapped forcefully around her neck. "We won't be long. We've come for Alexis and then we'll be on our way. If I take my hand off your mouth, are you going to scream or do anything stupid to alert the rest of the crew?"

Genevieve tasted the saltwater on the gloved hand still stifling her mouth and making it difficult to breathe. Unable to speak, she shook her head.

"Good." He pressed the barrel of the MP5 into her back hard, for good measure. "No need for anyone as pretty as you to get hurt."

"Thank you," she whispered, subserviently.

"Now I need you to call for Alexis. We know she's down here." He relaxed the pressure of his left arm on her throat.

"She's no longer on board," Genevieve said. "She went over to the *Antarctic Solace* with one of the other members of our crew."

"Oh, that's too bad." The man tightened his grip on her neck. "Because that means we're going to have to go over there to get her and I'm afraid we can't have you tipping anyone off about us coming — so I'm going to have to kill you."

Genevieve felt the barrel move up to her chest and said nothing.

"It sure is a waste to destroy something so beautiful!"

"Stop it!" Alexis screamed and crawled out from behind the

couch. "Leave her alone. I'm the one you need."

"Right you are, Alexis."

Two of the five men quickly grabbed her. The other two guarded the exit. The fifth person, the one who still held Genevieve, barked the order, "Bind her wrists, and attach the weight—then we're out of here."

The two men holding Alexis bound her wrists with cable ties. The shorter of the two then removed three lead dive weights from his dive belt and bound them to her ankles. He then released a large amount of air from his buoyancy control device so he would remain neutrally buoyant.

Alexis wriggled. "No. Please, I don't want to drown!"

"Quiet!" The Frogman next to Alexis demanded. "You're not gonna drown. Not just yet, anyway. You're too important to HIM!"

Genevieve looked at Alexis as two Frogmen dragged her towards the exit. Her mouth set hard; bile rising in her throat. "Sit tight, Alexis. We're going to get you back to us—that's a promise."

The man holding her throat laughed. "That's cute. Real cute. I doubt it's true though—not once you see where we're taking her. No one's coming for her."

"No?" Genevieve said. "Are you sure about that?"

The now-boiling saucepan of minestrone soup bubbled over, sending hot splutters of scalding water on to both her and her attacker's legs and arms. Genevieve threw herself backwards as they were both burnt. In the process, her right hand gripped his dive knife, which was attached to his chest by a short nylon lanyard.

"Shit!" The Frogman held her tight. "Stupid bitch tried to burn me. Pretty stupid. What did you think you were going to do, use the boiling water to disarm the five of us?"

The other men laughed at her.

"No. Of course not." Genevieve shook her head meekly.

"That would be impossible with a pot of boiling water."

"Then what did you expect to achieve?" he asked.

Genevieve didn't say a word. Instead she drove the short dive knife along the inside of her attacker's thigh. It sliced his femoral artery. Blood spurted wildly. The man dropped to the floor, releasing her in the process, as his automatic response was to apply direct pressure. By the time his hand reached the inside of his thigh, Genevieve drove the sharp end of the knife along the underside of his throat.

She grabbed the commander's Heckler & Koch MP5 and fired five shots without waiting for him to bleed to death. The first went into the head of the frogman guarding the door. The second killed the man next to him. The third and fourth went wide. And the fifth killed the person holding Alexis.

"Holy shit!" The remaining frogman swore and grabbed Alexis; using her as a human shield. "Who the fuck are you?"

Genevieve firmly lodged the butt of the MP5 into the crook of her shoulder and took aim. The frogman ducked behind Alexis and began dragging her out the door and on to the deck. She watched him struggle with the weight, but continue to remain protected by Alexis. She could just make out part of his arm. Genevieve squeezed the trigger.

Blood and bone fragments scattered from the end of his elbow. The man screamed furiously, but somehow maintained the fortitude to keep Alexis in front of him. "Who are you?"

"Someone you shouldn't have fucked with," Genevieve said. She then aimed at his left boot which was now visible and squeezed the trigger. A single shot fired. The man whimpered as blood quickly drained from the hole where his toes had previously been.

The frogman grunted and heaved Alexis backwards. Genevieve was too late to notice the boarding gate on board the *Maria Helena* had been left open, giving him the unhindered ability to reach the water.

"No!" Genevieve ran forwards to catch her.

There was nothing she could do. The frogman fell backwards into the ice-cold waters of the Weddell Sea — taking Alexis with him.

Genevieve reached the edge of the deck. With lead weights attached to her ankles, Alexis quickly sank into the crystal clear waters. The frogman, who appeared to be even more negatively buoyant, dragged at her ankles like a tormenting demon to the depths below.

Through nearly a hundred and sixty feet of perfectly clear water she watched as Alexis was dragged down towards the mouth of a large black monster. Unable to make out the full shape, she watched in abject horror, as the two blurry figures were swallowed whole.

CHAPTER 62

S AM HEARD THE SHOTS AND ran. By the time he reached the deck of the *Maria Helena* with two teams of Navy SEALs and the Secretary of Defense by his side, Genevieve was lying face down on the deck of the *Maria Helena* staring at the water. She didn't even flinch when he arrived.

"Gen—where's Alexis!" he yelled.

She stood up. Her mouth set hard. "They got her, Sam. I tried to stop them, but I wasn't quick enough."

Sam looked over the edge of the ship. The visibility was so clear he could make out the vague outline of the seabed nearly two hundred feet below. He looked up at her. "What happened, Gen?"

"They came for Alexis, tied her wrists and ankles together. Then weighted her down with lead and dragged her off the side of the ship."

"They killed her?" Sam shook his head. "It doesn't make any sense. They needed her!"

"No," Genevieve said. "I saw one of them shove a regulator in her mouth once she was in the water."

"Well, there goes that hope." The Secretary of Defense stepped back from the ship's balustrade and crossed her arms. Her mouth set hard with a cruel display of pragmatism. "I thought we might have gotten lucky, and she drowned in the attempt."

Genevieve stood up and looked at the Secretary of Defense. "Would you like to explain to me why five frogmen just abducted Alexis?"

"No," Margaret said, defiantly. "But I'd like to know where they took her."

"You mean, where the submarine took her?" Genevieve said.

"Christ!" The Secretary of Defense turned to look at her. "Of course they needed some way to move her."

Sam nodded in understanding. "Genevieve. Run up to the bridge and tell Matthew to put the sonar buoys in the water. Tell him we're hunting the submarine which took Alexis."

"I'm on it," she replied.

There was a frenzy of action on board the *Maria Helena* as the Navy SEALS untied the mooring lines and Matthew took them away from the *Antarctic Solace*. Sam and the Secretary of Defense entered the living area where Alexis was abducted. Four dead frogmen were scattered throughout the room. There was a lot of blood. Three had been shot in the head. A fourth looked as though he'd had the main arteries of his right leg and throat severed. It was hard to believe so much blood could have come from just one person.

The Secretary of Defense looked at the scene of the massacre and then back at him. "Is there something you want to tell me about that young woman who was standing outside?"

"Genevieve?" Sam stopped climbing the stairs to the bridge. He shook his head. "No ma'am. I don't think you want to know—it will only mean you'd have to knowingly look the other way about another one of my crew."

"Good. I'd rather not have to put your entire ship and crew in the off-limits basket for surveillance or any investigations by the NSA, CIA, and FBI. Should I be worried about her?"

"Genevieve?" Sam shook his head. "No. We share similar enemies, and for the most part, she's here to cook and bring a feminine touch to the *Maria Helena*."

The Secretary of Defense looked at the swath of dead bodies and grinned. "I can see that."

"I've found she has some other useful skills that come in handy."

"Just make sure this doesn't come back to bite me. Pretending Elise doesn't exist is one thing. I do it out of necessity and because we need the services she provides for you." The Secretary of Defense looked around the stairwell, checking that no one was within hearing distance, and then lowered her voice. "And because of where she's come from, she must be protected."

Sam whispered. "I thought we agreed it was best to never mention her past? You know as well as I do her origins are going to come back to haunt her one day."

"I'm more worried they'll come back to haunt the lot of us."

CHAPTER 63

S AM ENTERED THE BRIDGE. MATTHEW stood at the helm and slowly increased power to the twin engines until she moved away from the *Antarctic Solace.* The computer monitor showed the results in real time of the sonar swathes, providing a clear image of the seabed below. Matthew pointed the *Maria Helena* in the direction that Genevieve told them she's seen the submarine move.

The active sonar began emitting pulses of sounds while a computer searched for the acoustic location of any target with a similar shape to a nuclear submarine—the Secretary of Defense had already provided the technical details of the nuclear submarine stolen ten years earlier and suspected of being used by Robert Cassidy.

Sam stepped next to Matthew. "Anything?"

"Look for yourself. The Weddell Sea is riddled with icebergs."

The Secretary of Defense stared at Sam. "We don't like icebergs?"

"Not if we want to find something," Sam said. "Think of them like a giant maze of mirrors found in an amusement park. The active sonar 'pings' hit the ice and bounce back. There's no way the submarine is out of range of sonar yet. My bet is it's waiting, hiding, somewhere below."

"But can you find it?" she asked.

"Sure we can. We've found things much harder than a moving submarine before. It's just going to take time. And our nuclear submarines are well designed to be hard to find."

The Secretary of Defense looked at him hard. "I'm afraid time's something we don't have."

Sam nodded. "We might get lucky. Would you like to tell me why they just abducted Alexis, ma'am?"

"Because Robert needs her to complete his Project."

"Why?" Sam stared at the sonar monitor.

"Because he's a religious man. Did you know he became a scientist to discredit the origins of Christianity?"

"No. What happened?"

"He found a closer relationship between God and Science," she said. "We think he's working on the belief that the book is telling him to return us to the times of Eden. He believes that if man can't learn to play nicely with each other, then we may as well just go back to fighting with sticks."

"I thought no one had anything powerful enough to produce the type of EMP required to destroy all electricity on the planet?"

The Secretary of Defense shrugged. "Sure we do. We have more nuclear armaments than a kind fool like you could imagine. But we're safe in that we know he won't be using a standard nuclear weapon."

"Why not?"

"To produce that sort of EMP you would need a rocket several times larger than anything ever built. In short, he doesn't have the resources."

"So why is Alexis dangerous?"

"Because she's the world leading expert on subatomic particles."

"And you think she knows how to produce something more powerful than a nuclear bomb using a particle accelerator?"

"Robert Cassidy thinks so," she replied. "And Cassidy's many things, but he's not stupid. If he thinks she has the ability, then I'm willing to be terrified. Christ, if we thought we could get him by nuking Antarctica now, we would, just to be certain."

"Holy shit!" Sam said. "I think I know where they're going."

"Where?" she asked.

"To a massive hadron collider that the scientists from Pegasus found beneath the East Antarctic ice sheet."

"They've already built one?" The Secretary of Defense stared hard at him with her piercing eyes.

"It would appear so," Sam said.

"Then time's already run out."

CHAPTER 64

S AM LOOKED AT THE TOPOGRAPHIC map. The opening to the ice tunnels leading to the Massive Hadron Collider was marked with a red asterisk. He measured the corresponding distance between the Dumont d'Urville Sea and their destination—it was just under a hundred miles. There was plenty of room to reach it by helicopter and make the return trip on a single tank of aviation fuel.

He looked up at the Secretary of Defense. "We'll take the Sikorsky."

She stared at him; her face unreadable. "It's going to be dangerous."

"It's always dangerous. What makes this any worse?"

"Robert Cassidy."

Sam smiled. "I've never seen you so openly concerned, ma'am."

"I've never had so much reason to be afraid." She straightened her military dress uniform. "Robert Cassidy may be insane, but he's one of the brightest minds to ever come out of the American education system. You've already seen how he can block radio channels by superimposing alternative radio waves over all frequencies, and you know what he's planning on doing—but you have to understand he has technologies that can confuse your electrical systems."

"Is that why they were using an old de-Havilland Tiger

Moth — because it started with a hand starter and then required no electrical input to fly?"

"How did you know they used an old Tiger-Moth?" She snapped. Her voice was quick and sharp.

"Yesterday, when Alexis and I were inside the Taylor Valley, and returning from the Pegasus, we were attacked by a yellow Tiger-Moth. I shot the pilot and the aircraft incinerated shortly after crashing."

"That confirms Robert Cassidy is behind this."

"You've seen them before?" Sam asked.

"Yes. When he first started on *The Island* we gave him four de-Havilland Tiger Moths. As you pointed out before, they were uniquely fitting for his research because they required no electronics to fly. Of course, they carried instruments to take a number of readings for his research, but there was no risk his research was going to cause them to crash." Through her glasses her dark green eyes confronted him. "Your Sikorsky helicopter, I'm afraid, has no such protection."

Sam sighed as realization dawned. "The hovercraft's lying dead in the Taylor Valley, so unless you have a better idea we're going to have to take the risk."

The Secretary of Defense remained silent.

"In that case," Sam said. "We'll take the Sikorsky."

CHAPTER 65

U NABLE TO LOCATE THE SUBMARINE, and with time running
out, the *Maria Helena* gave up the hunt and returned to
the *Antarctic Solace.* Tom met them at the makeshift dock and
lithely stepped onto the deck of the *Maria Helena.*

Sam shook his hand. "Good to see you, Tom. Where's Elise?"

"She moved to the Texas."

Sam turned to the Secretary of Defense. "What have you got
Elise doing on board your anachronistic battleship?"

"She's searching for the island using satellite imaging," she
replied, stepping off the *Maria Helena.*

"I thought you said it was impossible because Robert
Cassidy has a system which confuses the satellites by sending
signals to make cloud cover larger or smaller in order to block
the view of the island?"

"So did I," she said. "Robert Cassidy's a very smart man.
Few people get to beat him."

"Then what's Elise trying to do?" Sam persisted.

"It turns out Elise might be smarter. She's programmed the
satellites to compare meteorological data, such as synoptic
charts, wave height buoys, and sea water temperatures with
the images of clouds seen by the satellites."

"Okay. So what does that achieve?" Sam asked.

"Cassidy can create make believe clouds over his island as
much as he likes, but when Elise compares the two types of

data, his island is going to stand out like a neon light."

"Where are you going?" Sam asked.

"Back to the Texas — to hunt for *The Island*."

"What about the massive hadron collider? I thought you were going to join me with a team of SEALs to secure it."

She shrugged her shoulders. "Why would I do that?"

"Isn't that where they're taking Alexis?"

"No," the Secretary of Defense said. "My guess is they already have whatever subatomic particle they need. Right now, what they need is for Alexis to help make sense of it."

"But you said I should go to the location we found in the journal?" Sam asked.

"Yes," she confirmed. "You and Tom should. Be quick. Get in undetected and get out. Perhaps they've left something that might show us where *The Island* is."

"What about your men?"

"The SEALs?"

"Yeah."

"They're going to prepare for the worst and secure the bays. The island was here. You confirmed that for me. Cassidy's hiding it somewhere nearby, and my men are going to find out where. I'll stay on board the Texas and continue hunting."

"That's why you brought out the last relic from the steam powered battleship era of Dreadnoughts."

"Yes. Cassidy has worked on a number of low powered EMP devices that can stop a ship, or a helicopter dead in its tracks. We're going to get him this time. There's nothing essential to the running of the USS Texas that requires electricity to function."

CHAPTER 66

A LEXIS WOKE UP FEELING DISORIENTED. She opened her eyes and found herself in a single room carved into the volcanic rock known as pumice. She ran her hand along the rough, porous stone and tried to remember how she'd gotten there. There had been a problem on the *Antarctic Solace* — she was all alone, and then a man had come and saved her. *His name was Sam Reilly!* She felt pleased with herself to have recalled that much. Alexis stood up and instantly felt dizziness attack at her mind. Her hands were shaking and it was hard to balance — there was no doubt that they had drugged her. *But who were they, and why had they done this to her?*

She remembered the Pegasus ice station and discovering the truth about the Massive Hadron Collider that had illegally been built below the East Antarctic ice sheet. Then she remembered being on board the *Maria Helena* when a group of frogmen attacked. Someone on board had fought them off well. *Her name was Genevieve and she was more deadly than she looked.* She grasped at what she knew. Feeling pleased to even have that much information. Her memory was coming back in dribs and drabs, in an ad hoc and illogical fashion, but it was coming back to her — which meant whatever damage they'd done to her could be repaired.

But what happened after the frogmen attacked?

Suddenly she recalled being dragged overboard. The ice cold water pierced her skin with the resounding shock of a thousand fire ants attacking her. Somehow she tried to swim but couldn't. *Why couldn't I swim? I used to swim laps — why couldn't I make it to the surface?* Then it hit her — someone had tied her legs together and attached a lead weight. *They were dragging me to the bottom!*

Did I pass out? Alexis couldn't remember so she guessed she must have. She remembered someone shoving something into her mouth. She fought it, but wasn't strong enough. She tried, but eventually took a deep breath and then entered a blissful sleep. *Am I dead?* Alexis looked around the room again. *Some afterlife, hey? This's what I get for being an atheist is it?*

She tried to stand, but the ground beneath her trembled. She could feel the vibrations and hum of heavy machinery. She tried to stand again. She was definitely on a boat, or a submarine. *No. I'm not dead — they took me on a submarine and then they drugged me. Why did they drug me? What do they want from me?* Alexis struggled to reach the door at the end of the room. She tried the handle and it turned easily, which meant she could leave if she wanted. *But did she want to leave? Were there worse things waiting outside?*

Alexis didn't have to deliberate on her choice very long. Instead the door handle turned and a man walked in. He was slim with a trimmed gray beard. Deep lines creased his old face as he smiled warmly.

"Where am I?" she asked.

"You're on *The Island*."

"*The Island?* Which one? Why have you brought me here?"

"Just — *The Island*, I'm afraid. And I've brought you here because I'm afraid I need your help."

CHAPTER 67

W ITH HIS HANDS AT THE controls of the Sikorsky MH 60
Nighthawk, Tom glanced at the sea below, where the
Maria Helena rested completely still in the ice-filled Dumont
d'Urville Sea. He pushed his left foot pedal to the floor and
swung the helicopter around so that the ice sheet of East
Antarctica came into view like a frozen pond that stretched
infinitely toward the horizon. A moment later he moved the
cyclic stick forward and dipped the nose of the helicopter,
allowing the Sikorsky to fly at its most aerodynamic and fastest
speed. He slowly increased his height to an altitude of one
thousand feet and headed south.

Next to him, Sam stared at the topographical map trying to
achieve the impossible task of finding a visible landmark or
reference point to navigate from. After about five minutes Sam
shook his head and folded the map away.

Tom chuckled. "Couldn't work out where we're going in all
this ice?"

"Sure I could. Just keep the Trans Antarctic Ridge on your
left and when you start to see some big caverns open up below
it means we're close."

"How many are there?"

Sam sighed. "According to Pier's notes from the Pegasus,
there should be about a thousand of them."

"Any one of them in particular?"

"There should be five small ones lined up together, followed by a massive one. It's the massive one we're after."

Tom lined the Trans Antarctic Ridge up to a reference point on the left corner of the windshield and kept it there. "Okay, so we're looking for five needles in a frozen haystack?"

"That's sounds about right," Sam conceded.

"So how do we pick which one we're looking for?"

Sam grinned. "If they built the world's largest Hadron Collider inside, I would guess it will be one of the largest caverns. And even if I'm wrong, one thing's for certain—there will be large roads from the snow cats required to move all the materials to build it."

"Are you sure?" Tom asked. His face hard and focused.

"No, I'm just guessing, why?"

"It doesn't make sense."

"What doesn't?"

"You told me Alexis said something this size would have taken an army of engineers nearly two decades to build. That means ships coming and going, and large convoys of heavy snow vehicles moving complex equipment."

Sam nodded. "Yeah, that's right."

"Then why were the scientists of Pegasus the first to discover it?"

"I'll be damned. You're right. They must have had a better way to cover it up. That sort of operation couldn't have gone unnoticed for twenty years."

Thirty minutes later they reached the spot they were looking for. From the air, Tom could clearly make out the five ice crevices lined up in a row, each one pointing towards the largest of them all. There were no snow tractors, or obvious signs of manmade construction, but the image fit the description Sam had given him.

He moved the cyclic to the right and then dipped the nose

of the helicopter downwards to make a large circle of the area and allow a clear vision of the ice world from the cockpit.

Sam removed the map and double checked the markings. "This is it," he confirmed. "See, I told you we'd work it out once we got here."

"That's great, Sam. Now, where do you want me to put us down?"

Sam studied the landscape in a glance and pointed to a large flat area. "How about there?"

"I've got it."

Tom gently lowered the collective and dipped the cyclic stick forward to start their descent—a moment later, everything went dead. There was no flash, no sound of gunfire or explosions. Simply every instrument on board and the engine failed simultaneously.

CHAPTER 68

T HE SIKORSKY HELD ITS POSITION in the sky for a split second before losing its battle with gravity. Tom felt the cyclic stick lose all resistance as the main rotor blades lost RPMs and no longer created lift, meaning his controls were useless. The altimeter, which was based on air pressure, showed they were falling at a rate of two thousand feet per minute.

"Power's gone!" Tom said, as he lowered the collective all the way down, which allowed the main rotor blades to spin freely and pick up RPM speed and at the same time maintain a normal angle of attack similar to a glide position in a fixed wing aircraft. He then shoved the cyclic stick as far forward as it could go. With his right foot he pressed hard on the pedal in an attempt to counteract the sudden loss of torque normally provided by the engine, preventing the helicopter from entering a death spiral. The immediate result was that instead of an uncontrolled fall, Tom maintained control of the helicopter, as it fell rapidly from the sky in a process known as autorotation.

Sam flicked switches next to him in an attempt to restart the engine. "Power's not coming back."

Tom glanced at the altimeter. It read: 700 feet. "Copy. I've commenced autorotation."

Sam pointed at a suitable landing position. There were holes in the ice, giant caverns large enough to swallow the Sikorksy whole. A long cavern divided two main sheets of ice. A long flat section was visible on the western side of it. There wasn't a lot of room, but it would have to do. "Aim for there."

"I see it!" His eyes glanced at the RPM counter for the main rotor blades. The speed increased as the air started to flow up through the rotor system. He was still a long way off the speed required to land the helicopter. He turned gently to the left in order to set up for a landing into the wind and on to his final approach.

Sam read out his altitude and airspeed: "Sixty knots. Forty feet."

Tom nodded and pulled back on the cyclic stick to commence flaring. The nose of the Sikorsky lifted and their descent rate slowed from two thousand feet per minute to one thousand in an instant. At the same time forward movement reduced to zero. The helicopter stabilized to a level attitude approximately seven feet off the ground. Tom gently raised the collective pitch, causing the main rotor blades to decrease RPM speed but increase lift. A moment later the landing skids sunk into the snow.

"Nice landing, Tom." Sam patted him on the shoulder. He climbed out of the helicopter, slid a backpack over his shoulders and picked up his Uzi. Sam pointed to the opening in the distance. "The entrance should be a few hundred feet in that direction."

CHAPTER 69

S AM FOLLOWED THE EDGE OF the chasm towards the entrance of the massive cavern. The hardened ice was easier than snow to walk on because his feet didn't sink into it, but the downside was the hiking boots he wore were slippery and made him feel like he was going to fall off the edge at any moment.

Just before they reached the opening to a large tunnel Sam spotted something yellow. It had been pushed into a hollowed alcove in the ice. He recognized it instantly.

"That's the same type of yellow de-Havilland Tiger Moth which attacked Alexis and me!"

Tom grinned. "That's good news. It means we're at the right place. The downside of course is that now we know we have company."

Sam aimed the Uzi towards the airplane and searched for the pilot. "Yeah, let's just hope they weren't expecting visitors."

Confident the pilot wasn't still there, Sam quickly approached the small airplane. Recent snowfall had already built over the cockpit. Sam ran his hands over the engine manifold. It was still warm to touch. The pilot had only recently landed. Sam glanced past it, where a parallel set of footprints formed tracks entering the massive ice cavern.

"Shall we play follow the leader?" Sam asked.

"Sure. You're it."

Sam entered the cavern. A narrow parallel row of indentations in the ice showed the place had been well driven on with a small snow machine such as a snow scooter to form a road about four feet wide. There was nothing large enough to indicate anything like a snow caterpillar or tractor had ever entered. The footpath sized road crept along the ice-wall deep inside the cavern. The road could have gone for miles. On one side a wall of ice stretched to the surface. And four feet to the other side an abys like crevice reached deeper than their eyes could see.

They were running out of time. Sam picked up speed and began jogging. A mile in and the entire path came to an opening that descended deep into the earth, forming a dead end. A steel structure reached out of the ice like a jagged claw. He followed the structure to the end of the platform where an elevator cable dropped into the darkness below.

"So much for the theory it would have taken thousands of trips with convoys of snow trucks to build this place," Tom said, staring out into the vacuous ice cavern. "It looks like they carried everything in by hand and then used this elevator to where they need it."

Sam shook his head. "Something like this needed hundreds of tons worth of materials. There must have been another entrance."

"Or, someone else built it—before them?"

"You think they weren't the first to find the Massive Hadron Collider?" Sam asked.

"I don't know. I'm just saying it doesn't seem possible they built it all without anyone finding out about it. One thing's for certain, they didn't use this elevator to bring everything inside."

Sam opened his backpack and removed a LIDAR range detector, small hand held device resembling the type of gun law enforcement used to measure speed vehicles using a laser.

On one side were three round openings like a three-barreled gun, while the other side had a six inch digital display screen. Handheld light detection and ranging known as LIDAR provided an in-depth 3D image of areas up to ten miles away.

Sam switched it on and pointed it directly into the open cavern. "Let's see exactly what we're dealing with."

The cavern was massive. He slowly moved it around until he developed a clear picture of both its manmade and naturally forming structures. It showed the road continued only a few feet ahead, but looked as though it had been destroyed by a landslide years earlier. Had they been able to continue along the road, it zigzagged for a total of fifteen miles and would have taken them hours to reach the bottom.

Finally, Sam pointed the LIDAR gun below the elevator. The cable descended until it intersected with the road three miles below.

"I guess we're taking the elevator," Sam said.

"Oh great, we're taking a lift into the abyss. Talk about your journey to the center of the earth."

"You got a better plan?"

"No."

Sam stepped on to the elevator. "Then I suggest we get going. Three miles is a long way down."

CHAPTER 70

A LEXIS WATCHED AS ROBERT CASSIDY entered the room again. He brought breakfast with him—Bacon and Eggs Benedict with a large glass of orange juice. He seemed cheerful and sure of himself. He never tried to hurt her, or threaten her. The old man seemed to have the confidence of someone who knew that they had the winning card, despite it being obvious to everyone else in the room that he'd already lost—that was what made him so frightening.

"Good morning, Alexis," he said in his gentle and deep voice.

"Morning Robert," she replied, surprised how easily common civilities could be spoken between captor and captive.

"Now, I'm afraid we've arrived and it's time you helped."

She laughed. It felt insane, but came naturally to her. "Why would I willingly help you build a high energy yielding device so you can destroy the world?"

"Destroy the world?" He looked shocked, and angry. "Is that what you think this is all about? You think I'm crazy and I want to destroy the world?"

"That's pretty much what you said earlier. You want to cease all electrical activity on the planet—you want to return the human race to the Dark Ages!"

Cassidy shook his head vehemently. "On this island we once built weapons for your so called civilizations. Weapons so destructive I eventually had to accept the simple truth that mankind cannot demonstrate the responsibility required to maintain its role as the top of the food chain. I'm doing this because if I don't the inevitable outcome will see to it that mankind no longer has a place—Dark Ages or not—on this planet!"

She stared at the old man who'd taken such interest in her. He was clearly crazy, but there was no doubt in her mind he truly believed every word he said. "I'm afraid I couldn't help you even if I wanted to."

"Why not?"

"What you're asking is impossible in the time that you've given me. Do you understand how much equipment I would need from my office in CERN?"

"I have no idea, but fortunately for me my son has gone to great lengths to retrieve everything from your office so that you can commence work immediately." Robert Cassidy smiled. "He's on his way up—I think you two may have previously met. Did I mention he used to work at CERN, too?"

She looked up as the door opened wider and a man walked in. He had blond hair, and an almost sheepish grin. He remained silent as he carried her laptop into the room.

"Daniel!" she screamed at the man who she was meant to marry two weeks ago.

CHAPTER 71

T HE ELEVATOR CAME TO A stop at the bottom of the dark void. Sam had a powerful flashlight mounted with the scope on the barrel of his Uzi, which he shined around. Everything from the flooring through to the three mile high vertical ice cliffs rising to the roof of the chasm was ice. The elevator was the last remaining evidence of anything manmade.

"Now where?" Tom asked.

"No idea. Cover me, and I'll see if LIDAR can show us the way."

Sam slung his Uzi over his shoulder and then pulled out his handheld LIDAR gun. He switched it on and a moment later he was staring at a clear image of the entire vault. The place looked completely sealed—but no one builds a three mile elevator into a dead end for no reason.

Sam looked at Tom. "Can you see anything?"

Tom stared at it and then said, "What about this spot here?"

"The round hole?" Sam tried to enhance the image. "That's only a few feet wide."

"That's a few feet wider than anywhere else I can see."

"Okay, let's try it."

Sam held the LIDAR gun in front of him, searching for anything else. He was confident they were alone in the cavern—otherwise it would have detected the image of a person. A moment later, the elevator began returning to the surface.

"Shit!" Tom swore.

Sam moved to look at it. The controls were on the elevator. The bottom area where they'd gotten off had nothing except for a large pulley for the elevator's cables. There was no way to call back the elevator.

"Don't worry about it yet," Sam said, his voice calm and focused. Let's have a look at the tunnel you found. Maybe there's another way out."

They slowly walked deeper into the chasm until they reached the round opening carved into the ice. It was too perfectly formed to be anything but manmade. Sam put his LIDAR gun away and checked his Uzi. He then slowly crawled into the tunnel.

It went for maybe twenty or thirty feet and Sam found he was sweating by the end of it despite being surrounded by ice. A light shined on the opposite end of the tunnel. A beacon of hope they were on the right track. He climbed out the end of the tunnel head first into a well-lit room shaped like a rectangle and made entirely from hollowed-out ice.

The tunnel Sam had climbed through opened approximately midway down the longer length of the rectangle. A second tunnel ran through the middle of the two shorter ends. These tunnels were carved into the ice and shaped similarly to the one he'd just crawled through — only instead of being empty, these tunnels housed four blue rails, which were bolted into the ice and ran straight through the rectangular room and back out the other side.

In the middle of the room a single vehicle was fixed to the blue quad-rails by a series of wheels that gripped the rails at every angle. It was made of glass and ceramic materials and shaped like a cross between an elongated egg and a bullet. At a glance it was designed to seat up to three people. Sam thought it looked like a futuristic mining cart or great rollercoaster ride. Either way, there was no doubt about its purpose.

"Tom, you've got to see this!" he said.

Tom's head appeared out the end of the tunnel and his solid frame and large body followed behind. He looked up at the cart. "Where have you taken me, Disneyland's new ride for Frozen?"

CHAPTER 72

S AM AND TOM STRAPPED THEMSELVES into the five-point harnesses inside the strange vehicle. The door closed with a soft-pressurized latch and the internal climate control began to hum. Sam found a single white lever in the middle of his front seat. Sam studied it. A series of green markers were arranged next to a forward arrow and vice versa a series of red markers were arranged in the opposite direction.

Sam turned to face Tom behind. "It looks like I'm driving."

"Then let's go, driver."

Sam eased the lever forwards and the cart leapt forwards, pushing his back hard into the seat as the electric motor hummed. He immediately returned it to the neutral position, but the cart was already through the first tunnel and was descending steeply. It built up speed until Sam felt like he was freefalling into the dark below.

He pulled the lever backwards until the cart slowed to a stop. He found himself being supported entirely by the five-point harness, which meant they were now in a completely vertical shaft. He felt the blood rush to his head.

Tom tapped him on his shoulder. "You'd better get this thing moving before the brakes give out and we fall to our bloody deaths."

"Okay," Sam said, easing the lever back to the neutral position until they started moving again.

After a few minutes the tunnel evened out into a dark and level position. Sam slowed the machine to a stop again. "I can't see a thing."

Tom reached forwards. His long arm stretching past Sam and flicked a single switch on the roof, labelled, *external lighting*.

All areas surrounding their cart suddenly lit up with a powerful yellow light. They were in another cavern hollowed out of ancient ice, hardened and compressed over thousands of years. To the left of them was a vertical ice wall that reached both higher and lower than their lights could penetrate. The cart was made of glass above and below, allowing Sam to see that sections of the rails were suspended above a void so deep their lights couldn't penetrate. To the right was a stainless steel circular tunnel, like the ones Alexis had shown him of the Large Hadron Collider at CERN. Only this one reached nearly fifty feet in height compared to the one he'd seen in photos which were roughly five to six feet.

"My God, they did it!" Sam said, in awe.

Tom looked up at the giant structure. "Yeah, which means the Cassidy Project is close to completion."

"All right," Sam said, increasing speed again. "Let's see if this thing can tell us where The Island's going to launch the rocket from."

Sam pushed the lever forward and the electric motor instantly moved the elongated egg shaped tunnel cart faster. There were no speed instruments or any other way to determine how fast they were going. The craft felt stable as its multitude of wheels spun around the four tubular rails which formed the tracks. It followed the same tunnel as the Massive Hadron Collider, occasionally dipping or raising twenty to thirty feet to extend below or above protruding steel equipment and ice, giving Sam the feeling he was on probably the most expensive rollercoaster ride of all time.

"How long do you think this thing's going to keep going?" Tom asked.

"I don't know. Alexis said the Large Hadron Collider at CERN has a total circumference of seventeen miles, and this was meant to be a lot larger. Without a reference, we'd never know."

"Can you speed her up anymore?"

"I think so," Sam said. "I don't know how much this thing can take, but I'll give it a try."

He pushed the lever completely forward until the tunnel cart zipped through the quad rail tracks at jarring speeds like some horrific rollercoaster. Twenty minutes later, the ride came to a sudden halt as a series of magnetic slow down points forced it to stop.

Sam opened his eyes. The tunnel cart was inside a large work station. The lights were on and the entire cavern could be seen clearly. Computer monitors and diagnostic machines lined the walls. Computer screens displayed images of a number of security cameras inside the Massive Hadron Collider. A second tunnel could be seen descending in a perpendicular direction. An egg-shaped tunnel vehicle, like the one he and Tom were in, was stationary at what appeared to be the start of a separate track, built with quad tubular tracks, but yellow instead of blue.

Two workers stepped into the room.

They were both struggling to carry a single large canister, and were seemingly oblivious to Tom and Sam's arrival. Sam reached for the door. It didn't open. He hadn't thought to see how the door opened after closing it.

"Quick, we have to catch them!" Sam whispered in frustration.

The workers spotted them and lowered the canister. The one closest to the tunnel vehicle shook his head and said, "Leave it. We've got to go. We have enough!"

"Quick!" Sam said.

Tom pressed a green button he spotted at the base of the door and it released with a loud hiss as the pressure equalized. "Go!"

Sam climbed out the door. He aimed the Uzi at them. "Stop!

Both men had already climbed inside the tunnel vehicle. The smaller of the two men closed the door and the craft leapt forward. Sam squeezed the trigger, sending several bursts into the back of the tunnel vehicle before it descended sharply and disappeared.

Sam raced to the edge of the tunnel. He took aim to fire again and stopped — the railway tracks ran into a subterranean river and all that remained of the tunnel vehicle were the ripples where it had struck the water.

"Damnit!" Sam swore. He took a deep breath. The air was salty. He felt the yellow rounded material used to make the quad rails. It was tough as steel but flexible as rubber. He tried to pry at it with his knife, but it didn't move. "This thing must be designed with flexibility in mind to accommodate the small amount of movement as the height of the water changes."

"Don't worry about it. We stopped them from leaving with the canister." Tom's nostrils flared as he breathed deeply. "Is that seawater?"

"It would appear so."

Tom smiled. "Which means, we just worked out how they were getting in here for the past twenty years without anyone noticing."

Sam grinned. "And it also means we know where *the Island* must be hiding."

"We do?"

Sam pointed to the map on the wall which showed the directions and destinations of the tunnels. It showed exactly where the seawater-filled tunnel opened to the sea. He placed an asterisk with a pen on the map. "It's over here. If they were moving canisters out, it means *the Island* must be somewhere near this point."

"What do you think's inside the canister?"

Sam looked at the device. There were several in the alcove behind it. A thermometer gave the precise temperature as absolute zero. Sam shook his head. "Forget about the canisters. We have to find that island before the Cassidy Project goes into effect."

Tom stopped him. "What did you find in the canister?"

"This." Sam opened his computer tablet and pressed on an icon. He showed it to Tom—the image exactly matched the canister he was looking at.

Tom shook his head. "Where did you get this image?"

"Alexis sent it to me. It was her theoretical design to store and transport individual subatomic particles without letting them break apart or degrade over time." Sam swore. "I don't know how they convinced her to do it, but it appears they already have her technology to transport the God Particle. And that means Robert Cassidy is now in possession of the ability to play God."

CHAPTER 73

S am took a photograph of the map of the tunnels. He and Tom were approximately two thirds of the way through the circuit. If they continued along the same tunnel tracks they'd reach the first ice tunnel where they'd entered and could return to the elevator. Sam still didn't have a clue how to access the elevator, though. He studied the map to see if there was another way to the surface, but he never got the chance to find one.

The blue quad tracks began vibrating with the hum of an oncoming tunnel vehicle. Sam moved into the alcove with Tom. His Uzi was loaded with a new magazine of 32 rounds and ready to fire. Three tunnel vehicles came to a sudden stop following the series of magnetic speed reduction devices. Several people began climbing out, each with weapons in their hands.

Sam didn't wait to talk. There was no doubt about their purpose here. Unlike the workers he had seen before, these were dressed in military snow attire, and were clearly trained soldiers. Most likely, mercenaries or security guards. Either way, he didn't wait to find out. He fired a small burst of bullets into the first three.

Tom aimed the Remington 12 gauge shotgun at the second tunnel vehicle as it slowed to a stop. He fired and it blew a hole in the windshield. He then pumped the shotgun again and fired a second shot—killing everyone inside.

More tunnel vehicles arrived.

Tom fired another two rounds of 50 caliber, 12 gauge shotgun shells. "Let's not stay around to see who our next guests are."

Sam climbed into the front seat of their tunnel vehicle. He leaned out and sprayed the entrance to the workstation and loaded another magazine of thirty two rounds into his Uzi with a click. "Time to go."

Tom climbed in and closed the hatch. Sam didn't wait for the air pressure to equalize before he pushed the lever all the way forward. The egg shaped rollercoaster lurched ahead, hurling their backs hard against the seats.

Tom looked behind. Two mercenaries climbed into the stationary tunnel vehicle used by the first three unwanted guests to arrive. He heard the sound of gunfire as one of them destroyed the glass door. "We've got company!"

"Nothing we can do about it!" Sam yelled.

"We'll see about that," Tom yelled back. Three bullets raked the rear windshield, sending large cracks through the reinforced glass. Tom shoved the Remington Twelve Gauge shotgun through the crack and fired.

Tom missed.

Tom pumped the shotgun and fired again. The spray of shotgun pellets showered the front windshield of their attacker's tunnel vehicle. There was damage but not enough to break the glass completely.

Tom carefully aimed at the machine following and squeezed the trigger. The shot fired wide and missed by miles — as Tom felt his guts suddenly wrenched from his insides as the tunnel vehicle dropped down a steep decline, and he fell hard into Sam.

"You okay?" Sam asked.

"Never better," Tom replied. "You?"

"Fine, but you'd better hold on," Sam said. "I can see our

destination up ahead. I'm going to slam on the brakes, but you and I will only have seconds to get out before the guys behind slam into us."

"Go for it."

Sam pulled the lever all the way backwards and the magnetic brakes slowed them to a standstill in a matter of seconds. They were both out of the rollercoaster in another two seconds. And their attackers slammed into the back of their cart one second after that.

Sparks, and mingled fragments of glass, steel and blood shot through the dark tunnel ahead as the two tunnel vehicles smashed into each other.

Sam raced through the ice tunnel to where the elevator was thankfully waiting for them. On the surface they both kept a fast pace somewhere between a jog and a run. Time was running out faster than they could keep up. If they lost this thing, they'd need to wait another hundred years to use electricity again.

The sunlight opened up in the distance.

"I don't mean to bring a bit of a downer to your party," Tom said. "But given the Sikorsky has no electricals—how do you suggest we get out of here?"

Sam looked at the yellow de-Havilland Tiger Moth. "It looks like they kindly left us with transport."

CHAPTER 74

TOM CLIMBED INTO THE FORWARD cockpit of the Tiger Moth. The little bi-plane was painted a bright yellow and had tandem seating with controls at the forward and aft cockpits. "After what I saw you do with the tunnel vehicle, I think I'll fly."

Sam grinned as he moved to the single propeller at the front. "Sure, but may I remind you what happened to the last aircraft you flew?"

"Hey, the Sikorsky flew through some sort of magnetic field which shorted all its avionics!" Tom opened the fuel line. "All right, spin the prop!"

Sam spun it hard, but nothing happened.

Tom pushed the choke button all the way in and said, "Okay, go again."

He watched as Sam tried to spin the prop but the engine failed to fire. It was severely cold and it was a wonder someone had ever got the damned thing to fly in the area. "Try it again or I'm going to have to get out and push."

Sam pulled down on the outward blade of the wooden propeller — hard. The engine fired and Tom slowly increased the fuel pressure until it was running smoothly. The propeller pulled at the old biplane and Tom found the two front wheels failed to hold in the snow.

"You'd better hop on, Sam."

Tom eased the throttle back as far as he dared until Sam had climbed in and then pushed it forwards again. With the fuel line open, the aircraft began to hum as it moved forward. Tom taxied using the awkward tiller bar to steer the cumbersome tail dragger.

Once out from the edge of the ice chasm and onto the flat ice that made up the vast majority of East Antarctica Tom pushed the throttle fully in and the engine roared. Tom held the spritely aircraft on the ground until it couldn't take it any longer. He gently pulled the stick towards his chest and they were in the air.

He checked the compass and climbed in a northerly direction towards the *Maria Helena.* It took a few minutes, but he found himself starting to get used to the old controls. He remembered his training pilot in the Corps telling him the Tiger Moth had proved to be an ideal trainer once upon a time. It was simple and cheap to own and maintain. The control movements required a positive and sure hand as there was a slowness to control inputs. His trainer had told him that during Second World War instructors preferred these flight characteristics because of their effect at weeding out the inept student pilot.

Tom flicked the radio on. Immediately, the sound of Gloomy Sunday began playing loudly. He went to switch it off again.

"Wait!" Sam yelled just above the sound of the engine.

"What?"

"Turn the radio back on!"

Tom switched it back on. "We can't pick up anything or communicate with the *Maria Helena*—that stupid song is still playing."

"I know."

"So why do you want to listen to it?" Tom grinned. "You don't think our situation is that bad, do you?"

"No. I just saw the old Radio Direction Finder—on the

right."

Tom adjusted the radio's loop antenna. It was basically a small loop of metal wire mounted so it could be rotated around a vertical axis. At most angles the loop has a fairly flat reception pattern, but when it is aligned perpendicular to the station, the signal received on one side of the loop cancels the signal in the other, producing a sharp drop in reception known as the "null." He slowly rotated the loop and looked for the angle of the null. He stopped when he found it. "Well I'll be damned. There was a reason that noise has been playing constantly. Someone's trying to provide a bearing."

"I think we just found our way to *the Island*."

CHAPTER 75

T OM CONTINUED TO FLY THE old de-Havilland Tiger Moth on
the bearing for Gloomy Sunday, hoping that it wasn't a
sign for the likelihood of their success. It took them past the ice
sheet of East Antarctica and into the Dumont d'Urville Sea.
Twenty miles out Tom started to get worried, the biplane was
simple and had a good reputation, but it was old and the
further it went from land the more worried he became.

When he was close to turning around Tom stopped turning
the signal loop. He no longer needed to. All directions moved
him further from the source. *The Island* was below them.

He turned his head to face Sam. "I think we just found *the
Island*."

"Well done. Can you see anything?"

Tom banked to the left, making a slow and wide circle
around the source of the signal. "No, not a thing."

"Really? Because I can see *the Island* the USS Texas is
hunting."

Tom examined the water below. He put his polarized
sunglasses on and saw it straight away. In a world filled with
dark blue water, an area of roughly five square miles appeared
unnaturally green. There was either some extremely shallow
water below or they had indeed found *the Island*.

He grinned. "We'll I'll be damned. What do you want to do
now?"

"Take us back to the *Maria Helena*."

Tom straightened the biplane and leveled it for a direct heading towards the *Maria Helena*. When they reached it he flew low and circled the ship until Matthew came out on to the front deck with Sam's sniper rifle.

"Shit!" Tom swore, lifting the nose of the Tiger Moth. "What the hell was he going to do, shoot us down?"

"It's all right, Matthew's a terrible shot. He was probably just trying to scare us while he got a better view. You'll be happy to know he's recognized your ugly mug and is signaling to come around and land."

"You're certain?"

"I'd bet my life on it," Sam replied.

"In that case, that's exactly what we're doing."

Tom took the Tiger Moth down in a glided descent. He pulled back lightly on the stick and flared just above the ice flats and landed simultaneously on all three wheels. A perfect landing for a tail dragger, which has the main undercarriage as two front wheels and a very small wheel aft to stop the tail dragging on the ground.

Matthew met them with the zodiac rubber tender and transferred them to the *Maria Helena*. Tom was the first one up the ladder and on to the deck of the *Maria Helena*. It felt like it had been beached because the water was so placid. Genevieve embraced him like she hadn't seen him for a year, wrapping her arms and legs around him in a massive hug.

"Jesus, when I saw the yellow biplane I thought you were dead," she whispered in his ear.

Tom smiled, wanting nothing more than to kiss her lips. "I'm made of tougher stuff than you give me credit for." He moved to kiss her lips, but she turned her head and jumped down to give Sam a big hug.

Sam looked like he was relishing the offer and lifted her off the ground in the process. "I missed you, too," he said in a mocking voice.

Matthew was the last to climb the ladder. "What did you find?"

Sam looked at him. "They have the weapon. We found *the Island* where it's going to launch. Its twenty miles north-east from here."

"Good. You'll need to get a message to Elise on board the USS Texas. We don't have anything with anywhere near enough grunt to destroy *the Island!*"

"Do you know where the Texas currently is?" Sam asked.

"Satellites show her another forty miles east of the coordinates you gave for *the Island*," Genevieve said.

"Okay, here, send this to Elise," Sam handed Genevieve the coordinates.

"Sorry, Sam," Genevieve replied. "The radios are still blocked by that depressing music."

"That's okay. I want you to send it via Morse code."

Genevieve stared at Sam with a vacant expression, but said nothing.

"Okay, change of plans." Sam took the piece of paper with the coordinates out of Genevieve's hand and placed it in Matthew's hand. "New plan. Matthew, I want you to send these coordinates repeatedly to Elise."

"Via Morse code?" Matthew asked.

Sam took a bite out of an apple. "Yes."

"But the radios are still down."

"What happens every time you try and make a radio transmission?" Sam asked.

"It makes an interruption in the radio waves that sounds like incomprehensible static." Matthew smiled. "But a series of interruptions makes Morse code—I get it."

"Exactly," Sam said.

Tom looked at them both. "What makes you think Elise is

listening to the radio at all?"

Sam grinned. "Because Elise's computer is always listening. It will identify the Morse code immediately. Then Elise will read it and notice it's a standard set of GPS coordinates, and put it all together. The Texas will head there with its quad fourteen inch guns."

"Okay, Sam." Matthew looked at the coordinates. "Are you going to wait for them?"

Sam shook his head and started walking down stairs. "No. It's too far. They're at least another two hours away at best. Robert Cassidy may have launched his rocket by then. We might have to take a look at *the Island* ourselves."

Matthew followed him. "What do you want us to do?" Matthew's voice was tense and sharp. "There's nothing we're carrying capable of destroying *the Island* before it launches!"

"Tom and I are going back in the de-Havilland Tiger Moth."

"Why?" Matthew looked startled. "*The Island* is twenty-five miles out to sea and deeply sunk. It's not like you're able to land there."

Sam grabbed a dry diving suit, a military grade rebreather, dive mask, fins and an MP5. "You're right. Then I guess Tom and I had better be prepared in case we crash into the ocean . . . intentionally."

CHAPTER 76

A LEXIS STARED AT ROBERT CASSIDY after he told her that he had already replicated her canisters and had almost fifty stable Higgs Bosons stored inside.

"You've actually done it?" Alexis's heart raced with a mixture of excitement and guilt. "Nobody's ever seen more than one Higgs Boson in the same place before!"

"Do you want to see them?" He asked, more like a doting father, than a maniac who was willing to sacrifice everything to destroy the planet.

"Yes," she answered immediately.

"Follow me then."

She followed him through a series of tunnels, hollowed out of the same porous volcanic rock found in her room. Cassidy stopped inside a large laboratory. An individual canister stood on a table and a powerful electron microscope was perched above it. Sitting at the table was Robert Cassidy's son, her ex-fiancé—Daniel.

Robert was the first to speak. "We've been able to insert two Higgs Bosons inside the canister, but the instant we introduce a third the Higgs field loses its strength and the Higgs Bosons degrade."

"Why would you be trying to introduce three?" she asked.

"Not three, but thirty-six!" Robert laughed. It was warm and kind. "My dear, Alexis—I thought you were following my plan? I've engineered a model of Higgs Bosons, which I believe will specifically weaken the Higgs field specifically related to electricity. It will be strong enough to stop major electrical activities such as computers, communications, and robotics, but not damaging enough to destroy the world or the tiniest electrical impulses that drive a person's heart. How did you think I was going to remove electricity from the world?"

Alexis stared at Cassidy. Her green eyes, hard and piercing. "It can't be done. What you want is impossible. The Higgs field affects the mass of all electrons on the outskirts of any atomic particle. Don't you see, even if you could design a field to remove one part of the field, the Higgs Bosons used to build it would already degrade before you reach a stable model."

"My son seems to think you may have a solution?" Robert said.

Alexis's eyes darted towards Daniel, who quickly looked away. "It can't be done, Daniel."

"You once believed it could," Daniel said without looking at her. "In fact, you showed me your theory. I tried my best to understand it, but I couldn't. I couldn't make sense of it."

"Did you ever think that maybe you couldn't understand it because it wasn't possible?" she asked.

"You think you were wrong and I was right?" Daniel shook his head. "You're just trying to get out of helping us."

Robert Cassidy stood up. "The Battleship USS Texas is hunting for us with depth charges specifically designed to destroy *the Island*. The time for squabbling over who can do what is over. If you can build the model that I showed you, Professor Schultz—I suggest you do."

"I'm not going to help you destroy the science that has taken us thousands of years of evolution to reach. Why do you keep suggesting I will? You may as well kill me now. You have nothing to offer that's going to be more valuable than the livelihood of the planet's billions of human beings."

"Come with me." Cassidy grabbed her by her arm. "Let me show you what I must do if you can't make this work!"

Alexis followed him through another two long tunnels. Daniel walked with them and remained silent, but mimed the words, "I'm so sorry."

"Sorry for what, Daniel? Sorry you couldn't keep your dick in your pants, or sorry your father's insane and plans to destroy the world?"

"I'm sorry I hurt you. You must understand we needed you. I never meant to be around long enough to nearly marry you — I really am so sorry."

She laughed. "Christ, Daniel. That's you in a nutshell. You've been so timid all your life. We're about to destroy the planet, and you're worried about my feelings after I caught you fucking my best friend on the night before our wedding? You're more insane than your father!"

Robert unlocked the door and all three of them stepped inside a room that reached nearly a hundred feet into the air. There were two massive rockets standing upright. At least thirty people worked around each of them, testing, analyzing and preparing for the imminent launch.

"Professor Schultz," he said using her title. "This is what the inside of a nuclear missile silo looks like. Those are both based on the Thor W40 Rockets used during the early high altitude nuclear tests taken in 1962. Both have the potential of bringing about my great plan and returning earth to the way God chose it to be. Back to before humans felt they had the right to infinite knowledge and the power to destroy everything. To a time before electricity. The one to your left requires the energy derived from thirty-six Higgs Bosons."

Alexis stared at him. Her eyes vacant with fear. "You're crazy!"

Cassidy ignored her words and continued. "The one to the right is the largest nuclear bomb ever constructed. This will cause the Van Allen belt to vibrate in the right frequency using sound waves to destabilize all electricity around the world. Of course, the downside is the fall out of nuclear radiation will most likely kill most living human beings. There will be survivors and I'm willing to take that risk, if you leave me no choice. Like I said, I would let you choose to help me, and I think you'll make the right choice. So, what would you like to do?"

Alexis swallowed hard. "I'll build your stupid thirty-six Higgs Bosons model."

CHAPTER 77

O N THE BRIDGE OF THE USS Texas Elise had been working
hard following her program which compared dark rain
clouds picked up on satellite imaging with real-time
meteorological observations, such as water temperature, wave
height, wind speed and direction. The theory was simple. If
Robert Cassidy was triggering the satellites to imagine a cloud
was there that didn't exist in order to conceal the Island, it
would become obvious when compared with other weather
patterns that could be verified. Ergo any anomaly would most
likely be the Island. There was just one problem with her
program — it had found eleven such weather and satellite
anomalies.

Elise blinked hard. She had been analyzing her computer
readouts for thirty-six consecutive hours without a break.
When she opened her eyes a message was flashing in the
bottom right hand corner of her laptop screen. She clicked open
and read the contents of the message. She swiped the laptop
screen to the left until she reached a radio App. She opened it
and listened to the current radio message.

Elise grinned. "Margaret!" Elise was the only person who
felt comfortable calling her by her first name and not by her
title as Secretary of Defense. Margaret had somehow been
involved in her life since she was a baby. "You need to listen to
this."

"What is it?" The Secretary of Defense asked.

Elise pressed play. "Just listen."

The depressing sound of Gloomy Sunday played. Margaret frowned. "You know why Robert chose that song, don't you?"

"No. Why?"

"When Rezső Seress wrote it in 1933 some say he was challenging the Great Depression and increasing fascist influence in his native Hungary. The basis of Seress's lyrics is a reproach to the injustices of man, with a prayer to God to have mercy on the modern world and the people who perpetrate evil. Cassidy is telling us our greed has failed and he is going to make us repent."

"Really?" Elise wasn't convinced the Secretary of Defense wasn't reading too much into it.

"Why did you want me to listen to it anyway?"

"Forget the song. Can you hear the static interruptions?"

"Yeah. What about them?"

"They're a series of on and offs making the signals found in Morse code."

"What do they say?"

"They don't say anything. They simply repeat the coordinates for a certain location."

"Do you think it's a trick?" Margaret asked.

"No. I think it's Sam." Elise brought up the digital map and marked the coordinates. "And I think we'd better reach this point here as soon as possible if we want any chance of sinking *the Island* before Robert Cassidy launches his weapon."

CHAPTER 78

T HE YELLOW DE-HAVILLAND TIGER MOTH circled the submerged island. Sam placed the military grade rebreather mask over his face. It recycled oxygen and scraped carbon dioxide from his exhaled air. It was the first time he'd ever piloted an aircraft and SCUBA dived simultaneously. Tom tapped him on the shoulder to say he was ready.

Sam gave the all-okay Q symbol with his right hand and then pointed downwards with his thumb. He reduced power and placed the aircraft into a glide. He banked left onto the downwind leg and reduced altitude to 1000 feet, before turning left onto a short base run before banking into the wind for the final approach.

Sam pushed the stick forward and gradually lowered the nose of the aircraft. He increased flaps to full and the sea slowly loomed closer. The stall speed on the Tiger Moth was twenty-five miles an hour, but even at that speed if he landed poorly he or Tom could still end up breaking their necks. He took in a deep breath ten feet off the ground. Then slowly exhaled as he pulled the stick towards his chest, lifting the nose up until it flared and stalled as the front landing wheels struck the sea.

Seawater flew across the windshield and in an instant the aircraft dipped gently below the water as though it had been carefully dropped. Sam's head jolted forward in the process, striking the instrument panel. He wasn't injured, but a slight crack formed on his full-faced dive mask. He turned to see Tom

341

grinning and making the okay symbol with his right hand. A moment later the Tiger Moth began its journey to the seabed below.

Sam and Tom rode the sinking Tiger Moth to the seabed forty feet below. Bubbles of air from the cockpit and engine manifold rippled across their faces. Both men remained still as possible, mindful someone from *the Island* could be watching for survivors.

The old aircraft landed gracefully on the icy seafloor on a solid block of ice. Less than fifty feet away Sam could clearly see a submerged manmade runway—proving they had reached *the Island*. Sam grabbed the Heckler & Koch MP5, a preferred weapon by frogmen around the world for its ability to fire just as well after submersion. He then pulled on his fins and freed himself from the cockpit.

Tom swam up to him, pointed at the runway and wrote on his dive tablet: *BAD LANDING. NOT EVEN CLOSE TO RUNWAY!*

Sam laughed, wiped the chalk note off and then wrote: *SORRY. YOU OKAY?*

Tom nodded and then wrote below: *FINE. WATER'S FREEZING. LET'S GO.*

Sam brought up the digital version of the schematics for *the Island* which the Secretary of Defense had given him. She'd explained that Robert Cassidy had probably made some changes, but the main tunnels were unlikely to change and would provide the best chance of gaining access to the interior of *the Island*. He drew a line across his digital tablet and marked the main entrance, where the nuclear submarine most likely docked.

It had been a while since the two had relied on hand gestures and written notes when they dived. Their "push-to-talk" diving radio was blocked by the same depressing song the rest of Antarctica had to bear currently. Even so, he could understand what Tom was thinking—it's time to get out of the cold and to do that, they needed to gain access below.

Sam took the lead and swam to the end of the flat surface of *the Island*. He descended sixty feet, opening his jaw several times in the process to allow his ears to equalize. At the bottom he entered a large cave that extended halfway across *the Island* and moved in an upwards direction.

He followed the opening inside. A large air pocket existed above and he was able to surface. The cavern opened up to a dry area roughly the size of a football field. The place was well lit with high powered, UV emitting lights — designed to make the place feel like a beach. A subterranean sandy beach rested sixty feet away. It looked like the real thing, right down to palm trees, beach chairs, and a volley ball net. A long jetty ran out to where a black Benjamin Franklin class nuclear submarine was moored.

Tom surfaced next to him. His eyes wide with wonder. "Well, what do you make of that?"

CHAPTER 79

"FOLLOW ME," SAM SAID, RELEASING air from his buoyancy control device so he could dive again.

"Where are you going?" Tom replied. "I thought we needed to make it to the area beneath the surface of *the Island?*"

"We do. This won't take long."

Sam quickly swam to the side of the nuclear submarine. He placed a small circular device on the side of its hull and then turned the main chamber, causing it to create a vacuum and stick to the submarine's hull like it had been welded there. He turned and swam along the beach, before surfacing again.

Tom followed him. "What was that for?"

"A homing beacon. The Secretary of Defense said she'd be most obliged if we were able to make sure we didn't lose her submarine again once we found it." Sam removed his face mask and his fins. "The last thing any of us wants is to beat Cassidy only to have him, and the rest of his scientist buddies escape on their stolen sub. We'd spend the next twenty years trying to find him again."

Sam reached the edge of the beach and quickly moved to a set of palm trees next to a tunnel. It provided the most amount of concealment available. There were several tunnels. He removed his diving equipment and stripped out of his dry suit. Sam thoroughly dried his MP5, removed the bolt and pulled the trigger. The firing mechanism activated with a click.

Confident it would work if needed he reassembled the weapon and zipped up his dive boots again.

He stared at the six new tunnels leading out from the beach since his map had been drawn and then up at Tom who'd already reassembled his own weapon. "Any preference which tunnel we're going to take?"

"Nah, you choose," Tom replied, locking the magazine in place. "What did the map say?"

Sam grinned. Of course the map had changed since his government was in possession of *the Island*. "It said there was just one tunnel from the beach."

"Right. Let's take the biggest one. Goes to figure if they were moving nuclear weapons and large rockets, they would need more room to do so."

Sam nodded. "That's as good a theory as any."

Sam entered the tunnel first. It led upwards in a constant twenty degree pitch. It made sense given that everything inside *the Island* would need to be above the beach in order to remain dry. The tunnel was made from porous stone. Lights had been intermittently imbedded into the ceiling, but otherwise the island seemed entirely natural.

After climbing approximately twenty-five feet in elevation the tunnel opened to a medium sized room, with several large computers. No one was inside, but it was clearly a main hub for the everyday workings of *the Island.*

Sam looked at the first computer screen. It displayed the remote video surveillance from the beach. He quickly scanned the monitors looking for attackers.

"Tom, where would you place security if you had any?" Sam asked.

"Here," Tom replied without hesitation. "This looks like it's the main entrance to the Island. Looking at your old map, all intruders would have to pass through this point before reaching the inner levels of *the Island*."

"Exactly. So where are they?"

Tom studied the area. Most of the monitors showed views from security cameras. On the far left a computer showed the current position of all their resources. It included the location of three other de-Havilland Tiger Moths, five snow-caterpillars, and the Benjamin Franklin Class nuclear submarine in its dock. He shrugged. "Beats me."

"Me, too," Sam said. And he didn't like feeling confused during any raid. He wouldn't have been too keen to have been met by an army of mercenaries, but it would have at least made more sense.

Sam put his hand on the third computer monitor, which was running a screen saver. The touchscreen opened to the digital image of an analogue clock. The clock only had one arm and it was moving in a counterclockwise direction, as though someone was trying to turn back time.

He was about to dismiss the image and continue searching for any clue that suggested where they should go, when he noticed there weren't twelve numbers left on the face of the clock. Instead there were only five.

Five hours or five minutes?

The clock ticked backwards and the number of markers left were just four. It was working five minute intervals and had four intervals remaining.

Tom looked at the process and the number zero where the twelve would ordinarily be. "Twenty minutes on the clock."

"Until what?" Sam asked.

"Given Robert Cassidy already has the subatomic particles he needs to complete the project, I think this clock is telling us we've got twenty minutes to find him and stop him, or get real used to living without electricity."

CHAPTER 80

S AM FOUND A MAP OF the security cameras on the main computer. It showed a missile silo built into a large room closest to the surface of *the Island*. The Thor Rocket itself stretched sixty-five feet from her fin to the nose cone, extending from the lowest level through to a section just below the surface of *the Island*. There was no way to reach the base of the rocket in time because it had been secured by watertight doors. The only option left was to reach the upper end of the rocket, where the main ignition computers were stored.

He checked the fastest route before he and Tom started running through the series of tunnels and hatches until they reached it. Neither gave any thought or concern about defenders. Most, by the looks of things, had already left. Without electricity, *the Island* was going to be nothing more than a very cold, inhospitable and deserted environment. Obviously, Robert Cassidy had thought that much through and instructed many of his followers to leave before the world truly changes.

He would have liked to know where they had been moved to, but Sam had other priorities. In the back of his mind, he recalled Veyron explaining to him that the *Antarctic Solace* had its diesel engines and lighting all retrofitted to run without electricity. Robert Cassidy must have been planning on using it for their escape. The question was, now that Robert no longer was in control of the *Antarctic Solace* — where did he plan to go?

Sam turned the final corner and raised his right hand with a clenched fist, giving the silent message for stop. He heard voices. He recognized Alexis's but the other one he'd never heard before. It was deep and erudite, like the owner had once lectured. By the sounds of things he was still lecturing.

"Alexis," the stranger said. "You have done a great thing today. You should be proud of what you've helped me achieve. Without you, none of this could have been possible."

Sam guessed he was listening to Robert Cassidy. Even the Secretary of Defense agreed he was a supremely intelligent man.

"That's supposed to make me feel better?" Alexis said. "I'm going to be responsible for destroying nearly every major scientific breakthrough since 1752 when Benjamin Franklin decided to prove the existence of electrical current by famously flying a kite with a copper key during a thunderstorm! Do you really believe the world would have been better off if Thomas Edison decided candle light would suffice?"

Sam felt sick. The contents of his last meal rumbled in his bowels and his throat ached. *What could Cassidy have possibly done to convince her to sacrifice the world?* He didn't have time to wait and listen. He switched his Heckler and Koch MP5 from safety to full automatic and stepped inside.

"Robert Cassidy," Sam said, aiming directly at him. "It's over."

CHAPTER 81

S AM DECIDED ROBERT CASSIDY LOOKED more like he belonged in a nursing home than at the dangerous end of conspiracy to change the world. He had very little hair left and what remained was entirely white with the exception of his full beard, where some gray remained. If Cassidy was surprised by their sudden arrival, he didn't show it. Instead he smiled warmly, as though some unexpected guest had arrived to share in his delight.

Cassidy had a gun in his right hand. He held it with a casual indifference. Not at all like a trained soldier, but more like someone who'd stopped at a commercial shooting range and thought he'd have a go at whatever weapon was on offer. In this instance, it was a .38 caliber Smith & Wesson Model 10. Sam guessed it was most likely service issued back in 1958 when Cassidy had first joined the Starfish Prime project. It was old, but that didn't make it any less dangerous.

Sam's hard, piercing blue eyes darted between Cassidy and Alexis. He could easily shoot Cassidy dead in an instant — *but would the old man have the stubborn tenacity to get a shot off in the process?*

The ground beneath him began to move. His left hand instinctually reached for the side of the door frame for balance, while his right remained on the MP5. Sam sighed. A deep sense of impending doom unfolding in his gut — has *the Island begun its movement to the surface?*

"What are you going to do, Cassidy?" Sam asked again. "It's three against one here. You can't kill us all. It's over."

Cassidy slowly turned to face him. His gray eyes full of intelligence. Like a chess player, he was determining his final move for the game. Cassidy then smiled and lowered his handgun. "You're right, Mr. Reilly. It is over. We're about to surface. The Thor Rocket, carrying a weapon designed to alter the Higgs fields is set to launch automatically in just a few minutes!"

Sam snapped the gun out of Cassidy's hand. "Stop this. Abort the launch now!"

"I'm afraid I won't do that." Robert smiled, warmly.

Tom stepped in, placing the barrel of his Remington shotgun against Cassidy's face. "And I'm afraid we really are going to insist."

The room suddenly echoed with the sound of thunder.

"It's already done," Cassidy said, calmly. "That's the first stage of the Thor Rocket's liquid oxygen and kerosene fuel cells being ignited. The process can't be stopped now. You may as well learn to live without electricity. At least for the next hundred or so years."

Tom kept the Remington shotgun pointed at Cassidy's face. "Even so, you won't live to see it."

"No. But that's okay." Robert smiled. "As you can see I'm an old man. My life's work is nearly over. I can die happy knowing I made the world a better place."

CHAPTER 82

E LISE STARED AT THE STILLED water as the USS Texas reached the coordinates she'd found hidden behind the depressing song on the radio. The water looked dark blue in the overcast sunlight, making it impossible to determine how deep the seabed lay. The Texas sounded the depth at nearly five hundred feet.

Margaret stood next to her. "It appears *the Island* is missing."

"It will be here," Elise said, her voice confident.

Margaret frowned. "The depth sounders are reading 500 feet below our keel in all directions!"

Elise stood up and spoke to the commander of the battleship. "Your ship's instruments are wrong. Robert Cassidy has made a name for himself as a magician, capable of applying magnetic fields to falsely provide any readings he wants. This is how he's survived three decades without detection. Keep the guns ready to fire—we may only have one chance at this."

The Commander nodded. "Yes, Ma'am. Forward guns ready to fire."

"We should drop depth charges now!" Elise said.

Margaret placed her hand on Elise's left shoulder. "Are you certain? If you get this wrong we're about to give away our exact position and the only chance we might ever get at stopping Robert Cassidy."

Elise grimaced. "That's if their sonar pings haven't already.

If I get this wrong, we're all going to have to get used to life without electricity."

The Commander looked at the Secretary of Defense for confirmation. She nodded her head and said, "Go ahead, Commander."

The Commander nodded. "Fire depth charges on my mark."

CHAPTER 83

S AM HEARD THE ROCKET BAY doors above him open in preparation. The Thor Rocket would be released from its confines in a matter of seconds. Free to wreak the sort of damage unimaginable by its original creators. A circular window, with hardened glass allowed him to see the rocket, which extended through every level of *the Island.*

Seawater had already flooded into the forward firing bay. Like a modern nuclear missile from a submarine, it was capable of being launched from the protection of shallow water without *the Island* ever reaching the surface. He was filled with rage and frustration that despite the rocket being no more than a few inches away from him, there was nothing he could do to destroy it or prevent it from launching.

The rocket began to move.

Sam, Tom, Alexis and Robert watched as the rocket picked up speed and cleared the launch bay. The trailing rocket's exhaust plasma seared the glass window, sending heat throughout the room. Each of them turned to run in an attempt to survive the intense blast of radiant heat.

Robert Cassidy closed the heavy steel doors to the room they had been in, the second they were outside it. Sam saw Robert's hand flick the watertight security latch downwards when he heard the sounds. This time it was more like the clap of several massive thunder strikes, followed by a shockwave that resembled the epicenter of a grade nine earthquake.

Sam hit the deck. He rolled a couple feet and instinctively shielded Alexis with his arms. She tried to shout at him, but it was impossible to hear what she was trying to say above the roaring explosions. It all lasted less than a minute and then their world was filled with silence.

Sam grinned as he and Alexis managed to find their feet. "The USS Texas must have deployed her depth charges!"

Robert Cassidy turned to face him. His eyes vacuous and his jaw rigid with disdain. "No! It was our only hope!"

"It's over Robert—the Cassidy Project failed," Sam said.

Robert looked up at Sam, his eyes turning to hatred and a deep-rooted sense of loss. "What have you done? What have we all done?"

The silence then gave way to a new series of violent eruptions. *The Island,* after having the majority of its ice-filled surface damaged, was no longer able to maintain buoyancy. It was torn between the powerful forces sending the levels built in hollowed ice to the surface, while the heavier lower sections and nuclear reactor were dragging *the Island* to the bottom.

Robert Cassidy was the first to realize what had happened. He grabbed Sam by the shoulder, stared at him with cold gray eyes and said, *"The Island* is breaking apart!"

CHAPTER 84

F ORTY FEET AHEAD OF THE Texas, seawater began to move in a counterclockwise direction, forming a whirlpool as it sucked away at the surface of the otherwise stilled water. *What the hell is that?* Elise thought. An instant later the sea bubbled before rising into the air like a geyser. A few seconds later *the Island* broached the surface of the Dumont d'Urville Sea like a humpback whale.

The USS Texas rocked heavily under the changing sea. Elise held the edge of the bridge to steady herself. For a few seconds the majority of *the Island* became visible. A massive conglomerate of ice, volcanic stone, and machinery floating high in the seawater. The frozen surface, like an iceberg, concealed the size of the main livable part of *the Island*. The depth charges and Thor Rocket had shattered most of the ice into fragments. Elise stared in horror as those fragments now pulled away from each-other. The ice made up two thirds of the size of *the Island,* and almost all of its buoyancy.

Elise looked at Margret. "It's breaking apart!"

CHAPTER 85

T HE THIRD DISTINCT SOUND SAM heard was the bulk of the ice
separating from *the Island.* With the removal of the top of
the Island, air was no longer trapped inside, and water was free
to gush into the tunnels from below. They were now blocked
from their dive equipment and any chance of escape. Air
whipped through the surrounding tunnels around them. The
tunnel they currently occupied would protect them for a while
from the influx of water, but as *the Island* sank, the pressure
would increase and break through the watertight doors.

Sam looked at Tom and Robert — their hardened faces told
him they recognized the sound and knew their time was nearly
over. Sam squeezed Alexis's hand. "I'm sorry. This is it."

She squeezed it back and smiled kindly at him. "It's okay.
Not your fault."

Robert Cassidy broke their embrace. His eyes were wide and
filled with adrenaline. "Follow me. There may still be time."

"Time for what?" Sam, Tom and Alexis said in unison.

"To survive, of course!" Robert grinned madly as he began
moving along the tunnel. "Sam Reilly, I believe you must
continue my research. You understand how important it is?
Mankind must not be allowed to keep making the mistakes the
way they have."

Sam had no idea what Cassidy was talking about. It seemed
outrageous the old man wanted him to try again with the

Cassidy Project. Even so, telling the only person who knew of an escape route that he was a fool seemed like a poor decision. Consequently, Sam simply nodded and followed.

"Mankind must be allowed to carry on!" Cassidy continued.

"Yes," Sam replied, "of course!"

It took nearly five minutes of hard running before they reached the next door. Sam felt his ears pop several times. He equalized them by opening his jaw and then looked at Cassidy. "We're sinking, aren't we?"

"Yes. And fast." Cassidy looked kindly at them, quickly unlocking the bolts in the watertight door. "We'll be nearly to the bottom by now. Almost a thousand feet."

"There's no way we can reach the surface from there."

Robert shook his head. "No way at all. It's a good thing the three of you aren't going to the surface."

CHAPTER 86

T HE DOOR OPENED AND THE four of them raced into the next compartment. Sam grinned in pleasure. A small tunnel vehicle, similar to the one he and Tom had discovered in the subterranean Hadron Collider, made of glass and ceramics stood at the water's edge. It had four sets of three angled wheels. Each one mounted on the edge of the futuristic mine cart. The type he'd imagined were placed on a rollercoaster to protect it from falling off despite the severe speeds being achieved. It was attached to the quad yellow lines. Sam recognized them as the same ones used by the workers inside the Hadron Collider when they escaped earlier.

"Well, friends—what do you think?" Robert opened the hatch. "This is how we built the subterranean Hadron Collider. This will take you inside the bowels of the ice cavern in the main work station."

Sam knew the place. He'd been there less than twelve hours earlier. "Why didn't the tracks break?"

"They're made out of a high tensile and flexible composite material we developed. Even though *the Island* has spent the last decade locally, in these frigid waters, it often rises and falls with the tide. It was important for us to have a stable means for accessing the Hadron Collider. I'd love to explain it all to you, but the line is only so long. If we sink much further the track may snap under the strain!"

Sam looked inside. There were only three seats, and even then it was going to be difficult to fit three adults inside. "It doesn't look big enough for the four of us."

"No." Robert smiled effortlessly. "But the three of you should be able to squeeze inside."

"You're not coming with us, are you?" Sam asked.

Robert Cassidy shook his head, his gray beard surrounding his kind smile. "No. I'm old. I've been fighting this war against the stupidity of the human race a long time. My solution may have been radical and may have been wrong, but it was the only one I had and I believed it was the best way for the rest of the inhabitants of this planet to survive, as well as for mankind. I still do. The battle's lost, but I believe the three of you should take up the next generation of fighters. My time is over."

Sam looked at Cassidy. The man may have been crazy and spent his life trying to achieve the destruction of the human race as we know it, but his beliefs were honorable. Sam held out his hand. "We'll try our best."

Cassidy took it and gripped it warmly. "God speed, friends."

Alexis and Tom climbed into the middle and back seat. Sam climbed in last and closed the hatch.

"One more thing!" Robert said. "If you follow the green line you'll find the rest of the residents of *the Island*, the surviving crew from a B52 Bomber who unfortunately landed here in 1983, and the rest of the crew from the *Antarctic Solace.*"

CHAPTER 87

T WO WEEKS LATER ALEXIS WORKED on her laptop on board the *Antarctic Solace*. She had been given the green light to manage the Massive Hadron Collider. There would be a lot of legal red tape as well as feasibility studies to overcome before it could be used again. In general though, all members of the Antarctic Treaty System were unanimously in favor of continuing its work with her in control. There was a lot of work to be done, but she'd never shied away from hard effort.

She felt the *Antarctic Solace* rock as another ship pulled along her portside. Alexis got up and stepped out to see if the man she was waiting for would come to her. Sam Reilly had been consumed by the rescue response and she hadn't seen him since the fateful night *the Island* sank.

A man in his mid-fifties walked up the gangway, slowly moving towards her. He'd only just arrived from the latest trip made by the *Maria Helena* which had spent the last two weeks ferrying the rest of the survivors from *the Island* in East Antarctica back to the *Antarctic Solace*. It was the last trip the *Maria Helena* needed to make, and she watched with disappointment that it wasn't Sam Reilly who walked up the gangway. All the passengers from the *Antarctic Solace* were already aboard, and the original scientists and small community from the Island had all been taken to the USS Texas for investigation into their potential involvement in the Cassidy Project.

So the question nagged at her mind — *Who is that man? And where did he come from?*

The answer to that question was going to arrive shortly as he approached her. Despite his age, he looked at her with the uncertainty of a man unaccustomed to talking to a young, beautiful, woman.

The man bent down to speak closer to her, as though he were hard of hearing. "Are you Alexis Schultz, Ma'am?"

"Yes," she nodded.

He held out his hand to introduce himself. "My name is Able Rigby. A long time ago I was an aft gunner on board a B52H Bomber Stratofortress, named *Maverick's Menace.*"

Alexis gasped at the name and threw her arms around him. There were tears in her eyes as she embraced the stranger.

"My Commanding Officer was a Major James Maverick. To this day, I believe he was the kindest, most intelligent and decent man that ever lived." Able smiled warmly. "And I believe you were his one and only niece. He spoke about you often. You were his one big regret. He used to say he'd lived a good life, but he wanted to see you grow up."

"What happened to my uncle?" she asked.

"He died only recently. Pneumonia of all things. Can you believe it? After all he'd been through? I just wanted you to know that he was good man. Someone you should be proud of." Able handed her a red leather bound journal. "This was his journal. He wrote every day. Not much, but something. He wanted you to have this. He hoped that from it you might come to understand why he decided to support Robert Cassidy."

"Thank you," she said. Wet droplets were running freely down her freckled cheeks. "Thank you for your duty, for supporting my uncle and for giving me closure."

"You're welcome."

Alexis watched as Abel Rigby walked away. He hadn't left her sight before she untied the leather bindings and opened her uncle's journal. She flicked through until she found the first page he'd written in and began reading.

Dear Alexis,

If you ever find this journal let me begin to explain the circumstances surrounding our commitment to a man named Robert Cassidy and a Project that commenced back in 1962. You see, you have to understand I lived in a time when the world had gone mad. The two superpowers, the United States of America and the Soviet Union were never engaged directly in full-scale armed combat against one another, but they were heavily armed in preparation for a possible all-out nuclear world war. Each side had a nuclear deterrent that deterred an attack by the other side, on the basis that such an attack would lead to total destruction of the attacker. Both sides focused on the doctrine of mutually assured destruction if either party attacked.

We were all mad. In a world filled with madmen, sometimes the only person to turn to is a mad man. That was how I came to trust my friend, and ally, Robert Cassidy.

In September 1983 Robert Cassidy had attempted peaceful de-escalation negotiations with low level representatives of both the U.S. and Soviet Union. Shortly after the clandestine meeting a passenger plane was accidentally shot down by the Soviets while carrying one sitting U.S. Senator. President Ronald Reagan feared the Soviets were in the process of attempting to steal the Cassidy Project and would use it against them with the most gravest of outcomes for the U.S. Consequently, Ronald Reagan ordered the destruction of the Island and betrayal of his long term friend, Robert Cassidy.

This was part of that assassination attempt, and as you read the rest of my journal, I hope you'll understand why, I too, decided to help Robert Cassidy.

CHAPTER 88

S AM SMILED AS HE SAW Alexis. He knew Able Rigby had given Alexis her uncle's journal — he had given her the truth. At a glance he guessed her tears were a mixture of pride for who he was and of loss of what he could never be. Sam wanted to be there for her. In whatever capacity she needed him. Alexis stood up to meet him. She stepped forward and wrapped her arms around him. At first Sam thought she just wanted to be held. Needed to be comforted. And then he felt her lips on his. It was gentle at first. Tentative. And then filled with strong, passionate and drawn-out kisses. Afterwards Sam sat down next to Alexis, holding both her hands in his.

She smiled. Her green eyes were full of intelligence and life. "You've been busy."

"There were a lot more people down the green tunnel than we expected. Robert Cassidy created a unique, self-sustaining community. But it's done now."

"Where will you go?" she asked.

"From here we'll return to Florida. The *Maria Helena* is due for an overhaul, not to mention repairs for our helicopter and the replacement of the hovercraft. I might take a vacation. Do you want to join me?"

Alexis sat up. She fidgeted. *What doesn't she want to say?* "I can't. They've given me the go ahead to lead a team of scientists to determine the feasibility of utilizing the Massive Hadron

Collider in East Antarctica. By the sounds of things, the signatories of the Antarctic Treaty System are willing to go for it."

"That's great news." Sam squeezed her hand and watched her eyes turn away from his. "But something's not right."

"I spoke to Aliana Wolfgang this morning."

Sam smiled. "Wow. You know Aliana?"

"We were Rhodes Scholars together."

"You went to Oxford, before Harvard? Talk about being an overachiever."

"Yes," she blushed at his complement.

"How is she?" Sam asked with genuine interest.

"She sends her love and hopes you are well. I called her because something about your name sounded familiar. It wasn't until *the Island* had sunk and we got the internet running again that I googled your name and it all came back. I remembered Aliana talking about this really great guy the last time I saw her — that was about twelve months ago."

Sam squeezed her hands. "We broke up amicably. She has her research and I have my projects. The two kept us pretty far apart."

Alexis brought his hand up to her lips and kissed it tenderly. "You know I can't do this again?"

"Because of Aliana?" Sam asked.

"No. She told me about your situation. I'm with her — I couldn't be with someone I was always waiting to find out wasn't ever going to come home. The world needs heroes, Sam — they do. The problem with heroes though, is there are very few who live long enough to grow old with someone. You know that, don't you? Luck only lasts so far."

"I understand what you're saying."

She smiled at him, leaned close. Closed her eyes and kissed him again. "But I'm really glad you showed up when you did."

"Am I likely to see you again, sometime?"

"Probably not."

He looked a little crestfallen. "I understand."

"It's not that, Sam. I'm staying here in Antarctica."

"You liked the cold that much?"

"Yes. The cold helps with the overall running of the world's largest Hadron Collider."

"They're going to let you keep it?"

"It will take years to overcome the red tape, but yes — I think we'll get there. The world needs new energy sources if we're ever going to colonize space."

"We have to colonize space?"

"Course we do. Colonization is built into our genes. It's part of human existence. Think of all the wars in the world. We just aren't difficult to get along with, the human race is genetically programed to propagate and expand. Like locusts, we inevitably destroy the environment while we flourish. If we want to survive, one day we're going to have to colonize the stars."

"You'll never live long enough to see it through."

"Someone needs to start the steps so that generations thousands of years down from us can lead better lives."

"You're an amazing person."

"So are you."

He kissed her again. "Next time I'm down this way I might just look you up and take you out on a date."

"I look forward to it."

EPILOGUE

S TEVE CACHIA SAT IN THE corner of the tiny bar in the small town of Port Stephens in West Falkland Island. His second glass of locally brewed beer stood untouched; a book on the rare birdlife of the small island on the South Atlantic archipelago laid on the table next to it. He'd left the book open with such frequency he was almost certain he'd begun to know what was inside. Three guys took turns playing rounds of pool at the other end of the room. The barman, an entirely bald man with heavily wrinkled skin poured himself a shot of strong liquor. He drank it and then continued drying recently washed glasses with a hand towel.

It was hard to maintain a certain level of anonymity under the circumstances. Steve grinned. It had been two months and whoever he was waiting for still hadn't showed. He slumped his heavyset shoulders forward. His eyes were vacant, casually watching some gameshow on an antiquated television in the background. At his prime he used to be two hundred and thirty pounds of solid muscle. Once a top detective with New York's finest, he'd been given a pension after twenty years of exceptional service. Now fifty, he was still two hundred and thirty pounds, but the ratio of fat to muscle had changed places. Even so, he could move quickly if he needed to and there was a lot more strength in his arms than anyone would have given him credit for.

Like many before him, he'd found the pension less than

what he was used to living on and the life of early retirement unfulfilling. Consequently, he'd started his own private detective agency. That's how he came to find himself exceedingly bored on this small island in the middle of nowhere. His current case was as boring as it was ridiculous. If it wasn't for the money some fool was throwing at him he would have never taken it, let alone stayed this long.

Oh well, beggars can't be choosers.

In a world of digital espionage, smart computers, drones, and cameras no larger than your thumbnail it was hard to believe it was still important to put men on the ground for such surveillance. But technology was only so useful without having the people to act on it.

His phone vibrated. Steve pulled it out of his trouser pocket, opened it and looked at the single message.

Active movement inside the tunnel.

Someone had returned. He had set up a series of hidden cameras and motion detectors inside the tunnel at the end of the blowhole, along the surrounding areas of the island, and at the airport. He downed the second glass of beer, nodded his head politely at the barman, and walked outside.

In the next twenty-four hours he would earn the cost of his exorbitant fees. He could abduct the man within the hour, but that wasn't what he'd been paid to do. Instead, he was to follow the person. See where he goes and report. No mistakes. If the man thinks he or she is being followed, the entire game would be over and there would be no chance of a retake.

Steve settled into his hired Range Rover and casually headed north. Steve followed the man he'd been waiting for who drove north toward Port Howard. There was no rush. He kept a good five miles behind the man. He kept him on constant visual via satellite. Not that he even needed that. It was clear where the man was going. He'd come in by aircraft and he would need to leave via one, too. From West Falkland Island he would need to catch the ferry from Port Howard to New Haven that was due to leave at three p.m. and once there he had the option of flying out of Mount Pleasant Airport or Port Stanley Airport. Both flew international.

Steve made a quick call to both of them. He paid thousands of dollars in bribes over the past two months to tin pushers who worked at both control towers. Neither had any commercial jets flying out today, but Mount Pleasant had a privately owned Gulfstream G650 that was booked to fly out today.

"Where's it headed?" he asked.

"They've filed for a direct flight to Rome, Italy."

"You're certain?"

"Yes, absolutely."

It was impossible for Steve to get a flight for another forty-eight hours. The man who'd hired him was going to be pissed off, but what could he do about it? There weren't any flights arriving, let alone leaving before then.

He quickly made a call to some agents in New York. They were booked on the next flight to Rome and would be there with plenty of time to prepare for their guest. Steve wished he was able to be there in person. The last thing he needed was for his team to lose the guy. It was all over if they stuffed it up.

Steve looked at his phone — *do I make the call now?* He decided not to. His job was to get the information. Find out who the guy was and where he came from and then pass it on. The person who'd taken out the contract told him under no uncertain terms that once the man from the hidden tunnel had been located he would deal with it on his own.

It would take him nearly two days using the necessary stop overs of commercial flights to reach Rome from the Falkland Islands. It took the man he'd been paid to locate just nine hours by private jet.

Ten hours after he watched the Gulfstream G650 take off, Steve received a phone call from his second in command in Rome. "Tell me you have him!"

"Relax. We've got him, but I'm not sure you're gonna like where he went."

Steve listened to the whole story. His mouth was incredibly dry, and his mind blank. At the end of the story he hung up and swore several times. The sort of curses that'd make a hooker blush. *Now what the hell am I supposed to do?* Steve didn't have a clue. So he dialed the number.

The man on the other end of the line answered before the second ring. "Tell me you have something for me?"

Steve took a deep breath and began his report, keeping to the facts and specifics only. "Mr. Reilly. I have video footage of the man who entered the ancient tunnel inside the blow hole in Port Stephens. He took a direct flight to Rome by private jet. The jet was leased by a company that specializes in corporate and elite air transport. Once there, he was picked up by a private taxi and taken to the Vatican. He was immediately greeted by the Swiss guards, who all recognized him on sight. From there he approached the private chambers, where the Pope came out to greet him individually. A moment later he disappeared into the vault. My team has set up a surveillance surrounding the Vatican. When he leaves, we'll know where he's going."

"Thank you, Steve." Mr. Reilly said. His voice, cold and unemotional. "Do you know his name?"

"He flew under a passport issued by the Vatican, but it doesn't sound like a real name."

"What is it?"

"Testimonium Architectus."

"Witness to the Builders," Sam translated the Latin words. "Forget about the surveillance. I will deal with it from here. Send your completed invoice, including additional expenses for your team's travel to Rome. You'll be paid in full. I've been very happy with your services, but they are now no longer required."

<hr/>

Sam ended the cell call. His eyes no longer drifting out of the bridge of the *Maria Helena* towards the open ocean. "Elise, get me the live video feed from inside the blow hole."

Elise tapped on her keyboard and the dark image of the secret room became displayed. "There you go."

"I want lighting so I can see it!" he demanded, urgently.

"Coming up."

The background light made the secret alcove come alive. It was empty except for the book, which had been left open two months earlier, when he and Tom had found the place. Hidden inside a secret obsidian chamber at the end of an ancient blowhole on West Falkland Island, was a book which documented the major events in a history that spanned more than two thousand years of history. There was no way Sam could read what had been recently added to the book.

"Tell me you can zoom in close enough to read the latest entry in the book," Sam said.

"I'll try." Elise zoomed in until the newly written words were clearly visible.

Sam read the words out loud, *"The Book of Nostradamus has been found."*

The End

Want more?

Join my email list and get a FREE and EXCLUSIVE Sam Reilly story that's not available anywhere else!
Join here ~ http://bit.ly/ChristopherCartwright

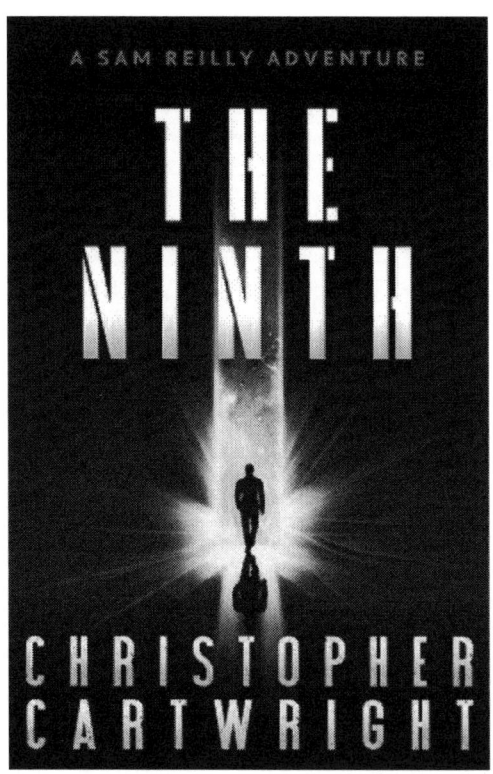

Printed in Great Britain
by Amazon